Elizabeth Hawksley has been writing since she was six. As a child she had free run of her grandfather's well-stocked nineteenth-century library and, as a result, has always felt at home in that century.

She has a degree in English from the University of Sussex and gained a distinction in her MA in Victorian Studies from Birkbeck College, University of London. As well as writing, she teaches English part-time at Barnet College of Further Education.

She has a grown-up son and daughter and lives in London.

6

CROSSING THE TAMAR

Cornwall 1808: in Selwood Priory the dying Sir Walter is watching a cockfight on his bedroom floor. His daughter, Dorothea, is planning the next Selwood smuggling venture, which the sinister Bram Gunthorpe is manoeuvring to take over when old Sir Walter dies. Then there are Sir Walter's numerous bastards, two of whom live at the Priory with their mother, Sir Walter's mistress — to the horror of the local gentry. Into this situation comes the new heir, the Reverend Veryan Selwood, a reclusive Oxford don with very rigid notions of propriety . . .

Books by Elizabeth Hawksley
Published by The House of Ulverscroft:

LYSANDER'S LADY
THE CABOCHON EMERALD

ELIZABETH HAWKSLEY

CROSSING THE TAMAR

Complete and Unabridged

ULVERSCROFT
Leicester

First published in Great Britain in 1998 by
Robert Hale Limited
London

First Large Print Edition
published 1999
by arrangement with
Robert Hale Limited
London

Cover Credit: Treryn Castle from Port Carnow Cove,
Cornwall 1832, in the author's own collection.
Photograph David Ridge.

British Library CIP Data

Hawksley, Elizabeth, *1944 –*
　　Crossing the Tamar.—Large print ed.—
　　Ulverscroft large print series: romance
　　1. Cornwall (England)—Fiction
　　2. Historical fiction
　　3. Large type books
　　I. Title
　　823.9′14 [F]

　　ISBN 0–7089–4147–8

Published by
F. A. Thorpe (Publishing) Ltd.
Anstey, Leicestershire
Set by Words & Graphics Ltd.
Anstey, Leicestershire
Printed and bound in Great Britain by
T. J. International Ltd., Padstow, Cornwall

This book is printed on acid-free paper

To my goddaughter
Alix
with love

Acknowledgements

I should like to thank Mr Ian Martin of the King's Arms, Torpoint and Mr Bernard Baker, fisherman, of Port Isaac for their help and hospitality. Special thanks go to Maggie Cook who acted as my guide and interpreter in Cornwall and whose help and encouragement went far beyond the call of auntly duty. Lastly, I could not have written this without the resources of the wonderful London Library — where else could I find *The Times* of 1808 and books on Cornish Mail coaches and a history of cock-fighting all under the same roof?

1

The west bedroom in Selwood Priory was of a sort of slovenly magnificence that was typical of its owner. The huge four-poster, which held the dying Sir Walter Selwood, had deep-red damask hangings, now split and frayed. Four bulbous finials surmounted each post, but only one of them was upright, the others were leaning at various crazy angles. What had once been a sumptuously embroidered quilt was holed and patched.

Sir Walter himself echoed this mixture of shabbiness and splendour. His deep-brown eyes were sunken, his high-bridged nose was etched sharply in a worn and lined face, and he wore, askew, an elaborately curled, but dirty, wig and a stained brocade dressing-gown.

The room itself had an arched roof and a pair of grotesquely carved corbels on either side of a Gothic window. Faded tapestries depicting the rape of Europa hung on the walls. They moved gustily in the draughts which whistled through the window and along the floorboards and made the bull's muscled flanks ripple suggestively. A dozen or so candles flickered and were reflected in a number of mirrors.

Neither of the two occupants appeared to notice the state of the room; Sir Walter because he had never cared, his money had always gone on his drinking and his gambling and, in earlier years, his whoring; his daughter, Dorothea, because she had never known anything else.

Dorothea was now thirty and, in most people's eyes, a confirmed spinster. Her practical grasp of estate matters and her ability to run Selwood Priory for Sir Walter's benefit, made her far too useful for her father ever to have attempted to marry her off. Besides, he told himself, who would want her? She was thin, almost bony, with no figure to speak of, and had pale, washed-out hair and incongruously dark eyes. Some of the country people, misliking such an oddity, called her a witch.

She was dressed in an unbecoming grey woollen dress with an old shawl draped round her shoulders against the draught. Her hands, with long, delicate fingers, were clasped in her lap and she was staring thoughtfully into the fire.

'The *Maria* is yours, of course,' said Sir Walter, his voice slurred.

Dorothea had inherited her mother's

fortune of £7,000 which was supposed to have been safely invested for her in the Funds. Unfortunately, her father, the sole trustee, had used the money to commission the *Maria*, a cutter of 100 tons and twelve guns to be specially built in Mevagissey to enable him to indulge in smuggling more profitably. Provided his daughter got her income of £350 year, what did it matter what the money was in, he told himself? In fact, the cutter had cost only a thousand or so to build and fit out, but there was no record of what had happened to the rest of the money. Doubtless, it had gone into Sir Walter's pockets and supported his gambling or his game-cocks.

There was nothing Dorothea could do about it. If the *Maria* were ever captured she would be either sold or broken up and that would be the end of her inheritance. She could only pray that that did not happen.

'Otherwise, it all goes to the heir, damn him,' finished Sir Walter.

'What about Fanny and the children?' asked Dorothea, in a worried tone.

'Fanny has the two thousand I settled on her.'

Fanny Potter had been Dorothea's own governess until, after the death of Dorothea's mother, she had succumbed to Sir Walter's demands and become his mistress. Now there were two love children as well and they all lived — to the horror of the local gentry — in Selwood Priory with Dorothea and her father. What sort of provision was a hundred a year, for that was all Fanny's money would bring in? Horace, now seventeen, still needed educating and setting up in the world. Thirteen-year-old Sylvia's position was even worse; who would want an illegitimate wife, unless she had a dowry to offset so serious a disadvantage?

'And the children, Father! What about Horace and Sylvia?'

Sir Walter didn't answer. Fanny had long ceased to interest him. He had allowed her to stay simply as a means of repelling interested matchmakers from trying to find him another wife after the death of Dorothea's mother. Fanny's presence meant that no lady could possibly visit Selwood Priory. That this had isolated Dorothea from all but the most distant contact with the local gentry concerned him not at all.

Dorothea's thin fingers plucked the fringe on her shawl as she contemplated the future. The heir was an unknown cousin, the Reverend Veryan Selwood, currently holding a fellowship at New College, Oxford. Her father had only met him once and had come

4

back spitting, 'Prissy parson, ha!' and refused to have his name mentioned.

'Damned entail,' growled Sir Walter, turning restlessly in the bed. 'If it weren't for that I could have left the place to Horace.'

Dorothea held her peace. Sir Walter could perfectly well have married Fanny and Horace would have been legitimate. He had refused to do so.

Sir Walter found his daughter's silence as infuriating as any comment.

'Marry an unchaste female? I, a Selwood!'

'She was chaste until she met you,' Dorothea pointed out.

'She fell like a ripe plum.'

His companion bit her lip. What chance did poor Fanny, a governess on thirty pounds a year, have against her employer with his two thousand a year? Morally, of course, it was wrong. But Fanny had seen it as her one chance of escape from a dreary future and a destitute old age — who could blame her for that?

Dorothea had once dared to say something of the sort to Mrs Gunthorpe of Quilquin Hall and that lady had been duly horrified. 'Miss Potter should have left the moment she knew her virtue was threatened,' she had pronounced. 'I am sure I would have done all I could to have found her a position in a truly Christian household.'

Dorothea had looked sceptical.

'I am shocked that you, Dorothea, should so far have forgotten yourself as to condone such a lapse of virtue. Consider your own position at least. I cannot even visit you at the Priory whilst that female is there. Good heavens! My dearest Isabel might be forced to meet her.' Isabel was Mrs Gunthorpe's daughter.

Dorothea did not care for Isabel, finding her like her mother, priggish and censorious. On the whole she could not regret the Gunthorpes' absence. Unfortunately, this embargo did not extend to Bram Gunthorpe, Isabel's brother. Bram was Dorothea's own age, of dissolute habits and with a ruthless streak, who enjoyed nights of drunken debauchery with Sir Walter. So far as was possible, Dorothea tried to be absent whenever he came over. Her concern was further increased by his recent growing interest in Sylvia, who, at thirteen, was beginning to find a man of Bram's reputation dangerously intriguing.

One advantage of this unknown cousin in holy orders, thought Dorothea, was that he would surely not countenance Bram's visits.

Sir Walter had fallen into a doze. Dorothea

remained where she was, gazing into the fire, and considered her future. She could sell the *Maria* outright: there were many men, merchants in Plymouth or gentlemen from the surrounding estates, who would be only too glad to snap up a swift and reliable cutter. But financially she would lose heavily. If she got £1,000, including the goodwill, she would be doing well. And that would not help their dependents: the money brought in by the *Maria*'s activities contributed greatly to the local income.

She could hire out the ship. That way she would at least keep some control over things and ensure that local people benefitted. But that could be risky too. She had known and trusted the captain, Daniel Watson, all her life. What would happen to him if she hired out the *Maria*? And what would happen to Horace and Sylvia, for it was becoming plain that her father had procrastinated for too long: he had always meant to provide for Horace and Sylvia — when he had some spare money. That time would now never come.

With her father gone and this unknown cousin inheriting, what was left for her anyway? Veryan Selwood was a parson. He would probably not want Fanny and the children. Even if she herself were tolerated, how would she pass her days? Now she had an active life. She ran the estate, organized the household and cultivated the herbs in her herb garden, which was her pride and joy. With a new owner her presence would be, at best, endured.

Ahead of her stretched a narrowed future.

An apple log fell in the grate and sent a shower of greenish sparks up the chimney. Sir Walter woke up with a start.

'Thea?'

'I'm here, Father.'

'You'd better write to this damned parson. I want to see him.'

★ ★ ★

The Reverend Veryan Selwood, the object of Sir Walter's censure, had just celebrated his thirty-second birthday. He was a tall, very thin man (he often forgot to eat) who stooped. His fair hair flopped untidily over his collar and his blue-grey eyes peered out at the world from behind metal-rimmed spectacles.

Today, in this year of Our Lord 1808, he sat in his book-lined study in New College, Oxford. Outside, a sharp March wind was blowing, but inside it was warm and snug. The fire was lit and pleasantly warm, the

8

coal scuttle full. He only had to ring the bell for the scout to bring him tea or coffee. He could dine in hall with his fellow dons, enjoy a good meal, excellent port and agreeable intellectual conversation. In short, he led a chaste, blameless and unhurried life, and if some people thought it too boring and narrow for a healthy young man, all Veryan would say was that it suited him.

Veryan was escaping, as part of him well recognized, from a bleak childhood with an invalid mother and a brutal father. His life and his sanity had been saved by his nurse, Matty, who had given him love and support; she had encouraged his love of learning, had comforted him when he was ill and did her best to shelter him from his father's wrath. Mr Selwood thought his only son a milksop, a mother's boy, who should be whipped soundly and toughened up if he were ever to grow up into something his father recognized as a man.

'I shall never be the sort of man my father is, Matty,' Veryan had said when he was about eight. 'I don't really like killing things.'

'You'll be a fine man, Master Veryan,' replied Matty. 'You've a good heart and you think about other folks. I don't know what more makes a gentleman.' She would not directly criticize Mr Selwood to his son, but Veryan was an intelligent little boy; she hoped that he would understand her.

Veryan had thrown his arms around her neck and hugged her.

'There, there, my lamb,' said Matty. She kissed him briskly and added, 'Now, what about those verbs you were learning? Do you want me to hear you?'

It was Matty who wrote him weekly letters when he was sent away to Winchester at thirteen, but she and his mother had both died within months of each other when he was fifteen. In her last letter to him, Matty had written, 'Use your brains, Master Veryan. That is your way out.' The next three years at Winchester, having to bear his father's savagery and violence in the holidays, were, without doubt, the most hellish of Veryan's life. If it hadn't been for his godfather, Mr Marcham, who frequently invited him to stay, he did not know how he would have survived.

But he had taken Matty's advice. He had worked hard and gained one of the special Fellowships to New College, Oxford, which were reserved for Wykehamists. What vacations he took he spent with the Marchams and the only time he returned to his childhood home was to attend his father's funeral. There he learned, without surprise, that his father had been living on his capital for years and that there would be only a few hundred pounds left after all his debts had been cleared. Veryan arranged for Matty's grave to be given the sort of headstone he thought she would have liked and gave the rest of the money to the church, on the understanding that they looked after her grave. He then returned to Oxford.

As well as his fellowship of £200 a year, Veryan had inherited his mother's fortune of £6,000 and now lived a scholarly and reclusive life with enough money to finance his only extravagance, books.

His days were spent translating poems from the *Greek Anthology* into careful English verse. He was not so much interested in the verse as poetry, but in being able to capture, as far as was possible, the exact nuances of the Ancient Greek. He was currently at work on Meleager, and he saw no incongruity in his position as a Fellow of the college, in holy orders, translating a man whose poetry was blatantly erotic.

Whereas another don might be the subject of ribald comment at his choice of poet, Veryan was exempt from such mockery: it was perfectly obvious that in his case it was a purely intellectual pursuit.

11

On this particular afternoon he had a visitor, his friend Toby Marcham. Toby was the son of Veryan's godfather and one of the few people outside Oxford's cloistered world with whom Veryan kept in touch.

Toby, at twenty-five, was seven years younger than Veryan and of an outgoing temperament, but in spite of these differences they had always got on well, each regarding the other as the brother he had never had.

'You can't shut yourself up all the time in this stupid way,' Toby was saying. 'Come and stay. The pater's always asking when we'll see you.'

'I'm busy. I have a new monograph coming out,' said Veryan impatiently. He had a surprisingly deep, mellifluous voice, which seemed at odds with his ascetic appearance.

Toby waved away the monograph. 'But what about life?' he protested, looking, it must be said, with some complacency at his handsome reflection in his friend's mottled mirror over the mantelpiece. His carefully dishevelled brown hair and laughing grey eyes satisfied him, and he turned back to Veryan.

'I have the life I want here.'

'Life! What about getting out? Seeing the world? Women? Dammit, Veryan, you live like a monk. It's not healthy.' Toby's own

12

amorous adventures were many and usually ended in disaster, as Veryan well knew.

There was a knock at the door and the college boy appeared. 'A letter for you, Mr Selwood. One and fivepence it cost.'

Veryan took it gingerly and fumbled in his pocket for some change. He found nothing.

'Here.' Toby flicked a couple of shillings at the boy, who ducked his head in acknowledgement and left.

'I don't often get letters.' Veryan ran one hand in a worried way through his hair and turned the letter over. 'Whoever could be writing to me?' He had always disliked the unexpected. He sat down and reached for the paper-knife to break the seal.

The writing was in a firm hand and the spiky black ink seemed ominously insistent.

Dear Mr Selwood
My father, Sir Walter Selwood, has asked me to write. He wants you to come immediately to Selwood Priory which, as you know, will be yours when he dies, which cannot now be far off.

You are to take the Royal Cornish Mail to Torpoint, which leaves London from the Swan with Two Necks in Lad Lane. The Oxford to Southampton stagecoach goes through Whitchurch, and you should be

13

*able to pick up the Mail coach there.
Mr Hooper, who runs the King's Arms
in Torpoint, will be instructed to provide
you with a horse and guide for the rest of
your journey.*

*Please excuse the peremptory style. The
orders are my father's, not mine. Acquit
me of any discourtesy.*

*Yours etc.
D. Selwood*

Veryan adjusted his spectacles and pulled a
candle closer. He reread it carefully and then
handed the letter to Toby. Toby scanned
it.

'Congratulations, Veryan. An estate! A
good one, I hope?'

'I've no idea.'

Toby looked up. 'You are not serious?
This D. Selwood seems to think you know.
Who is she? I assume it's a female otherwise
the estate would be hers.'

'I don't know!' Veryan sank his head in
his hands. 'Honestly, Toby, I don't know.'
He sounded desperate. 'I met Sir Walter
once, about ten years ago now. An appalling
man — one of those loud, hard-drinking,
hard-gambling fellows.' He had reminded
Veryan, most unpleasantly, of his father.

14

He had gone to the Mitre to meet Slr
Walter and during the evening his host
had become drunker and drunker and, to
Veryan's extreme embarrassment, ended by
thrusting his hand up the barmaid's skirts
and pulling her onto his knee. Veryan could
not recall the girl's raucous squeals and
Sir Walter's red-faced laughter without a
shudder. He had left shortly afterwards,
pursued by Sir Walter's taunts.

'Milksop! Damned parson. You're a mealy-
mouthed Miss Molly. Couldn't get it up for
a woman if she were offered you on a plate,
I warrant.'

Veryan had never spoken of this episode
to anybody and had done his best to erase
Sir Walter from his mind.

'But you must have known you were to
inherit?'

'Yes. No. Sir Walter must have said
something, but I dismissed it. I didn't want
anything to do with him. He was a lecherous
old goat and I thought that he'd make sure
he had an heir. He didn't care any more for
me than I did for him.'

'But the estate, Veryan. Where is it?
How much is it worth? You must know
something!'

'I don't. Cornwall, I suppose. I really don't
know.'

Toby looked at him in affectionate exasperation. Veryan's obliviousness to his own material advantage was, no doubt, admirable, but, in Toby's opinion, hardly sane. 'You'll go, of course.'

Veryan frowned down at the letter. 'I cannot see why I should.'

'Veryan! This is a dying man's request.'

'Sir Walter can die perfectly well without me.' Veryan's mouth set in a stubborn line that Toby knew all too well. If pushed, he could be as obstinate as a mule.

Toby was silent for a moment. He remembered Veryan's father who had bullied and stormed at his only child; Veryan's sole defence had been silent rebellion. He had been shaken, beaten and kicked and still he said nothing; a wilful stubbornness that had driven his father to further blows. Veryan would not give in. No wonder the poor fellow had chosen this cloistered existence, thought Toby.

'Perhaps you're right,' he said lightly. 'Sir Walter is a tartar. If this Miss Selwood gets into trouble, too bad! Why should you humour her?'

Veryan's mouth relaxed. He smiled suddenly — an unexpectedly impish smile which crinkled the corners of his eyes and made him look much younger.

'Do you imagine that I'm taken in by this sudden about turn? You think I should go, don't you?'

Toby laughed and spread his hands. '*Touché*. But I'm not saying another word on the subject.'

'Damn you!'

★ ★ ★

Dorothea moved quietly round her herb garret and checked the parsley seedlings, which she had planted in trays a couple of weeks ago. They were now on a trestle table in front of a south facing window. Even in Cornwall, where the climate was mild, they could not go out yet awhile.

The garret was at the top of the old Priory gatehouse, one of the few buildings remaining from before the Dissolution, which was when a Tudor Selwood had got his hands on the property. He had 'lent' some money to King Henry, knowing full well that he would never see it again, but in due course he was rewarded with this small priory and the hand of an heiress who, so far as Dorothea could see, had been given little choice in the matter.

It was Lady Amicia who had taken over the old gatehouse and she had dried her herbs up here, just as Dorothea now did. Dorothea could understand why Lady Amicia had liked the room. It was a thirteenth century stone building which arched over the drive entrance. The windows were mullioned and let in a flood of light. The room was whitewashed and the roof beams had once been painted with a green and red pattern of flowers and leaves, still just discernible. They had hooks in them to hang dried herbs. The place smelt faintly and pleasantly astringent.

Oak shelves ran round the edge of the room and held Dorothea's stoneware jars for seeds and dried herbs. Other pots and bottles were for ointments and potions, for the herb garret was strictly utilitarian and Dorothea's salves and medicines much in demand. On the north side, facing the house, there was a marble shelf, a pair of scales with a brass tray, cast-iron weights, pestles and mortars of various sizes, chopping boards and a stone sink with a bucket underneath it.

Dorothea worked automatically, her mind partly on the herbs and partly on this unknown cousin. He was a very distant connection, she knew. The Selwoods were not a prolific family, at least, not where legitimate heirs were concerned. Sir Walter was the only surviving child and his father had had only the one brother. That hadn't stopped either of them making inroads into the local female population. Dorothea's grandfather, indeed, had exercised a sort of *droit de seigneur* on the estate and many local families bore the black eyes and aquiline noses of their Selwood inheritance.

Her hands moved busily, pricking out the parsley seedlings. The Reverend Veryan Selwood, what would he be like? Dorothea imagined an old man, wearing breeches and gaiters and with a parson's wideawake hat. But what would he do about Fanny and the children? Would he see the necessity of educating Horace properly, given his illegitimate status? And Sylvia? Would she be expected to become a governess in due course as her mother had been, slaving away for a paltry thirty pounds a year and subject to the same dishonourable intentions of the master of the house?

Father should have fulfilled his obligations, thought Dorothea, on a sudden spurt of anger. He should have made proper provision. It had only been at Dorothea's insistence that Horace had had any schooling worthy of the name. He attended a boarding-school in Exeter. Sylvia was educated at home by her mother.

Dorothea regarded her father with a

sort of weary tolerance. He was selfish and autocratic, but he was not vicious. Providing it didn't interfere with his comfort he allowed Dorothea her own way. Things were undoubtedly easier when she had taken over the running of the estate shortly after her seventeenth birthday. At least the servants knew that they would be paid. But Sir Walter's outgoings far exceeded his income, and the gap was bridged by smuggling — or free-trading, as Sir Walter preferred to call it.

What on earth would Mr Veryan Selwood have to say about that?

She gazed out of the window, a frown creasing her brow. The view from the mullion window was splendid, for there was the sea sparkling in the sun not a hundred yards away. To her right, she could just see the village of Porthgavern, with the higgledy-piggledy roofs of Delabole slate going down to the harbour. She scanned the horizon rapidly. Her cutter, the *Maria*, was due, though she would not venture in until nightfall. Then she would weigh anchor near the little cove almost opposite the gatehouse and unload the casks of brandy and geneva, the oilskin packets of lace and the bales of tobacco. There would be a handsome profit on the goods, and it was needed, for Sir

Walter liked to gamble and he currently owed Bram Gunthorpe 300 guineas. Money, thought Dorothea savagely, which could have gone towards making poor Fanny's position a little more secure.

A movement caught her eye. A young boy, aged about ten, was coming up the hill. Dorothea left her parsley and went down the spiral stone staircase.

'Diggory, what's the news?'

Diggory pulled off his cap. 'Father do say to tell 'ee the *Maria* be in this evening, Miss Thea.'

Dorothea nodded. 'Tell him, usual arrangements. And I want somebody to go over to Polperro. We don't want any trouble from there.' There was a Customs officers station at Polperro and they had a small Revenue cutter which would be only too pleased to take the *Maria* and her cargo. She looked at Diggory and smiled. 'Are you hungry?'

Diggory nodded.

Dorothea led the way upstairs to the herb garret. 'Don't touch! Here.' She reached inside one of the jars and handed him a couple of barley sugar twists.

'Thank'ee, Miss Thea.' He ducked his head at her and left. Dorothea watched him go. Diggory's father, Abel Watson, was one of Sir Walter's by-blows. Diggory had the

Selwood dark eyes and his dark hair stood up in tufts much as Horace's had done at his age. She sighed. She would have liked to have started a school in Porthgavern so that children like Diggory could have a better start in life, but her father was against it.

She locked the herb garret and went downstairs.

* * *

The stable block at Selwood Priory occupied what had once been one side of the cloisters. The Tudor builders had seen no reason not to use perfectly good stone and each loose-box had lintels of curiously carved columns and there was a broken bit of tympanum embedded in the wall above the saddle room. The stables were surprisingly well appointed, considering the dilapidated state of the Priory itself. There were five horses and Sylvia's pony in the various loose-boxes and several enclosures which contained Sir Walter's precious duckwing game, both the golden and silver varieties and his red-breasted black game, for he was a keen enthusiast of cockfighting and bred champions.

Horace, the elder of Fanny Potter's children, was in the end loose-box with his new three-year-old filly, Beauty. He had come back from his school in Exeter, partly because of the Easter holidays, but also because of his father's illness. Horace hoped he could stay away for good — beastly place, and the food was disgusting. The boys, of course, had found out that he was illegitimate and had ragged him unmercifully.

Horace was at that stage of gawky adolescence where he looked as though he had been stretched. He was now a gangly six foot and had the Selwood dark hair with his mother's hazel eyes. He was seventeen now, and he wanted to be out in the world. What was the use of fusty Latin verses or knowing the names of the Roman emperors?

Horace was not overburdened with intro-spection, but even he recognized that things were going to change. This unknown cousin would inherit all. A parson to boot!

'Horace?' It was Dorothea's voice. Horace poked his head out of the loose-box. Dorothea undid the half-door and stepped inside, closing it behind her. The filly whickered gently and pushed at her pocket where experience told her there might be an apple. Dorothea smiled, produced the apple, one of last year's windfalls, and stroked the silken flank.

'Father?' Horace put down the curry comb.

Dorothea shook her head. 'The *Maria*. Abel's sent word. She should come in this evening.'

Horace's eyes lit up. 'Good. Things have been damned flat recently.' Horace knew his father was dying and he was as sorry as he could be, but it all took such an age. Waiting around was never Horace's strong point. 'I like a bit of excitement.'

'Excitement is the last thing we need,' Dorothea said dampeningly. 'Father's in no case to oversee this and nothing must go wrong.'

'Don't fuss, Thea.'

'Smuggling is a capital offence, Horace. And I should remind you that Bram Gunthorpe is a Justice of the Peace.'

'Bram would never split on one of us!'

'You think not?' Dorothea's tone was sarcastic.

Horace laughed uneasily. 'Bram's up to his own neck in smuggling, Thea.'

'Do you imagine he would object to increasing his share once Father dies? Some feeling of chivalry towards the widow and orphans, perhaps?'

Horace shifted uncomfortably. 'He's a bad lot, I grant you. But there'd be an uproar if one of us was taken.'

'I'm not thinking of you, Horace; it's

24

people like Abel I worry about. You'd probably get off with a warning; Abel would hang or be pressed. Once anybody of ours was sent to the Quarter Assizes in Bodmin, what could be done? Bram could wash his hands of it. I don't like you being mixed up in this and I never have. You have courage, but you don't think before you act.'

'You have a damned cutting tongue, Thea,' said Horace resentfully.

'And need it,' snapped Dorothea.

Horace saw that she was seriously ruffled and set himself to reassure her. He'd be sensible, he promised. No tricks on excisemen, no quixotic acts.

Dorothea looked sceptical but said no more.

'What do you want me to do, Thea?' Horace gave the horse one last pat and opened the stable door for his sister.

'The usual. Customers warned of a shipment. Requirements noted. You'd better call on Mrs Pascoe, she mentioned she wanted some lace. Oh, and mention it to Josh if you see him. I daresay he knows already, but it's better to leave nothing to chance.' Josh was Sir Walter's groom and general factotum. He had been with Sir Walter since they were both boys and what Josh didn't know about Sir Walter's affairs was not worth knowing.

Horace grimaced. 'Boring stuff.'

Dorothea shrugged. 'Father gambles. He owes Bram three hundred guineas and it must be paid. God knows what this parson cousin of ours would do if he knew of this.'

'Lord, yes,' grinned Horace. 'I never thought of that. When's he coming?'

'I hope to God not before this shipment's safely out of the way,' said Dorothea with feeling. 'Take the cob, Horace. Less conspicuous. People might remember you on Beauty.'

She watched him go towards the saddle-room and went back to the house. She entered by the back door which gave onto a passage leading on one side to the scullery and the kitchen and on the other to the dairy. Noises from the scullery told her that Mrs Kellow, the cook-housekeeper, was there chivvying one of the housemaids.

Mrs Kellow had been with the family all her life and was now a cheerful, rosy woman well into her sixties, with wispy white hair and bright blue eyes. She wiped her hands on the apron when she saw Dorothea and nodded dismissal to the maid.

'The *Maria* be back then, Miss Thea?'

They discussed it with the ease of long

practice. Miss Potter would be given her nighttime chocolate with a teaspoonful of tincture of opium. Sylvia would be sent up to bed early.

If anything went wrong Mrs Kellow's good sense could be relied on. The secret cellar was kept clean. There would be fresh water and some bread in a stone crock and an oil lamp with a tinder-box. The straw mattresses must be taken out and shaken. Dorothea would see that there were bandages and enough laudanum to quieten anyone. Once, when Dorothea was a little girl, two men had been hidden there for four days while excisemen prowled round. On that occasion there had been no food and water and both men had been wounded. One of them had died. She had never forgotten it.

'Men!' said Mrs Kellow comfortably. 'They do 'ave no sense. 'Tis as well to be prepared.'

★ ★ ★

Later that afternoon Sir Walter was in a foul temper. 'When's that damned parson coming, Thea?' His voice was slurred and his cheeks more sunken than before.

'I don't know, Father. I wrote the evening you asked me and Josh got it to the Mail.'

'He should be here by now.' Sir Walter attempted to shout and was stopped by a coughing fit. Dorothea held a glass of brandy to his lips, mopped him up and settled him back against the pillows. 'I'm done for, Thea. But I want to see him before I slip my cable.'

There was silence. Then, 'The game-cocks. I want to see the game-cocks fight.' Dorothea said nothing. 'Now!' There was another prolonged coughing fit.

'The *Maria*'s due in tonight.' Dorothea spoke reluctantly. 'Everybody will be wanted at the cove.'

'You damned well tried to keep it from me,' rasped Sir Walter.

Dorothea opened her mouth and then shut it again. It was true that she had hoped to keep it from him until it was safely over.

'Where's Josh?' Sir Walter pulled himself up. 'Get Josh! Now, damn you. Can't leave all this to some half-witted woman.'

Dorothea compressed her lips.

★ ★ ★

Veryan spent two horrific nights on the road. The Royal Cornish Mail proved to be something of a misnomer — the landlord of the posting inn at Whitchurch professed

28

not to have heard of it. Finally, Veryan caught the Exeter Mail and managed to secure an illegal seat on the roof by dint of bribing the guard, an action which he hated and made him feel, if anything, even more resentful towards Sir Walter and this unknown cousin. Then it rained. Not a downpour, but a steady drizzle which gradually soaked though Veryan's greatcoat, the drips from his hat trickling down his neck. By the time they reached Exeter, Veryan was cold, wet, miserable and thoroughly fed up.

At Exeter he found the Royal Cornish Mail, which he discovered terminated there. The proprietors were thinking of extending its route, he was told, but there wasn't much call for it at this time of year. So much for Miss Selwood's information, thought Veryan savagely.

He spent an uncomfortable night at Foote's Hotel in Exeter. Veryan was unused to sleeping in inns and the landlord, spotting a greenhorn, promptly put him in a poky room, with damp sheets and a smoking chimney. The room overlooked the stableyard and Veryan's sleep was constantly broken as coaches arrived and departed. When he did sleep he dreamt he was reliving the jolting and rattling of the previous day's journey. His temper was not improved the following morning by the boot boy refusing to clean his boots.

'Boots go outside your door at night,' the boot boy told him. 'It ain't my place to clean boots now. Besides, I'm wanted in the tap room.' He waited hopefully, clinking the change in his trouser pocket, but Veryan was oblivious to hints and dismissed him. The boot boy shrugged and slouched off.

But the new day brightened up and the scenery was interesting. The road skirted Dartmoor and to his right Veryan glimpsed the forbidding moors with their menacing stone tors and every now and then a small herd of shaggy Dartmoor ponies. To his left, the countryside seemed kinder and more fertile. There were cider orchards and everywhere astonishingly red earth. His spirits began to rise. If this was like Cornwall, he thought, perhaps it wouldn't be so bad.

Cornwall, when it came, was a shock. At Plymouth, the horses were unharnessed and the coach pulled onto the Torpoint ferry and made stable with chocks. Fresh horses would be waiting at the other side. Veryan and the other passengers were glad to get out and stretch their legs. Veryan stood by the gunwales and watched the water slide out from under the bows. The tide was on the turn and Veryan could see the ferrymen straining at the oars. Ahead lay Cornwall.

It was not the sunny red-earthed uplands of Devon. No, Veryan realized with a shiver, this was an older, alien land. The soil was different, the landscape had none of the softness he had left behind. Crossing the Tamar was like going to a foreign country.

The very weather was changing and heavy cloud was rolling in from the west. A few spots of rain began to fall on the deck. He should never have come. This country did not mean him well. He should have stayed away. He stared apprehensively at the sullen country ahead.

' 'Ee be new to this part of the world, then?'

Veryan turned round. The coachman was standing behind him and nodded at the approaching harbour.

'Yes.' Veryan pulled himself together. 'My mother came from this part of the world, but I have never visited it before.'

' 'Ee got family hereabouts, then?' The coachman seemed determined to be friendly.

'Sir Walter Selwood,' said Veryan reluctantly.

The coachman whistled. ' 'Ee be mortal bad, I hear.'

Was this a moral or a physical statement, Veryan wondered? 'I'm on my way there.'

'Everyone do know Sir Walter,' said

the coachman. ''E'm got quite a name hereabouts.' Again the tone was ambiguous.

What's that supposed to mean, thought Veryan irritated. He turned away and fixed his gaze on the fast-approaching shore.

★ ★ ★

Ten o'clock on a chilly March night and the small rocky inlet of Morvoren Cove was full of men. They had arrived by twos and threes and each gone to his appointed task. Two had taken a small boat out to Morvoren Rock and were sitting there with a lantern at the ready. Others had swept the beach clear of seaweed and piled it carefully to one side to be used later to cover their traces. A number of galleys, long narrow rowing-boats, were pulled up on the beach. These would transfer the contraband from the cutter to the shore. They were extremely fast and could outmanoeuvre any sailing boat. There was the occasional soft whinny from a string of mules and Goonhilly ponies, each one bearing a wooden pack saddle with crooks.

Josh, a thickset man of well over sixty, with grizzled hair and wearing stout leather boots, was making a mental note of who was there, for they would all have to be paid when the night's work was done. Every now and then he glanced out to sea. There was a thin sliver of moon, and it was windy. Smuggling was best carried out on dark nights: the two men on Morvoren Rock would light the dark lantern, which was so shaded that it cast a light only out to sea and was not visible from land. Daniel Watson, the captain of the *Maria*, would weigh anchor as close to Morvoren Rock as was safe and prepare to transfer their cargo to the galleys. But the *Maria*'s sails would be only half furled and she would be ready to sail at a moment's notice. Daniel would take no chances.

Dorothea, wearing a dark dress and her head covered with a grey woolen shawl, came down the path behind the cove. Josh looked up.

'Be 'ee ready, Miss Thea?'

She nodded. The goods would be stored in the crypt underneath the gatehouse. It ran under the drive and the entrance was through an arched door in the side of the building, a wall which had long been covered with carefully cultivated ivy.

'Where be Master Horace?'

Dorothea found herself going cold suddenly. 'I thought he was with you.'

''E said 'e be going to give 'ee a hand.'

Dorothea clenched her hands. 'Oh the damn fool!'

''E'm gone with Abel over Polperro.' Josh knew that Abel had plans for the Polperro Revenue cutter if it should think of trying to stop and board the *Maria*. 'Don't 'ee fret, Miss Thea,' he said unconvincingly, 'Abel'll see that 'e don't come to harm.'

'If I were Abel I'd drop him in the nearest creek,' snapped Dorothea.

But there was no time for more. Out on Morvoren Rock a tiny light flashed briefly in their direction. The *Maria* had arrived. The men ran to the galleys, pushed them out and jumped in. Straining her eyes in the darkness Dorothea could just make out the bulk of the cutter.

In spite of herself, she was caught up in the excitement of the moment. Immediately all was bustle. In a surprisingly short time the galleys returned and ankers and half-ankers of brandy and geneva landed, bales of lace, tobacco and tea were thrown onto the shore and then the galleys went back for more. Speed was essential. The casks were swiftly rolled along the sand and loaded onto the patient animals. Immediately a group of six animals were loaded they set off.

Dorothea saw Diggory, knee deep in the water, struggling with bales of tobacco and oilskin parcels of precious lace. He waved. Dorothea raised her hand briefly and then turned to the pack-animals. Her job was to see the goods safely bestowed. If anything happened, she must see that as much as possible was hidden.

'Ready, Miss Thea?' It was Michael Cross, a small, balding man with several teeth missing where he had lost an argument with an excise officer. He was Abel Watson's half-brother, though they had never got on and seldom talked. Dorothea had seen him earlier, raking the seaweed.

She nodded and they set off. Over her shoulder she could see other ponies ready to follow them.

'Is my young brother with Abel, Michael?'

Michael glanced at her uneasily. Earlier, Abel had gone over to Polperro to keep an eye on the movements of the excisemen. He had plans for a decoy if they should have got wind of the landing. Michael didn't know the details.

'Don't 'ee fret about Master Horace, miss,' he said reassuringly, ''e'm be brave as a lion. Just like 'is father, I reckon.'

'And with half his sense,' retorted Dorothea. But she smiled.

They reached the gatehouse by the little cliff path and Dorothea went forward to open the ivy-clad door. She would stay here now, directing the men to store the casks carefully, for this was a big consignment and all the space would be needed.

There was a brief lull after the first dozen or so ponies and mules had been unloaded and Dorothea busied herself pushing the casks as close together as possible and putting the bales of tobacco and the lace on the shelves. This lot should pay off Bram, she thought. She went to the door and glanced down the cliff path. Another string of ponies was coming up now, but it would be a few minutes before they reached her.

She took the gatehouse key from her pocket and went up to her herb garret. There was only a thin crescent moon, but it was a clear starry night and in the room the light shone cold and silver and the jars on the shelves threw inky shadows on the walls. The early evening clouds had vanished and it was too bright for safety. She crossed to the window. She could not see down to the cove, for the angle was too steep, but she could see out to sea. And there, on the horizon, was the smudged shape of . . . It was still a long way off, but could it be the Revenue cutter?

She ran down the stairs and beckoned to Michael who was returning with another load.

'Tell your men to unload as quickly as possible. Come with me, Michael.'

He followed her up the stairs and to the window. She pointed. 'The Polperro Revenue cutter?'

Michael tugged at his ear and shook his head. 'Wrong size. Anyway, she be too far out. Don't 'ee fret, Miss Thea.' He avoided her gaze and cleared his throat once or twice.

Michael left and Dorothea stood there for a moment. Something was not quite right, but she couldn't place it. Michael was plainly uneasy. Worried, she went out of the garret and up a further flight of steps onto the leads. Yes, there was a cutter of some sort and she was heading towards them.

Dorothea ran downstairs to the crypt. Young Diggory had just come up leading a string of Goonhilly ponies. He grinned at Dorothea, plainly delighted to be allowed in on the evening's activities.

'Diggory,' said Dorothea swiftly. 'Run down and tell Josh there's a cutter out to sea. At about two o'clock. She's coming this way. Oh, and if Josh tells you to go home and stay out of trouble, you're to do as he says, do you hear?'

Diggory made a face but nodded.

Work was proceeding swiftly down at the cove. Most of the casks were now unloaded and the small beach was full of bales and packets. Josh was directing operations, every now and then glancing out to sea. It all looked safe, but one could never be sure. Then a light flashed in their direction. It was one of the men on the Morvoren Rock. He had climbed to the top and raked the horizon with a telescope and must have seen the same boat and flashed a warning. The two men could be seen scrambling down the rock and into their boat. The *Maria* had seen them too, for there was a sudden frenzy of activity; the anchor was dragged up, ropes pulled, sails lifted.

On shore, the stuff had to be got to a safe hiding-place as soon as possible. The ponies and mules were swiftly loaded up and the men took the remaining bales.

'Diggory! Get that there seaweed raked out. And look sharpish!' Josh issued orders fast.

The men from Morvoren Rock were now heading back towards Porthgavern. Josh ran up the cliff path and scanned the horizon from the top. It was the Polperro Revenue cutter all right. Someone, thought Josh savagely, had tipped them off. The *Maria* was slowly getting away. Once her speed was up she could outpace any cutter, but would she get up enough speed before the cutter was upon her? Fortunately, she was now clear of contraband. She might be suspected, but nothing could be proved.

A warning shot rang out and fell some thirty yards short of the *Maria*. Too damn close, thought Josh. But there was nothing he could do. He ran back down to the cove. His job was to see that the place was clear and the goods safely bestowed.

Diggory and another couple of lads had finished rearranging the seaweed. Josh took the brooms.

'All right, lads, that's it. Best get home. Diggory, I be wanting to see your dad in the morning.'

The last of the ponies had gone up the cliff path. Josh followed, vigorously sweeping any droppings into the gully. In the cellar, Dorothea was organizing the unloading. The place was almost full and the men worked swiftly. She looked up as Josh came in.

'Was that a shot?'

Josh explained, 'There be nothing we can do for the *Maria*. I just pray she'm not impounded on suspicion.' It would be a serious capital loss as they both knew. Out to sea came more shots, much closer this time. The ponies and mules, unloaded now, were being trotted away into the surrounding moors. They would be dropped off in their various owners' stables and no one would

39

be a penny the wiser. If anyone did chance to meet them, most folk would know better than to ask questions.

' 'Tis done, miss.' Michael Cross came over. His face was strained.

Dorothea locked the door and rearranged the ivy. 'We could go up to the roof of the gatehouse,' she offered. 'We could see what's happening. Do you want to come, Michael?'

She unlocked the gatehouse door and climbed past the herb garret, up a second flight to the leads. Josh's telescope raked the sea. It was too damn bright, he thought. There, a few hundred yards off shore was the *Maria*; she was gathering speed, but not fast enough. The Revenue cutter was plainly visible now and, as they stood, a couple more bursts of fire flared in the dark. The *Maria* would never be able to get away.

Then, suddenly, as if from nowhere, a small fishing-boat appeared, tacking to and fro over the waves, apparently oblivious to the cutter. Any one with half an eye could see that she was 'creeping', that is trying to raise a previously sunk cargo with grappling hooks.

'Oh my God,' breathed Dorothea. She glanced at Michael whose knuckles were white as he grasped the edge of the coping.

Dorothea did not need to be told that this was Abel's boat and, in all probability, Horace was on board.

The cutter swung round and again came the crack of gunfire. The fishing-boat seemed suddenly to have realized the danger and there was much frantic movement as she slowly pulled round. The *Maria* was well under way now. The cutter hesitated and then decided to pursue the fishing-boat. Josh handed Dorothea the telescope. She adjusted it and looked. There were three men on board the fishing-boat: Abel's stocky form was easy to spot; the second man was probably Tim Wilcox, the blacksmith, and the third was Horace.

The fishing-boat had turned and was now heading back towards Porthgavern. A warning shot landed within a few yards of her stern. The boat was stopping. She would be boarded by the Revenue men and held on suspicion of smuggling . . . Dorothea couldn't bear to watch.

2

Veryan spent his first night in Cornwall at the King's Arms in Torpoint. It was pleasantly welcoming with a glowing fire in the public room and clean sand on the floor. The tables were of well-scrubbed oak and there was a general air of prosperity about the place. Behind the bar, Mrs Hooper, the landlady, rinsed some tankards and hung them up on brass hooks above her head. Her ample bosom was rigidly corseted and she wore a stiffly starched apron. She appeared to be the sort of woman who would stand no nonsense. She looked up as Veryan entered.

'I am Mr Selwood.' Veryan assumed an authority he did not altogether feel. 'I believe I am expected.'

The landlady gave him a slow up-and-down stare. It was a look which she had perfected over a lifetime of raucous Saturday nights and it had made many a man behave himself and helped give the King's Arms its reputation for being a decent sort of place. 'Mr Selwood?' She turned her head to someone in the back room. 'Husband! Somebody who calls hisself Mr Selwood.'

Damned suspicious lot, thought Veryan. The pleasant glow initiated by the fire vanished. He reached into his breast pocket and produced his card case. The landlady took the card gingerly by one corner and handed it to her husband.

The Reverend Veryan Selwood, read the legend. Mr Hooper looked at it carefully, then threw back his head with a loud guffaw. 'He'm a parson! A Selwood, a parson! Oh, my eye!'

Veryan's lips became a thin line of displeasure. He resented being greeted like a cross between a criminal and a comic turn. He'd do his duty by Sir Walter, but when the estate came to him he'd hand the whole thing over to an agent to run. He certainly didn't want to live in this benighted part of the world.

'When you've finished,' he said icily, 'would you be so good as to show me to a room? I shall not be travelling any more today.'

Mr Hooper's laugh died. 'Sorry, sir. But our orders be to provide you with a horse and guide at once.'

Veryan's mouth took on an obstinate line. 'I am not moving another yard today.'

The Hoopers exchanged worried glances. 'But Sir Walter . . . '

'Sir Walter may order you, but he has no control over me. If you cannot provide me with a decent room I shall go to the Ferry House Inn.'

A few minutes later, his boots off and borne away by the boot boy for cleaning, a decanter of excellent brandy on the bedside table, Veryan lay on the oak half-tester, his hands behind his head, and contemplated the ceiling. The room was a great improvement on the inn in Exeter. There was a modern sash window, sprigged wallpaper on the walls and a blue and white ewer and bowl on the washstand in the corner. Mrs Hooper was now attentive and obliging. She had offered to take his greatcoat, promising to remove the mud splashes.

Veryan's spirits rose. He should have asserted himself more in Exeter, he now saw.

Later that evening, having sent up the mackerel, boiled potatoes and spinach of their guest's choice, and Mrs Hooper's marmalade tartlets and the cheese-board with a barrel of biscuits, Mrs Hooper turned to her husband.

'You shouldn't laugh at'm. 'E did take it badly.'

'A Selwood, a parson!' Mr Hooper gave another stifled guffaw.

''E do seem very unworldly-like,' said his wife. ''E were asking what to do about 'is boots! 'Ee'd think 'e 'adn't left home before.'

'Gunthorpe'll make mincemeat of 'e.'

'Oh, I do 'ope not. Mr Selwood be a gentleman. 'Ee can see that.'

Hooper grunted. 'Us don't need fine English gentlemen. Foreigners!'

''E be a Selwood,' his wife reminded him.

'A Selwood? 'E bain't like no Selwood I've ever known! Well, blood will out and us'll see.'

'I hope somebody'll warn 'm agin Gunthorpe, though,' said Mrs Hooper soberly.

★ ★ ★

Just off the new coaching road that led from Torpoint to Liskeard there stood a small tumbledown bothy. During the summer it was sometimes used by shepherds during shearing, but now, on this chill March evening, a lone man occupied it. He was plainly waiting for somebody, for every now and then he went to the door and looked out into the darkness, listening intently to the night sounds. Although there was a lantern by his side, it was not lit; he seemed content to sit in the dark.

Bram Gunthorpe, for it was he, was a tall thickset man, dangerously close to running to fat, with strong, rather fleshy features and a bullet head set on a bull-like neck. His hair was fair and close-cropped and his eyes a cold blue. There was a certain aura of danger about Bram which made some ladies agreeably flustered — a fact Bram was well aware of and used to his advantage.

His mother had always doted on him and, as his father had died when he was only eleven, Bram had been allowed, even encouraged, to be the man of the house. Mrs Gunthorpe had refused to send him away to school, which might have knocked some sense into him. He was an indulged only son with far more power than was good for him. None of this would have mattered with a sweeter-natured child, but Bram had always had a brutal streak.

The nearest male who might have checked him was Sir Walter Selwood, but Sir Walter had only laughed at Bram's youthful excesses and encouraged his debauchery rather than otherwise. Selwood liked to show off his own hard head and to boast of his amatory conquests to an admiring younger follower and applauded Bram's experiments with the bottle and the serving maids up at Quilquin Hall.

'Get 'em on their backs, boy,' advised Sir Walter. 'That's the only suitable position for women.'

Nevertheless, for all his boasting, Sir Walter was a man with a heart. It never stopped him seducing the village girls, but he always gave them money for their babies and he could be relied on to support his illegitimate offspring and, when they grew up, to help with a loan for a fishing-boat or provide a dowry for a girl wanting to get married. He assumed that Bram would do the same.

Bram did no such thing. When Mary Pengelly, a 14-year-old housemaid up at Quilquin Hall became pregnant, she was turned out by an outraged Mrs Gunthorpe. Bram only shrugged: Mary was getting to be a bore anyway. The girl hanged herself. Sir Walter was genuinely shocked, but, by then, it was too late. Bram knew that he was feared and relished it. Prudent mothers avoided sending their daughters to work at the Hall.

Mrs Gunthorpe realized too late that she had reared a man who would stop at nothing to get his own way. Her dowry of £8,000 had been settled on her on her marriage and, in due course, the money would go to Isabel, but increasingly Bram was demanding 'loans' from the income it provided and he was not above using violence if he did not get them.

What Bram wanted was greater control of the lucrative smuggling in the area, but his estate was inland and had no direct access to the sea, which made things difficult. He was part owner of a small smuggling lugger in Cawsand, but a fifth share could not begin to satisfy Bram's urgent need for money. He had tried to entangle Sir Walter in gaming debts with the aim of forcing him to sell him some land with a harbour, but his opponent was too wily for that.

Recently, Bram had interested himself in the Polperro Revenue cutter — if the excisemen could remove the *Maria* in the course of their job, that would deal the Selwood smuggling a blow from which it might not recover. He would have to play a very careful game indeed and keep himself removed from any direct action, for no Cornishman would forgive treachery by one of their own. The excisemen were not local: no local man would dream of betraying another Cornishman to them — unless he were blackmailed to do so. And lately, in his capacity as Justice of the Peace, Bram had saved a local man from transportation . . .

A twig snapped outside. Bram went cautiously to the door. He could see nothing.

Then came the faint cry of a nightjar, '*cu-ic, cu-ic*'. Bram made an answering call. A few moments more and a figure appeared.

'Well?' Bram demanded abruptly.

'I be sorry, sir. It didn't work.' The newcomer was plainly nervous of Bram and spoke reluctantly.

'Why not? Didn't they see the *Maria*?'

'They been decoyed. Some fishing-boat were nearby. They thought she were 'creeping' but it turned out she were picking up lobster pots.' The man spoke in a low voice and kept looking over his shoulder nervously.

'Lobster pots at Morvoren Cove! They must be greenhorns to believe that. Damn them! What's the use of sending coastguards down from Sussex? They need local men who know the coast.'

The other was silent. No local man would take on such a job, only a wretch like himself who was under Gunthorpe's thumb. He wished he'd had the courage to hang himself like poor Mary.

'Who was in the boat?'

'The boat?'

'Yes, damn you.' Bram's fingers were round the man's throat. 'Who was in that fishing-boat?'

'I . . . I didn't see, sir.'

'Didn't see?' Bram was squeezing tighter.

'Come now, I cannot believe that.'

The face was turning purple; a choking sound gargled in his throat. Bram flung him to the ground. It was some minutes before the man could speak. 'Abel, and Tim Wilcox and a lad.' The names were barely whispered.

'What lad?'

'A local lad.'

Bram picked him up roughly and hit him hard on the jaw.

'It were Master Horace, sir. But 'e be only a bit of a boy.'

'Horace,' repeated Bram, in a voice that made the man on the ground shiver. 'All right, you've squealed like the coward you are. Now get out.'

When he'd gone, Bram stayed on in the dark, thinking.

Quilquin Hall was not a particularly wealthy estate, though a gentleman of quiet habits and modest ambition could live very happily on its £1,200 a year. But Bram was neither quiet nor modest in his ambitions.

Several times a year he went up to London and had a month or so on the town. At first he was lucky and managed to win more than he lost, but last time he'd visited a new, fashionable gaming-hell in King Street and had lost heavily, scattering IOUs like confetti.

Even after bullying his mother and squeezing his tenants, he still owed 900 guineas.

A lucky evening with Sir Walter had netted him 300 guineas. But then Sir Walter had fallen ill and, so far, Bram hadn't seen his winnings. He had no compunction about threatening anybody who owed him money, but even he couldn't threaten Sir Walter on his deathbed.

An attempt to cajole Horace into playing with him had failed. Horace had refused, and in such a way that Bram was left in no doubt that Horace suspected him of cheating. Master Horace, thought Bram, was getting too cocky. He needed to be taught a lesson.

Bram had even considered marrying Dorothea, but that would be a last resort. She was like a dried old stick, he thought sourly, and the only use he would have for her was her £7,000. (If he had guessed what Sir Walter had done with his daughter's inheritance, he would have been more enthusiastic.) Dorothea had always treated him with courtesy, but somehow, her disapproval was quite plain and those black eyes of hers could be uncomfortably disdainful. Bram dismissed her from his mind and turned to pleasanter things.

There was that delicious little nymph

Sylvia, for example, just beginning to unfurl her petals and given to blushing whenever he spoke to her. Bram indulged himself in a satisfying fantasy of a submissive Sylvia — he preferred his sex violent, that way he knew he was in control — but reluctantly pushed it away. He had no scruples about taking a 13-year-old girl, but she was openly acknowledged by Sir Walter and was, by upbringing at least, a lady. She wasn't accessible enough. Yet.

But Sir Walter was dying and that meant change. Change meant new possibilities. There would be a vacuum created by Selwood's death both in the smuggling and in access to Sylvia. He would go over tomorrow, he decided, pay his respects and see how the land lay.

For the moment he would have to contain himself with whatever patience he could muster.

* * *

Fanny Potter, a pleasantly rounded woman in her late forties, was sitting in the drawing-room with Dorothea. She was tearful and anxious about the future. Twenty years ago her plumpness had attracted Sir Walter, who liked curves on a woman, and Fanny's soft hazel eyes and becoming blushes had all played their part in egging him on. At the time, Fanny had been conscious only of a sort of fluster whenever she met Sir Walter.

Lady Selwood, Dorothea's mother, was dying and Fanny was fully occupied with trying to make her last days comfortable, teaching Dorothea and, during her scanty leisure, worrying about what she should do when Lady Selwood died. How proper would it be for her to remain in a widower's household?

In the event Sir Walter decided things for her. If Fanny deceived herself into thinking that Sir Walter would propose when his year of mourning was over, she had only herself to blame, as Sir Walter pointed out: he had never promised her anything beyond a settlement of £2,000. By the time she had recognized that marriage was highly unlikely, it was too late and she was carrying Horace.

'I should not have allowed it,' she wept. 'But I so wanted a home and children . . . '

'I don't suppose Father gave you much choice,' observed Dorothea. She had been only ten when her mother had died, but even she had noticed her father's gallantry towards her governess. For one thing, he came into the schoolroom, something he'd never done before; he took Miss Potter out riding and she'd return flushed and smiling.

'I wonder you don't despise me,' wept Fanny.

'Nonsense,' said Dorothea. 'You saved me from a lonely childhood. I was delighted when I knew you were going to stay.'

'But you were only ten, dear. Too young to know how wicked I was.'

'Come, Fanny. This is morbid.' Dorothea had never begrudged Fanny her modicum of happiness. She had had a far more comfortable life than she could ever have hoped for as a governess. Doubtless she had paid for it when Sir Walter gradually lost interest in her and returned to pursuing other women. 'It takes two, you know. Father should have married you, I've often thought so. Then we wouldn't have all this fuss over this parson cousin.'

'Oh dear.' Fanny dabbed at her eyes with a corner of her cambric handkerchief. 'In holy orders! He must dislike my situation and I'm sure I cannot blame him.'

'Your situation is nothing to do with him, and so I shall tell him,' stated Dorothea. She was determined to put Mr Selwood in his place if he attempted any holier-than-thou attitude.

'You must be conciliatory, Thea,' begged Miss Potter. 'I'm sure I do not know where we shall go if we are turned out.'

'You won't be turned out! Anyway, where is the man? He should have been here a day or so ago.' It was just as well he hadn't come earlier, in view of the arrival of the *Maria*, but that didn't stop her resenting Mr Selwood's non-appearance.

The door opened and Sylvia bounced in. She was a pretty girl with curly, nut-brown hair and hazel eyes and she was growing fast in all directions. She wore a blue, high-necked round gown in a soft wool and her wrists were shooting out of the sleeves. The hem had plainly been let down once already for the old hemline was disguised by velvet ruching. Her slight breasts strained at the bodice.

Dorothea looked up. 'Close the door please, Sylvia.'

Sylvia raised her eyes to the ceiling and pushed half-heartedly at the door with her foot.

'Properly.'

'Oh all right.' The door was banged shut and Sylvia flounced onto the window seat and began biting her nails.

Dorothea glanced across at her but said nothing. Fanny, not so wise, said, 'Sylvia, darling, a lady doesn't bite her nails.'

Sylvia tossed her brown curls. 'I'm not a lady, am I?'

'Of course you're a lady,' said her mother. 'You're a gentleman's daughter.'

'Huh!' retorted Sylvia. 'So's Martha, come to that.' Martha was one of Sir Walter's by-blows whose mother cleaned pilchards in Porthgavern: Sir Walter was nothing if not eclectic in his choice of conquests.

Fanny gave a moan of distress and Sylvia tossed her head again and turned to look out of the window. A bullish figure in a bottle-green riding coat was riding up the drive. He had a whip in one hand and every now and then he flicked it irritably at the horse's rump. The horse's bit was covered in lather. The man wore his top hat at a slightly rakish angle and, as he approached, he happened to glance upwards and saw Sylvia. Immediately he raised his hat and bowed. Sylvia giggled, jumped down and went to the door. 'It's Mr Gunthorpe,' she said happily, and disappeared.

Fanny and Dorothea looked at each other. Dorothea rose. 'I daresay he wants to see Father,' she said. 'I'll go. Don't worry, Fanny, if Sylvia's there I'll stay with them.'

'Oh dear,' said Fanny inadequately.

Dorothea made a face. 'Who was it

wrote about trouble coming in battalions? Shakespeare?' She left.

Fanny sighed and picked up her discarded sewing. Try as she might she could not be at ease with Mr Gunthorpe. He always spoke courteously enough, but there was something in his tone, a touch of insolence, that Fanny had no way of countering. A stronger woman would have faced him down, but Fanny could only feel awkward.

Now he had bewitched Sylvia. There were no slammed doors and nail-biting when Bram Gunthorpe was around. Sylvia was all giggles and admiring glances. But there was something in Mr Gunthorpe's look which made Fanny profoundly uneasy for her daughter.

She folded up her sewing and rose. Mr Gunthorpe would have to be offered luncheon. She would go and speak to Mrs Kellow about it.

★ ★ ★

Veryan arrived at Selwood Priory at about six o'clock that evening, just as the sun was sinking in the west. The guide provided by Mr Hooper was a surly fellow who said very little, only occasionally spitting into the hedge. The horse was a steady plodder and shambled along on knocked knees. Veryan's travelling portmanteau was strapped onto a pillion behind his saddle. Veryan rarely rode in Oxford, though he had ridden as a child, and he soon found himself sore and aching from using unaccustomed muscles. A fine drizzle did not improve matters and the countryside looked bleak and grey.

He was astonished to see oxen ploughing the fields; in Oxfordshire they had long been superseded by the horse. It confirmed him in his view that the place was primitive beyond belief. He wished he'd never come.

They passed through the tumbledown village of Sheviock, all mangy dogs and decaying thatch, and turned off the coach road down a mule track and along by the sea. Veryan had not expected the sea to be so close and he looked warily at the track which ran only twenty yards or so from the edge. It was windswept up here and the drizzle began to harden into rain. Some thorn bushes, bent almost double against the prevailing wind, crouched over the road. A few blackthorns, their bare branches sprinkled with white flowers, provided a welcome touch of spring to come, but Veryan was in no mood to appreciate it.

He composed a stinging Latin couplet in his head about the horrors of this God-forsaken place, but even that did not cheer him up.

Eventually, the guide turned off down another bridle path that led to Porthgavern and jerked his head in the direction of Selwood Priory, whose chimneys could just be seen. Veryan pulled up his horse in amazement. But the place was huge, was his first incoherent thought; what seemed like an acre of twisting chimneys rose up in front of the old elm trees which lay at the back of the Priory. The guide grunted, nodded to the left and turned up the road to the gatehouse, the horses clopping over the ankers and half-ankers hidden in the crypt beneath their unsuspecting hooves.

Veryan looked up. Good God, a mediæval gatehouse! Perpendicular? No, earlier, surely? It reminded him of Oxford. They passed under the gatehouse and on up the drive. The house which now appeared was undoubtedly Tudor and, in the fading light of day, the stone looked warm. The Priory appeared to have been thrown together. What had once been the refectory was still recognisably there, and though some attempt had been made to secularize the front door, it still looked startlingly like the entrance to a priory, even

59

though the saints were long gone from their niches.

Veryan dismounted stiffly and the guide went to tug at the bell-chain. The place seemed deserted. There were no lights. Veryan could hear the bell clanging somewhere in the interior. Eventually a flustered Mrs Kellow arrived.

'Oh, Mr Selwood! Pray come in.' She turned her head. 'Jack! Do 'ee take Mr Selwood's luggage up to 'is room.' She turned to the guide. 'There be food and ale for 'ee round the back.' She nodded dismissal. The guide took the bridles of both horses and left.

Veryan removed his hat and stepped inside. He found himself in an arched hall hung with threadbare banners from long dead Selwoods and lit only by a couple of smoky candles. Mrs Kellow held a small lantern. She led him up an oak staircase with deeply worn treads and showed him to his room, lighting a branch of candles on the mantelpiece. 'I'll tell Sir Walter you be here, sir. And I'll send Jack up with some hot water.' She curtseyed and left.

Veryan looked round at the faded grandeur. Everything had seen better days. The brocade curtains were frayed, the ceiling darkened in places with candlesmoke. And yet, the taciturn guide had told him that the estate was a good one and worth some two thousand a year. Surely Sir Walter could afford to live more comfortably on that? So what had he done with his money?

He was soon to find out.

Sir Walter greeted the news of Veryan's arrival with irritation. 'He took his time, didn't he? Thea, ring the bell. Ask Mrs Kellow to send the fellow in.'

Dorothea moved quietly to the bell-pull, tugged it and then returned to her seat on the far side of the bed.

'Josh.' Sir Walter turned back to the matter in hand. 'Let's see how the golden duckwing performs. Now, there's a bird. Just look at how straight his keel is!' Josh and Ozzie, who helped Josh in the stables, were busily preparing a cockfight for Sir Walter's delectation. One of the large looking-glasses had been so positioned on the floor that it would reflect the fight without Sir Walter having to move from his position on the bed.

Josh handed the golden duckwing to Ozzie, who held it carefully, clasping its beak gently with one hand, the other making sure that the razor-sharp cockspurs were well away from his arm. Josh took out a second bird from another sack, this time a silver duckwing.

'Beautiful, this one be. Look at his good round bone, sir. My money be on 'im.' He tucked the second bird carefully under his arm and nodded to Ozzie.

Carefully, at the same time, they put both birds down on the Persian carpet by Sir Walter's bed, held them beaks touching and then let go.

The two game-cocks eyed each other, then one suddenly lunged, his sharp beak scoring the side of the second. Instantly the birds were fighting, the spurs gouging at their opponents, blood and feathers flying. The three men leant forward and became absorbed in the fight.

Veryan, guided to the room by Mrs Kellow, knocked at the door and opened it. The room was lit by dozens of candles, which, after the gloom of the corridor and his room, made him blink. Candelabra stood on every surface and were reflected in the mirrors. On the floor, on what had once been a magnificent Persian carpet, were two game cocks. As Veryan's appalled gaze travelled down to the blood and feathers at his feet, one of the cocks made a final rush at his opponent, scoring deep into his throat with the razor-sharp spurs. The other, blood dripping all over the carpet, staggered and fell. The victor leapt on his victim's shuddering body and uttered a triumphant crow.

'The silver does it,' Sir Walter croaked. 'A champion, Josh.'

Veryan raised his eyes. In the bed lay an old man, wig askew, with dark malevolent eyes and deathly pale skin. He was propped up on a number of dirty brocade cushions. A glass of brandy was in his hand. He had not noticed his visitor entering the room. It was a minute or so before Veryan recognized him as the man he had met at the Mitre in Oxford.

The colour drained from his face as he tried to take in the carnage on the carpet. Nobody took any notice of him. There was a thin, plain woman in an outmoded gown sitting in one corner. A nurse, wondered Veryan? She was sewing and remained oblivious to the fight on the far side of the bed.

'A good fight,' said Sir Walter, his voice slurred. 'I thought the golden would have put up more of a show. Take them away, Josh.'

Josh stepped up to the bed, picked up the victor and shoved him unceremoniously into the sack and slung the dead one through his belt, where it hung, eyes shut, blood congealing on its beak.

'Father, Mr Selwood has arrived.' Dorothea folded up her sewing and looked at their guest. She saw a tall, thin man who wore spectacles and stooped badly. His eyes were practically starting out of their sockets with horror. Well, she thought sourly, he will have to get used to such things.

'Selwood?' said Sir Walter vaguely.

His daughter came forward and held a tumbler to his lips for a moment. 'Veryan Selwood. You remember.'

The old man muttered and then let out a surprisingly loud, neighing laugh. 'Selwood, eh? The parson. And about time too.' He turned slowly and focused on his reluctant guest. 'Come here and let me look at you.'

Veryan stepped gingerly over the blood and feathers to the bed.

'Sit down. On the bed. Thea, bring me a candle.'

Sir Walter's shaky hand held the candle and passed it closely over his guest's face. Veryan could feel the heat of the flame and smell the wax which dripped onto the eiderdown. Sir Walter took no notice.

'Take off those damned spectacles.' Again the candle moved slowly across. 'Hm.' Another unnerving silence. 'You'll have to do, though I don't care for parsons, damned mealy-mouthed lot. I couldn't stand your father — he was a bully and a braggart.'

Veryan said nothing.

'Well, cat got your tongue?'

64

'I wasn't aware that you had asked me a question,' said Veryan. Sir Walter was something of a bully himself, he thought. And who was this female with the odd colouring? Veryan didn't like the unpredictable and the woman's black eyes and fair hair disconcerted him: it was unnatural somehow.

'So you have some spunk, eh?' Sir Walter did not seem offended. 'Selwood will soon be all yours. I wish you joy of it. But you're not to turn out Fanny and the children, mind.'

Veryan's face expressed bewilderment. He turned to Dorothea.

'Are you 'Fanny'?' he asked.

'I am your cousin, Dorothea Selwood. Fanny, Miss Potter, was my governess. Horace and Sylvia are her children.'

'And mine,' added Sir Walter maliciously, watching Veryan's face, whose expression changed to a mixture of moral outrage and distaste.

Miss Potter, thought Veryan, would be better placed in the local magdalen. What was Sir Walter about allowing a woman of that sort to be governess to his daughter? He glanced across at Dorothea, who was regarding him with a disconcertingly direct gaze. Bony, plain, with that mismatched colouring; he didn't care for her.

Dorothea caught his look and her black

65

eyes expressed a degree of hostility that Veryan found unnerving. Why the devil was she looking at him like that?

'I shall do whatever seems appropriate,' he said coldly.

Sir Walter gave a bark of laughter. 'Get rid of Fanny and matchmaking women will pour in to collar you from all over Cornwall.' Veryan, he noted with pleasure, was now looking appalled. 'Didn't think of that, I daresay. Yes, you'll be quite a catch hereabouts. Of course, you could marry Thea here and save yourself a lot of trouble. She's free. Nobody has wanted her up to now.'

Dorothea's hands clenched. She had schooled herself over the years not to react to her father's jeers on her looks or insinuations as to her undesirability in the marriage stakes.

'He is not serious, Mr Selwood. My father is trying to discompose you.' Her tone was expressionless.

Sir Walter shuffled irritably. 'Well, why not?' he blustered. 'He isn't married. You're at your last prayers.'

Dorothea swallowed and said nothing. In the distance a clock chimed.

'Father, we must leave you. Dinner will be ready soon. Mr Selwood, would you pull the bell, please? It is on the wall just behind you.' She rose.

Veryan stood up and reached for the bell-pull. He then held the door open for Dorothea, bowed slightly to Sir Walter, and followed his cousin out of the room.

'The drawing-room is downstairs, Mr Selwood. Left at the bottom of the stairs. I shall join you there shortly.' He caught a glimpse of her set, rigid face as she turned away from him and vanished down a corridor.

Dorothea went to her room, lit the branch of candles, sank down in front of her dressing-table and buried her face in her hands. Eventually she straightened up and stared at her reflection in the glass in front of her. Huge dark eyes, reddened by tears, stared back at her. Her fair hair was a pale blur. Was she really so ugly and unwanted? In happier times, when her mother had been alive, she was 'Mama's little fairy', and 'My pretty daughter'. How had she changed into this 30-year-old spinster, the butt of her father's jibes?

Her mother had been an intelligent, cultivated woman, much respected by the Gunthorpes and the other county families. She had endeavoured to ignore her husband's infidelities and Sir Walter had always treated her with courtesy: she was the exception to his view that women were mere playthings to be discarded when they no longer amused. Dorothea, coming under her mother's aegis, had also partaken of that respect.

All that had vanished with her death. Dorothea was left in a limbo world, with only a sense of her own integrity to guide her. Somewhere along the way she had made her choice. If being the despised unmarried daughter was the price she had to pay not to be a plaything, so be it. But occasionally, as this evening, when she was humiliated in front of Mr Selwood, the price was bitter.

Dorothea rose and went to wash her eyes with cold water and to change into something more suitable for dinner. At least she would not have to endure the slights that doubtless lay ahead for poor Fanny from this humourless, bigoted cousin of hers.

Veryan went downstairs more than half inclined to walk straight out of the front door and never be seen again. Duty, or possibly a sense of doom, prevailed. He turned left at the foot of the stairs and found himself in the drawing-room, a room shabbily magnificent, like the rest of the house. There was a large fire-place surmounted by a black marble mantelpiece, above which were the armorial bearings of the Selwoods heavily carved in stone. The effect was sombre and imposing.

The rest of the room was equally so. A couple of faded tapestries hung on the walls; in one, Jove sported with Ganymede in a manner that left little to the imagination — Veryan averted his gaze — and in the other, Bacchus was attempting, with obvious success, to seduce Ariadne. Some Jacobean chairs with needle-work cushions were arranged in solemn grandeur around the room. In one of these sat a plump, rather faded lady in a grey silk dress with a becoming Norfolk shawl draped over her shoulders. Her hair was a pretty brown, lightly sprinkled with grey, and arranged in a neat, modest bun. Veryan, who had been feeling more and more as if he had landed among savages, was cheered by this evidence of civilization.

She rose as he entered and came forward, holding out her hand.

'How do you do. You must be Mr Selwood. I do hope you had a good journey — the roads hereabouts can be shocking. I trust Mrs Kellow has made you comfortable?'

'Yes, thank you,' Veryan stuttered. He shook her hand with some reluctance; he didn't like being touched.

The lady caught his look and continued, 'Oh dear, I'm afraid you've been with Sir Walter. I know how exhausting that can be. Pray, let me offer you a drink. Sherry? I'm not sure where Miss Selwood is, but she will be down shortly.'

'Miss Selwood was with her father,' said Veryan, striving to equal her social tone. Who was this lady, he wondered? She had not introduced herself. Whoever she was it was a relief to meet with the normal social decencies. Such was Veryan's horror of any moral irregularity that he had already decided that Miss Potter would be a brassy woman with an underbred manner; that the woman in front of him could be she never crossed his mind.

He accepted the sherry and one of the Jacobean chairs and set himself to converse. Veryan usually avoided social occasions, but this lady asked just the right interested questions about his journey, and he found himself relaxing.

The fire was pleasantly warm, the sherry excellent, and his unknown companion was agreeably undemanding.

The door opened and Dorothea entered. She had changed into a brown silk dress and with her was a young man who was dressed in the height of fashion with an

70

absurdly high collar and carefully pomaded hair. He looked just like an undergraduate trying to cut a dash, thought Veryan. There was a bound and a thump from the hall as Sylvia jumped the remaining few stairs, and she, too, came in. She had changed into a white dress and she was twisting her coral necklace as she stared at him.

'I'm so sorry I'm late, Fanny,' said Dorothea. 'Father was being quite impossible.'

Veryan looked at Fanny, his eyes widening.

'Ah, Mr Selwood. You have met Miss Potter, I see. Good. May I introduce you to Horace and Sylvia FitzWalter? This is your cousin, Mr Selwood.'

Courtesies were exchanged. Dorothea noted, with amusement, that Mr Selwood was struggling for speech: doubtless he was striving for some moral indignation. Fortunately, at that moment the gong sounded. 'Shall we go in?' continued Dorothea smoothly. 'Mr Selwood, would you escort Miss Potter? Horace, open the door, if you please.'

Whatever Veryan had been going to do he now surrendered to *force majeur* and allowed himself to offer his arm to Fanny. In no time at all, it seemed, they were all seated in the dining-room and Mrs Kellow and the maids were bringing in the food.

Good, thought Dorothea. First hurdle

cleared. A man cannot be morally indignant whilst eating turbot.

The young FitzWalters, strictly primed by Dorothea, were on their best behaviour. If neither of them could understand why Veryan chose to surround himself with fusty books in Greek and Latin, they were too polite to say so. Horace was feeling particularly contrite (Dorothea had ticked him off soundly about his irresponsible behaviour in going with Abel and Tim Wilcox) and he now offered to show his new cousin some good rides and asked if he liked fishing.

Veryan could not be churlish with a schoolboy. 'I enjoyed fishing as a boy. Or were you talking of sea fishing?' What should he call him? The effrontery of calling themselves 'FitzWalter' — like king's bastards, he thought! 'Master Horace' was too servile and he was damned if he was going to acknowledge the relationship and call him 'cousin'.

'We have some pretty good fishing, I can tell you!' Horace enthused. 'Mackerel . . . lobsters. The Fawley boys and I often take out a boat.'

Sylvia had been studying Veryan. She could see that Dorothea didn't like him, but he seemed all right to her. She liked his voice, so deep and clear and he had a

72

lovely smile, even if his mouth went down most of the time. But why was he looking so disapproving? Of course, Bram Gunthorpe was her secret template of what a man should be, but this new cousin wasn't that bad, though he'd be better without those horrid spectacles and if he sat up straight.

'I hope you'll do something about Tamsin Wright's roof, Cousin,' she said. She wanted to show this new cousin that she could be grown-up and concerned about the problems on the estate.

Veryan turned. 'Who is Tamsin Wright, Miss Sylvia?'

'Tom Wright's widow. He died last year and she now lives in a little cottage in Porthgavern. But the roof leaks dreadfully and Father doesn't do anything.'

'You must not criticize your father, my dear,' said Fanny, after an apprehensive glance at Veryan.

'Why not?' asked Sylvia reasonably. 'He's not fulfilling his obligations as a landlord.' She sat back, feeling pleased with herself. That showed she had judgement about such things, she thought. She wasn't just an empty-headed miss, as her father believed.

'We don't talk of such things in company, dear,' said her mother.

'But Mr Selwood's family,' objected Sylvia.

And doesn't want to be, thought Dorothea. 'It is not fitting that you, in your position, should set yourself up against your, er, father's judgement,' said Veryan repressively.

You prig, thought Dorothea. You damned, self-centred prig. Sylvia, she saw, was bent over her plate trying to hide her tears, her face flushed with mortification. Horace was looking absolutely furious at this slight on his sister.

What on earth was going to happen when Sir Walter died? If this were an example of Mr Selwood's attitude, they were all in for a very stormy ride.

3

The evening was interminable. Fanny sent Sylvia up to bed the moment dinner was over and, for once, Sylvia did not protest. The rest of the company retired to the drawing-room and made stilted conversation, all except for Horace who turned his back on his cousin and absorbed himself in *The Sportsman's Dictionary: or, The Gentleman's Companion for Town and Country*. Dorothea couldn't blame him: she wished she might do something similar herself.

Had she but known it, Veryan had regretted his words to Sylvia the moment he uttered them and, as soon as he decently could, excused himself on the grounds of having had a long journey.

'Of course, Mr Selwood,' said Fanny in her gentle way. 'How selfish of us. You must be so tired. Do you know your way? Shall I ring for Jack to show you up?'

'Thank you. I confess I find the place very bewildering.'

'And some brandy, Mr Selwood,' said Dorothea, 'I'm sure you must be in need of it. I shall have some sent up to you.' It had suddenly occurred to her that Veryan's room overlooked the stable-yard and tonight was the night they had arranged to transfer the goods from the crypt to their several destinations. It would be better if Mr Selwood were soundly asleep.

It was much later, at around midnight, that Dorothea slipped a shawl over her head and went across to the stables. Josh was in the saddle-room sitting by the table where he usually cleaned the tack. There was a small lantern beside him. He was turning over a piece of paper in his hands.

'How did 'n go then, Miss Thea?'

Dorothea made a face. 'I see problems ahead.'

'We have problems here,' returned Josh. He handed her the folded piece of paper. She opened it. *Get Master Horris bak to skule.* Dorothea looked at it carefully. It had been printed, but whether to disguise the author's hand or because he or she could write no better, was not clear. It came from a torn poster advertising the auction of a wreck to be held shortly. There was one such poster outside the ship's chandlers in Porthgavern.

'How did this arrive?'

'Found 'n here when I came back from the cockfight. Ozzie and Joe say they don't know naught about it.' Ozzie and Joe were stable lad and gardener's boy respectively. 'I didn't let on about the contents.'

Dorothea sat down on an upturned box and tried to concentrate. The estate employed Bill Kellow, Mrs Kellow's nephew, as gardener with Joe as his assistant; Josh ran the stables and looked after the game-cocks with young Ozzie Tregair to help him. Inside, were Mrs Kellow, the two maids, Molly and Lucy, and Jack, who was boot boy, lamp boy and did various other odd jobs.

'Do you think it was one of ours?'

Josh nodded reluctantly.

'So somebody knows something we don't know and isn't telling. Too scared perhaps?' This was plainly more than an educational exhortation, she thought: it was a warning.

Josh looked down at the box containing the saddle soap and brushes, but said nothing.

'The warning must be about Bram Gunthorpe. He's never liked Horace and I must admit that Horace has been barely polite. I could believe that Mr Gunthorpe might wish to injure him in some way: he always was a vindictive man,' said Dorothea. 'But what is to be done?' Horace could hardly go back to school with his father dying.

Josh scratched his ear worriedly. 'Do us tell Master Horace?'

77

'I don't know. I'd rather not. Sheer bravado might make him do something foolish — like the other night. But I shall tell Mrs Kellow, she can keep her eyes peeled.'

'But what about they goods, Miss Thea? They be still in crypt. Your pa needs that money to pay off Mr Gunthorpe — 'e'm been proper worried about it. I've seen to mules and ponies for this evening, like you said. Do 'ee want 'n to go ahead?'

Dorothea nodded. Several dozen mules and ponies could not be hired without Gunthorpe knowing of it; indeed, some of them came from tenant farmers on his estate. Any alteration in the plans would only alert his suspicions that someone had given a warning. 'While Father is alive I think we're safe enough. Besides, Mr Gunthorpe wants his money.'

'I did think, what with Mr Selwood arriving . . . ' Josh jerked his head in the direction of Veryan's bedroom window which looked out over the stable-yard.

'Our reverend friend shouldn't hear a thing,' said Dorothea mischievously. 'I dropped some laudanum into his brandy.' She grinned suddenly.

Josh allowed himself a sour smile. 'I'll be getting on then, Miss Thea.'

'I'll need you to help me carry the money for Daniel,' said Dorothea. 'I only came for a lantern. Come to the library in about twenty minutes.'

Josh took down a spare lantern from its hook, lit it and handed it to her. She watched Josh disappear into the darkness and then went back into the house, holding the lantern under her cloak. She moved quietly to the library, the lantern making a small pool of light on the floor. All was silent save for the usual creaks of an old house and a mouse scuttling somewhere in the wainscot. The family had gone to bed and Mrs Kellow would have seen to it that the maids were in their attic rooms and Jack in his little cubby-hole.

Once in the library, she shut and locked the door and lit a branch of candles. Daniel Watson, the Captain of the *Maria*, would need to be paid for the goods. There was a wall safe to one side of the fireplace, hidden behind a painting of two game-cocks. Inside was 500 guineas in gold, carefully sewn into sacks of 100 guineas each. Dorothea took them out and locked the safe again. She then got down a red leather ledger with an iron clasp, unlocked that with a small key she wore on a chain around her neck, and made a careful note of the transaction.

If it hadn't been for the debt to Bram, she thought, there would have been nearly £700 profit.

As it was she would have barely £400 to finance the next trip. And continue she must if Mr Selwood's attitude towards Sylvia and Horace remained the same. The burden of their support was obviously going to fall on her, and this was the only way she had to provide for them.

Up in his bedroom, Veryan, wrapped closely in his dressing-gown, stood at the window. He had often been ill as a child and he recognized laudanum the moment he tasted it, even disguised in brandy. He had tipped his glass into a bowl of flowers. Why, he thought uneasily, did Miss Selwood, for it had been she who had smilingly handed him the brandy, want him drugged?

There was only a thin sickle moon, but it was a clear night and the moon together with the starlight enabled him to see well enough once his eyes became accustomed. He saw Dorothea go to the saddle-room and later come out with the lantern and return to the house. He watched Josh set off down towards the drive. Twenty minutes later Josh returned and went into the house. Veryan was just about to go down and investigate — surely Miss Selwood was not having a clandestine meeting with the groom? — when he heard a creak below him and the kitchen door opened and Dorothea's cloaked figure emerged, swiftly followed by Josh. They were each carrying something heavy. They both went down the drive.

Veryan stayed at the window for another fifteen minutes, but nothing further occurred. Still uneasy, Veryan bolted his door and made his way back to bed. Unfortunately, he had forgotten that he had put down his spectacles on a small table by his bed. In the darkness he stumbled, knocked the spectacles off the table and trod on them.

★ ★ ★

Breakfast the following morning at Quilquin Hall: Bram, his broad shoulders squeezed with difficulty into an olive-green morning coat in a fine kerseymere and wearing buff-coloured Bedford cord breeches, sat at the head of the table. His mother, dressed correctly but dowdily in a purple bloom round gown with a high neck, sat at the foot. With them sat Isabel, in a white poplin chemise robe with a light shawl draped over her arms, for it was a chilly morning. Her fair curls were piled up on her head in a classic knot and

81

fell in ringlets around her face. She had blue eyes like her brother and a small rosebud mouth. She looked apprehensively at Bram and hoped that he was in a good mood.

The meal was almost over, but neither lady ventured to move until Bram indicated that they might. Isabel had cut up an apple into very small pieces, but most of it remained uneaten. She sipped nervously at a cup of coffee.

'When did he arrive, Brother?' she ventured.

'Yesterday evening.' His voice was reassuringly normal.

Isabel thought she might risk a further comment. 'In holy orders too! I dare swear Miss Potter won't like that! Nor those so-called FitzWalters.'

'I think we shall soon see the last of Miss Potter,' said Bram. His informant had told him that Sir Veryan was very starchy in his notions. Good, that made his little plan all the more likely to succeed. He smiled, quite pleasantly, at his sister.

'I wonder if he is good-looking?' said Isabel.

'You'll be able to see him in church on Sunday, I daresay,' said Bram, reaching out for a couple of hazelnuts and the nutcrackers. It suddenly crossed his mind that if Selwood took a fancy to Isabel then perhaps matters with the smuggling might be 'arranged'. Plenty of the clergy connived at the smuggling, as Bram well knew, but a man from Oxford, a foreigner, would probably have strong objections. Bram would encourage them.

Mr Selwood as a brother-in-law could be decidedly useful: if he had any sense he'd look the other way while Bram took over the free-trading. Bram would see to it that Selwood's cellar was always well stocked and there would be some French lace for Isabel to keep them sweet. He shelled the hazelnuts and offered one to his sister and watched her maliciously while she ate it. He knew Isabel didn't care for hazelnuts. Mrs Gunthorpe smiled nervously.

Isabel would live at the Priory with her husband and Bram would be an attentive brother. Dorothea, of course, would have to go: Bram would instruct Isabel accordingly. Miss Potter and Sylvia could be found a cottage on the estate — Bram wanted Sylvia to hand, so to speak. He had other plans for Horace.

There was a scratch at the door and the butler entered with a letter on a silver salver which he presented to Bram.

Dear Mr Gunthorpe

If you would be so good as to come to Selwood Priory this morning at eleven o'clock, I shall have the three hundred guineas my father owes you ready for your collection.

Yours etc
D. Selwood

Bram scanned it briefly, scrunched it up and tossed it onto the fire. It was usually Dorothea who settled things and he resented it. She was damned efficient, too. Mrs Kellow was always there, ostensibly as a chaperone, but also as a witness and there would be a receipt waiting for him to sign.

He toyed with the idea of writing back and saying that the time was inconvenient, but he needed that money and he guessed that Miss Selwood knew it. Dorothea's attitude rankled. She was always perfectly civil, but those black eyes expressed a lack of appreciation that Bram was not used to. Once, when they were both about sixteen, he'd attempted to kiss her behind the church door and she'd bitten his ear lobe so hard that it still bore the scars. It was her loss, he told himself. Nobody would want to kiss her now.

'Bram,' said Isabel coaxingly, 'you will go to the Priory, won't you? Unless you do, you know that Mr Selwood cannot visit here.'

'Setting your cap at him?' said Bram nastily.

Isabel bit her lip and said nothing.

'I'll go this morning,' said Bram, as if conferring a favour. 'I should pay my respects to Sir Walter in any case.'

'What a kind brother you have, dearest,' cried Mrs Gunthorpe. She had just 'lent' her son twenty guineas and was dreading him gambling that away as well. Her tears had had no effect on him. At least, with Sir Walter dying, he couldn't gamble at the Priory.

★ ★ ★

At the gatehouse the previous night, everything had gone smoothly. The mules and Goonhilly ponies had trotted off in various directions and the money received had been placed in an iron chest and carried back by Josh and Daniel Watson to Dorothea's other hiding-place, this time in the herb garret. The trip had been a good one; the profit had been nearly 700 guineas, even counting the payment of a half-crown to each of the helpers. Dorothea gestured to

85

Josh and Daniel to sit down. She then drew the lantern closer and counted out the 300 guineas her father owed to Bram Gunthorpe and put them in a leather bag.

Dorothea had always liked Daniel Watson. He was a genial, burly man, with the dark eyes and hooked nose of his Selwood inheritance. His mother had been a laundress up at the Priory in the days when Lady Selwood was still alive. They lived in a little cottage next to the gardener's. Daniel was some six years older than Dorothea and she had always thought of him as a beloved elder brother, for she had seen much of him. She remembered him making her various things; a swing to go on one of the apple trees in the orchard, a whipping top when she was recovering from chicken-pox.

Daniel had been more fortunate than most of the Watsons, for his mother had been converted by a visiting Methodist preacher who had taught the boy to read and write and had preached the virtues of sobriety and self-reliance. Daniel had taken it to heart for, unlike most Cornishmen, he rarely drank and he proved calm and resourceful in an emergency.

'What about the damage from the Revenue cutter's guns?' asked Dorothea, when the business was done.

Daniel shrugged. 'The jib sail needed repairing and she took some shot in her bows. Nothing too serious, Miss Thea. She be lying now in Sutton Pool.'

'So you'll be off again in a week or so?'

'Aye. Abel will tell 'ee when.' He paused and added, 'You'm be letting me know about Sir Walter, Miss Thea?' He jerked his head towards the house.

'Of course. Josh will make sure you know. It can't be long now I'm afraid.'

Daniel said nothing, only put one hand briefly on Dorothea's shoulder. He then nodded to Josh and left.

It was strange thought Dorothea, not for the first time, how the web of kinship spread itself. She would trust Abel and Daniel Watson with her life if need be. They felt like family to her. The same, however, could not be said for Mr Veryan Selwood — obnoxious prig. She turned to Josh.

'I'll be glad to pay off Gunthorpe,' she remarked, lifting up the heavy leather bag and grimacing. 'Keep an eye on him, won't you, Josh? See who he talks to while he's here.' He tended to pinch the maids given half a chance; she'd tell Mrs Kellow to keep them busy when he came.

' 'Ere, Miss Thea. Let me carry that.' Josh took up the bag and left the herb garret.

Dorothea followed him and locked the door. Josh walked with her up to the house and handed the bag to her at the back door. Dorothea gave him back the saddle-room lantern and quietly let herself in.

The kitchen was warm and welcoming after the cold air outside. The fire had been banked, but still glowed redly under its cover. Mrs Kellow was there too. Earlier she had been sitting with Sir Walter and now sat, half-asleep, in the Windsor chair by the fire, a voluminous shawl over her nightdress. The draught of cold night air from the passage roused her.

'Oh, Miss Thea, your pa were took bad about half an hour ago. 'E been asking for 'ee. Miss Potter be with him. Let me get 'ee a hot drink, miss, 'ee look proper cold.'

Dorothea shook her head. 'I'll go up.' She gave Mrs Kellow a brief summary of events and the warning about Horace.

'It's that Mr Gunthorpe,' said Mrs Kellow without hesitation.

'So I think,' agreed Dorothea.

'That Molly,' went on Mrs Kellow, referring to one of the housemaids, 'now she'm a flighty piece and Jack sometimes do 'ave more money than he can rightly earn. Don't 'ee fret, Miss Thea, I'll be on the watch.'

Dorothea took a candle and the leather bag and went first to the library, where she put the money into the wall safe, and then upstairs to her father's room.

Fanny, looking pale and anxious, was hovering near the bed. Sir Walter, eyes closed, was lying motionless, breathing spasmodically.

'It came on just after two o'clock,' whispered Fanny. 'I've given him one of the calomel pills and applied mustard poultices, but I fear he's too weakened for more. Should I bleed him? I'm so frightened of doing the wrong thing.' She wrung her hands.

Dorothea felt for her father's pulse. It was fluttering weakly.

'Poor Fanny,' she said. 'You look exhausted. You should go to bed. Take some laudanum.'

Fanny wiped her eyes. 'I cannot bear a sickroom,' she whispered. 'It's not that I . . . but I just cannot bear it.'

Dorothea looked at her father. 'He may rally, but I think we should be prepared for the worst. Mrs Kellow will be up later. Go to bed, Fanny.' She gave her cheek a quick peck and pushed her gently out of the room before sinking down in Fanny's vacated chair.

She must have dozed off for when she awoke dawn was coming greyly through the curtains and she had cramp in one of her feet. She was also cold. Her father was sleeping, his pulse more steady. Dorothea massaged her foot, wincing as she did so, then went to replenish the fire. The noise of the poker in the hearth woke Sir Walter.

'Thea?' It was a thread of a voice.

'I'm here, Father.'

'You'll pay Gunthorpe?'

'Yes, Father. The money is ready and he's coming this morning. Don't worry about it.'

'Selwood, is he here yet?'

'Yes, Father. He came last night. Don't you remember?'

There was a pause. 'Doesn't like any of us,' her father said at last. 'But he'll do what's right.'

Dorothea held her peace. She doubted if Mr Selwood's ideas of what was right coincided with Sir Walter's. So far as she could see, her cousin would very likely throw out Fanny and the children the moment the funeral was over.

Sir Walter drifted off to sleep again. There was a knock at the door. This time it was Josh. He looked at Sir Walter and shook his head. ' 'Tis a sad time, Miss Thea,' he said. 'Man and boy I been with him these forty-five year. 'Ee better get some sleep, Miss Thea. You'm a deal to do today.'

Dorothea took one last look at her father

and left the room. Once in her bedroom she took off her shoes and dress, tumbled into bed and fell asleep almost immediately.

★ ★ ★

Breakfast the following morning was served early, at about ten o'clock. Usually there was much cheerful banter among the FitzWalters, but today they were subdued. Horace said very little and Sylvia kept wiping away tears with the back of her hand. Fanny was pale, but remained her usual hospitable self. She explained the situation to Veryan.

'Poor Dorothea sat up with him for most of the night,' she ended.

No, she did not, thought Veryan mutinously. He had not slept well. Selwood Priory's old timbers creaked and what sounded like a herd of mice had galloped about over his head. He had kept waking nervously, thinking that somebody was in the room. Then there was the problem of his broken spectacles. He doubted whether he could mend them, even enough to read with — reading was always Veryan's priority — and how on earth was he going to manage in company?

He explained the situation to Fanny.

'Oh, Mr Selwood, how unfortunate! I am so sorry. Thank goodness you didn't cut

91

yourself. I believe I have Lady Selwood's lorgnette somewhere. I shall look it out for you, then at least you may read. Now, may I pour you some coffee? Or would you prefer tea?'

'Coffee, thank you.' In the face of Fanny's gentle courtesies, Veryan found it impossible to remain ill-tempered. He relaxed slightly. Miss Potter was not responsible for trying to dope him, at any rate. Under her gentle urging, he allowed her to help him to some kippers. 'I can see them,' he explained. 'But I confess they look fuzzy.'

Dorothea entered at about half past ten, looking white and drawn. There were rings under her eyes and her face looked smudged with exhaustion.

'How is Sir Walter, my dear?' asked Fanny.

'Resting,' said Dorothea. 'He'd like to see the children when they've finished. No hurry; Josh is trying to give him something to eat.' She patted Sylvia gently on the shoulder and went to sit down.

'Good morning, Mr Selwood. I trust you slept well?' She thought there was something different about him, but was too exhausted to think what it might be.

'Not particularly,' said Veryan coldly. 'Strangely enough I was disturbed at about midnight by people moving about in the stable-yard. And then I broke my spectacles.'

Dorothea looked up and saw a pair of cold, blue-grey eyes glaring at her. So he knew. Her heart sank. Aloud she said, 'It's often difficult sleeping in a strange place. Father would like to see you too, Mr Selwood. Josh will send for you, if you wouldn't mind holding yourself in readiness.' She felt beyond coping with the spectacles.

Veryan bowed.

Josh would escort Veryan to Sir Walter's room the moment Bram Gunthorpe was spotted coming up the drive. Dorothea had no wish for her cousin to know about Sir Walter's debts, nor the source of the money.

Breakfast was finished and the FitzWalters left. Fanny offered Veryan some more coffee and Dorothea crumbled a piece of toast in her fingers. No one spoke. Eventually, the children were heard coming back down the stairs and Fanny rose and, with a murmured apology, left the room.

'I do not think it can be long,' said Dorothea eventually, as Veryan seemed determined on silence. He still said nothing. Dorothea took a deep breath and continued, 'I know that when Father dies all this will be yours. You may wish us to go. I hope you will allow me a little time to arrange things.'

Veryan screwed up his eyes in an attempt to focus and looked at her. 'I didn't want it! I didn't want any of it. And it's no wish of mine to be here. Why the devil didn't your father regularize his union with Miss Potter?'

'Selfishness,' returned Dorothea with equal asperity. 'He won't have to face the music, after all.'

Veryan's mouth took on its thin-lipped look. 'You should speak of your father with more respect.'

'Oh, why?'

Veryan couldn't answer. Nothing occurred to him. The whole situation was appalling in every way. 'A lady shouldn't . . . ' he began. Even to his own ears it sounded inadequate.

'Oh, do stop being so priggish,' cried Dorothea. 'I have managed ever since I was seventeen to do the best I can for all of us in very trying circumstances. I am not going to indulge in lies and evasions now.'

'Morality must be upheld, Miss Selwood.'

Dorothea gave an exasperated sigh. 'Truth must be upheld, Mr Selwood. And the truth is that Father is a monumentally selfish old man. Surely you can see that Miss Potter

94

is no adventuress? He took advantage of her vulnerability after my mother died. He has made no provision for Horace and Sylvia, who are entirely innocent and, by not marrying Fanny, he has deprived all of us of the normal social intercourse we might have enjoyed. I cannot find anything to respect in that.' He gambled and wenched too, she might have added. Mr Selwood would doubtless be horrified to learn how many 'Watsons' there were in the surrounding villages: it amused Sir Walter to give his name thus to his illegitimate offspring.

There was a knock at the door. It was Josh.

'Sir Walter would like to see Mr Selwood now,' he said. He exchanged a glance with Dorothea and gave a discreet nod.

Veryan's eyes narrowed. Something was going on, he was sure of it. But what? Surely Miss Selwood was not having an assignation with the groom? She had certainly been over to the stables the previous night. Dorothea's face held a look of tension. She had risen and moved towards the window. But Josh was holding open the door and Veryan had no option but to follow him upstairs.

However much his cousin might have lied about her whereabouts the previous night, when she said Sir Walter was dying she was plainly speaking the truth. It could not be long now, he saw. Josh ushered Veryan in and left them.

'Sit down.' The voice was scarcely more than a whisper.

Veryan sat and stared down at his hands. Sir Walter's fingers plucked at the eiderdown.

'Been thinking about you. You'll do.'

Veryan looked up.

'Aye. I know you don't like us, but you'll do. You go straight at your fences. Your father, for all his bluster, was a shirker.'

'Thank you.' Veryan could think of nothing whatever to say.

'I know I should have married Miss Potter, but I didn't and there's an end on it. The children are good children; you'll see to it that they don't suffer.' He would too, thought Sir Walter. He wouldn't like it, but he'd do his duty.

Veryan said nothing.

'Fawley's my agent, though Dorothea deals with most things. If you want to know anything, ask Thea.'

Veryan's lips tightened. He was damned if he would.

'You may go now.'

Veryan rose. He wondered if he should offer a prayer, but the thought was too embarrassing to contemplate.

'I don't need praying over,' said Sir Walter percipiently. 'Far too late for that. You could do with losing a few of those preachy ways of yours. Ring the bell for Josh and go away.' He closed his eyes.

Veryan bowed and left the room. He made his way down to the drawing-room. It was empty but the fire had been lit. There was a *Times* on the table, but it was over a week old. A couple of copies of *La Belle Assemblee* rested on a stool near Miss Potter's chair and there was a three-volume copy of *Evelina or The History of a Young Lady's Entrance into the World* on a shelf. Veryan, who was indifferent to what he ate or how he dressed, could not ignore the lack of reading matter.

Surely there must be books in the house somewhere? Didn't Miss Potter mention something about the library last night? He would go and find out.

He had just opened the door when he heard voices opposite. Another door had opened and there was Miss Selwood talking to an unknown gentleman. She'd been alone with him, quite unchaperoned!

'Is Miss Sylvia around?' the gentleman was asking. 'I promised her a ride on Brandy.'

'My sister is not available,' said Dorothea with finality.

The gentleman slapped his riding crop against his boot in an irritated gesture. 'Another day, perhaps.'

Dorothea made no reply. The visitor spun on his heel and walked away. Jack, who had been trimming the candles in the hall, went to open the front door. Veryan noticed that the gentleman carried a large leather bag. It looked as though it contained money — quite a lot of it too.

'Thank God that's over,' said Dorothea to somebody behind her. 'Where is Miss Sylvia, Mrs Kellow?'

'Don't 'ee worry, Miss Thea. She be with her ma in the prior's room.' Mrs Kellow went back to the kitchen and Dorothea returned to the room she'd just left.

So she wasn't unchaperoned, thought Veryan with a stab of irrational disappointment. Then he thought, what's the matter with me? Do I dislike my cousin so much that I prefer to put the worst construction on her behaviour? Veryan had never thought of himself as a vindictive man and he didn't care for this new view of himself.

He left the drawing-room and crossed the hall. The door was still ajar and he opened it. Dorothea was tidying some leatherbound books away. She gave a start as Veryan came in, but offered no explanation.

'So this is the library?' said Veryan, feeling obscurely guilty.

'Yes. Did you want anything, Mr Selwood?' He's seen Bram, she thought. What shall I say? She glared at him.

In a few hours' time, thought Veryan, this will be my library and I'm damned if I'm apologizing for walking into one of my own rooms.

'A book.'

'A book?' Dorothea stared blankly at him.

'Yes. I am a reading man, Miss Selwood. I am not accustomed to a house without books. I wanted something to read. Miss Potter kindly offered me Lady Selwood's lorgnette — unless you have any objection?'

'Of course not,' said Dorothea hastily. She made a vague gesture. 'These are my great-grandfather's books. I doubt whether anybody has opened them for nearly a century.'

Veryan peered at the shelves, selected Pindar's *Odes*, took it down and opened it. A cloud of dust flew out making them both cough. 'My great-grandfather too,' he observed.

'I'll get Molly to dust them properly,' said Dorothea, feeling ashamed.

'No! No! I'll do it.'

'But you can't! Molly will do it.'

'Certainly not,' said Veryan. 'These books

99

need the most careful handling. The binding is going in places. Molly may give them a gentle dust with a feather duster, but she is not to touch them.'

Dorothea began to be amused. This was the first sign of anything human she'd seen in her cousin.

'We are not a bookish family,' she explained. 'If I have any spare time I spend it in my herb garret.'

'Herbs,' said Veryan doubtfully. They looked at each other in mutual incomprehension.

★ ★ ★

Sir Walter died that night with Josh and Dorothea beside him. Mrs Kellow and Dorothea prepared him for burial, the Porthgavern ship's carpenter (another Watson) made him a fine elm coffin and for the next few days Sir Walter lay in state and the local people came to pay their last respects.

It was a strangely peaceful time for Dorothea. She spent most of it sitting quietly by her father's body, talking with surprising cheerfulness to the various mourners who had known him all their lives.

Tamsin Wright hobbled up from the village. ' 'E be gone then,' she said, peering

100

into the coffin, as if wanting the evidence of her own eyes. 'Aye, 'e were a lively chap when 'e were young, poor old bugger. ''Tis no fun being too old for a bit of frisk. Do 'ee have a drop of brandy now, me dear?'

Dorothea handed her one. Tamsin drank it with relish. 'I could tell 'ee stories, but 'twouldn't be proper 'im being your father.' Her old eyes held a decidedly knowledgeable twinkle.

'I've probably heard it all before,' observed Dorothea.

'Maybe 'ee have and maybe 'ee haven't. I'm telling no tales. But 'ow be the little maid?'

'Poor Miss Sylvia is taking it very hard.'

'She'm be a good maid. She'm trying to do something about my roof.'

'I know. I hope Mr Selw — Sir Veryan I should say, will see to it when things get sorted out after the funeral.'

''E be a parson, I hear. There'll be changes.'

Dorothea sighed.

The funeral was held a week after Sir Walter's death at St Petroc's in Egloscolom. The vicar, Mr Normanton, had marked the occasion by drinking steadily through two bottles of brandy the previous evening and was barely able to officiate. This, as the new Sir Veryan was to discover, was by no means unusual. The turn-out among the local people was surprisingly large. Sir Thomas and Lady Shebbeare and other gentry sent their condolences, though only Bram Gunthorpe appeared in person. Horace, with Josh in discreet attendance, accompanied Veryan.

Fanny, Dorothea and Sylvia, all wearing hastily dyed gowns, remained at the Priory and Fanny, eyes swollen with tears, read the funeral service in the drawing-room. It was not done for ladies to go to funerals, much to Dorothea's annoyance, for she wanted to keep an eye on Horace.

A large number of the local men were Watsons, several of whom, caps in hands, came up to Veryan and Horace introduced them.

'Abel Watson — Sir Veryan. Abel has a fishing boat and he and his wife run the chandler's shop in Porthgavern.' Did his cousin realize exactly who all these Watsons were, Horace wondered?

'I be sorry to hear about Sir Walter,' said Abel. 'A proper gentleman, 'e were.' His dark eyes flickered appraisingly over the heir and there was the suspicion of a wink at Horace.

They were interrupted.

'May I introduce myself, Sir Veryan? I am

102

Gunthorpe of Quilquin Hall, your nearest neighbour.' He nodded dismissively at Abel.

Veryan shook hands. At last, a gentleman amid all these hobbledehoys. A big man, but he carried himself well. There was something about him that reminded Veryan fleetingly of his father, an aura of brute strength, perhaps, emphasized by a jagged scar on his left earlobe as if a dog had savaged him. Mr Gunthorpe spoke pleasantly, saying a few friendly words to Horace, who scowled, before taking Veryan's arm and moving away a few paces.

'I hope that you will do us the honour of calling, Sir Veryan. My mother and sister would be delighted to make your acquaintance.'

Veryan bowed and expressed his eagerness to meet Mrs and Miss Gunthorpe, Sir Walter's words, 'matchmaking women will pour in to collar you from all over Cornwall' echoing ominously in his mind. However, there was no help for it. He would have to pay a courtesy visit at least.

Bram lowered his voice. 'Difficult situation. Mama and my sister cannot visit at the Priory. I'm sure you understand me.'

Veryan felt curiously ambivalent. As a man of the cloth he too deplored the presence of Sir Walter's mistress and children at the Priory, but a week or so in Miss Potter's company had made him less certain of his moral indignation. 'Indeed,' he said non-committally.

Bram's brows snapped together. If Selwood were going to prove difficult . . . He gave a cold smile. 'I am sure you will be kept very busy just now,' he said. 'I shan't look for you for a week or so. Sir Walter's affairs were always in something of a tangle. A number of the Watsons were engaged in the smuggling trade, I believe.'

'Watsons? Smuggling?'

'I hope I haven't been indiscreet? Sir Walter rather indulged himself amongst the women round here. Apart from our young friend,' he nodded in the direction of Horace who was talking to Abel, 'he had numerous other offspring — Watsons he liked to call them. It was his little pun.'

Veryan blenched. Suddenly, everything fell into place — the dark eyes and craggy faces he'd seen at the graveside were explained. 'Abel Watson is . . . ?'

'Oh yes. I believe him to be the eldest of the by-blows. It's a popular surname hereabouts, you'll find.' Bram enjoyed Veryan's consternation.

'And the smuggling?'

'Up to their ears, the lot of 'em — doubtless

with Sir Walter's knowledge, if not his connivance. I am a local Justice, I should know.'

'But . . . but this is dreadful. I had no idea! Rest assured, Mr Gunthorpe, I shall do my best to stamp it out. Smuggling! I can scarcely credit it.'

Bram was satisfied. Without Sir Walter's financial backing the enterprise would surely fold. Horace was too young to take over and Abel didn't have the authority to hold it together. If he played his cards right, the Selwood involvement would soon be history. 'I hear things on the bench,' he ended. 'I'll keep you informed, if I may. Perhaps we could work together on this?'

'I'd be grateful,' said Veryan.

★ ★ ★

The first thing Veryan did after the funeral was to arrange for Mrs Kellow to show him over the house, top to bottom. He followed her up to the attics, notebook at the ready and crawled, lantern in hand, into the lofts, inspected what he could see of the roof and guttering and so on down the house, ending up in the cellars, where he raised his eyebrows at the casks of brandy and wine.

The Priory, he realized, was in a state of

disrepair. Mice scuttled away as he poked about in the attics. There was wet rot in one loft and what looked suspiciously like woodworm in one of the bedrooms. Several window-frames needed replacing.

'We did our best, Sir Veryan,' said Mrs Kellow apologetically, 'but Sir Walter would never allow for repairs. The times Molly and Lucy have had to put up buckets to catch the drips!' She was torn between a wish to exonerate the servants from blame and a feeling of guilt that the house should be in so bad a condition.

'Yet there must be several hundred pounds' worth of wines and brandy in the cellar,' observed Veryan.

'I wouldn't know about that, sir,' said Mrs Kellow noncommittally. In fact, Veryan had not by any means seen all the cellar's contents, for she, Josh and Dorothea had been down the previous evening and removed what drink they could down to the secret cellar, whose entrance was through a trapdoor underneath one of the stone steps which led down into the cellars. The entrance was quite narrow, but Josh had been able to roll down several dozen of the half-anker casks of brandy and store a number of cases of Sir Walter's special port.

The following day, Veryan asked Josh to

show him round outside; the stable block and outbuildings, the garden with its potting sheds and greenhouses, but here he saw things had been better managed. He said as much to Josh.

'Sir Walter never spared no money on 'is horses,' replied Josh. 'And 'e were a man who liked 'is food, so you'm be finding things in better shape outside. 'Tis not Mrs Kellow's fault, Sir Veryan. Nor Miss Thea's neither: she did try 'er best.'

Veryan grunted. He was more than half-inclined to think that the state of the house reflected badly on his cousin. It did not occur to him that an elderly housekeeper and three servants was scarcely an adequate staff for a house the size of the Priory, which probably had as many as twenty bedrooms.

'The game-cocks will have to go,' said Veryan. 'I cannot countenance so brutal a sport — if sport it be. Who do you think would take them? Gunthorpe, perhaps? He seems a very pleasant gentleman.'

Josh drew a deep breath. Master Horace is not going to like this one bit, he thought. 'I'll make enquiries, sir. They be a valuable collection and worth summat, a hundred guineas or so.'

'A hundred guineas!'

'That be right, sir. We'm got eight cocks

and several dozen hens.'

'I'd like to see the gatehouse, too,' Veryan said next.

Oh my God, thought Josh. Aloud he said, 'You'll 'ave to ask Miss Thea, Sir Veryan. She be the only one with the key.'

'Surely you have a spare?' said Veryan suspiciously.

'No, sir. Miss Thea do look after her seedlings and such proper careful. She do 'ave a lot of dried herbs and her jars of medicines there. Some of them dangerous, she do say.'

Dangerous or not, thought Veryan obstinately, I mean to have a key to the gatehouse whether Miss Selwood likes it or not.

Dorothea watched all this in growing outrage. It would have been courteous for Veryan to have asked her permission even though, as new owner, he had every right to go wherever he liked. But he did not do so. When Josh told her about the gatehouse her wrath spilled over.

'How dare he?' she stormed. 'He's shut up every day with Mr Fawley, going over the accounts. I know, for Mr Fawley tells me. Poor man, he keeps telling Sir Veryan to ask me, but, of course, he won't. He can't understand how it is that the estate is so run down, repairs not done, and yet my father lived at three or four times his annual income. Ha! If only he knew.'

'But, Miss Thea, 'e be entitled to know. 'Tis now 'is estate.' Mrs Kellow, Josh knew, was half-reconciled to the changes; at least long-needed repairs were now being tackled. Sir Veryan had arranged for the defective guttering to be replaced and Molly and Lucy and several girls from Porthgavern were hard at work from dawn to dusk with brooms, mops and dusters.

'And now he wants my herb garret,' cried Dorothea, wiping away an angry tear. The herb garret was a place of refuge to her. She had hidden herself away there after her mother died and it was there that she had tried to come to terms with the restrictions on her life and learn to create something positive with her herbs and potions out of what looked like a dreary future.

' 'E didn't say nothing about wanting to take 'n over,' said Josh. Sir Veryan had not raised the matter again, so maybe second thoughts had prevailed.

'Ha!' retorted Dorothea, unconvinced.

4

Quilquin Hall had been built during the previous century by Bram's grandfather. Unlike Selwood Priory, it was a pleasantly regular house with a classical portico and symmetrical wings on either side. Inside, all was modern comfort, decorated with discernment and propriety. There were no suggestive tapestries here, only some landscapes of various Roman ruins brought back from the Grand Tour by Bram's grandfather and a few family portraits, including one of a simpering Mrs Gunthorpe as Perdita, complete with some tasteful sheep, decoratively arranged.

It was not until a couple of weeks after the funeral, in early April, that Veryan went to pay his promised visit to the Gunthorpes. In truth, he could have gone earlier, but he found himself procrastinating. Ladies, his mother had often told him, had sensitive natures that no mere man could hope to understand. This, coupled with the fact that (Matty being an exception) his life had been largely void of women, had left him with the vague feeling that they were alien creatures, whose nerves he would always jar and who were best avoided. However, the acquaintance could not be deferred forever and he must go.

The front door of Quilquin Hall was opened by a surprisingly ill-favoured maid. It was good of Gunthorpe to take her on, thought Veryan approvingly; the poor girl was badly scarred by smallpox and had a number of teeth missing. Veryan, much to his surprise, had discovered that he rather enjoyed having Molly and Lucy about the Priory, with their fresh young faces and pretty prints and he liked the way they bobbed curtseys whenever he said 'Good-morning' to them. The maid took his card and left him in a small saloon on the ground floor and went to fetch the butler.

Upstairs, in the blue drawing-room with its elegant cornice and elaborate ceiling-rose from which hung a Venetian glass chandelier, there was a sudden burst of activity. Mrs Gunthorpe had been reading Fordyce's *Sermons* and Isabel was trimming a bonnet when the butler entered with the card.

'At last!' exclaimed Mrs Gunthorpe. 'Show Sir Veryan up, Wade.'

Isabel flung the bonnet onto the window seat and rushed to the mirror, frantically

111

patting her hair into shape.

'He's taken his time,' she said resentfully. 'How do I look, Mama?'

'Like a lady, dearest,' said Mrs Gunthorpe approvingly. 'And I cannot but think that he will find it an agreeable change to be here after the hurly-burly of the arrangements at the Priory.'

Both ladies then sat down on either side of the fireplace, Mrs Gunthorpe, spine erect, bent her head devoutly over Fordyce's *Sermons* once again. Isabel picked up a neglected piece of sewing from her missionary basket and tried to look prettily engaged.

There was a pause of a few seconds after the butler announced, 'Sir Veryan Selwood, ma'am,' to allow their guest to appreciate the picture of pious rectitude and then both ladies rose to their feet.

'Sir Veryan, how delightful in you to call. Wade, tell Mr Gunthorpe that Sir Veryan is here. Pray, allow me to introduce my daughter.'

Isabel came forward and curtseyed. She had been waiting impatiently for this moment for more than a week and had taken every care with her dress. Her fair curls were pinned up *a la Madonna* and she wore a gown of blue-grey silk, cut demurely high, which matched her eyes.

She looked appraisingly at their guest. He was, naturally, in mourning. But black, she thought, suited him. His hair was rather longer than was fashionable but though he looked like a gentleman he did not, to Isabel's disappointment, look modish.

However, she smiled prettily and murmured a few suitable words of sympathy. Eligible gentlemen were thin on the ground and one couldn't be too choosy.

Veryan was not wearing his spectacles and, as well as missing the tableau offered, as he moved forward he tripped over a small footstool. Isabel hid a smile. Mrs Gunthorpe frowned at her daughter and urged her guest to be seated.

'So sorry, so clumsy of me.' Veryan peered down and tried to locate any other hazards. 'Am I about to sit on something?' Isabel quickly removed the missionary basket.

Veryan sat down gingerly. He should have remembered that ladies' drawing-rooms were full of knick-knacks. The ill-favoured maid came in with some wine. She was followed by Bram, who shook Veryan's hand and cocked a malicious eyebrow at his sister.

'I hope things are sorting themselves out at the Priory,' he began. 'You must know that your repairs to the roof are causing an immense amount of local interest. It can scarcely have been touched since old Prior Gilbert's time. But I am forgetting to enquire after Miss Selwood. How is her father's death affecting her?'

'Poor Dorothea,' said Isabel, with a palpable lack of sincerity. 'I pity her. What will she do now?'

'Once Sir Veryan has dealt with the Potter woman and her offspring, Dorothea can begin to lead the life of an ordinary gentlewoman,' said her mother with asperity.

Bram frowned down at his wine and tapped his foot impatiently. It was not a good sign and Isabel looked apprehensively at her mother.

Mrs Gunthorpe had not noticed and continued, 'As soon as I hear that Miss Potter and those children have gone, Sir Veryan, my daughter and I will visit you at the Priory. Other families too, the Shebbeares for example, will wish to make your acquaintance. It will be my duty to take Miss Selwood in hand. Poor girl, those clothes, that hair — such unfortunate colouring.' She smiled fondly at Isabel whose fair curls and blue eyes at least matched. 'She was looking quite distraught in church on Sunday.'

Isabel was watching Veryan. 'She has just lost her father, Mama. She may be allowed to look distraught at such a time.'

Veryan took another gulp of wine. He was feeling somewhat besieged. Miss Gunthorpe was all right, he thought, she at least had a kind heart, but her mother was something of a tartar. He certainly did not want Mrs Gunthorpe having *carte blanche* to visit. If he felt a twinge of sympathy towards Sir Walter's viewpoint, it was quickly suppressed.

Bram's eyes narrowed. He appreciated Isabel's wish to make her mark with Selwood, but Bram, too, had plans and they didn't include taking Sylvia out of his orbit.

'Have you thought of Pine Cottage for Miss Potter, Selwood?'

'Pine Cottage? No, where is it?'

'About a mile from the Priory. You must have passed it coming here. I believe it could be made very comfortable. It's a reasonable size and has a pleasant aspect.' And scarcely half a mile from Quilquin Hall to boot.

Mrs Gunthorpe sniffed. She had no wish for Miss Potter to be a mile nearer Quilquin Hall. Isabel shot a dismayed look at her brother who was smiling slightly.

Veryan's mouth took on its obstinate line. The occupants of the room might be fuzzy in outline, but he was well able to sense that he was being manoeuvred. Again there was this feeling of hidden information to which he was not privy. But he must be

115

wrong: Gunthorpe was merely being kind. What possible other motive could he have? He visited at Selwood Priory; he must know that poor Miss Potter was no Delilah.

'The best thing would be for Miss Potter to leave the neighbourhood entirely,' said Mrs Gunthorpe with conviction. 'Sir Veryan will scarcely wish to condone such immorality! I cannot risk dearest Isabel meeting her almost on our doorstep. Horace can be found a suitable situation. There are always clerks' positions in some business or other. The girl should go away to school for a year or so: I know of several charitable institutions. In due course she may be found a respectable position as a governess in some Christian household.'

'Poor Sylvia,' murmured Bram. 'What a fate.'

'What else is there for her?' put in Isabel sharply.

Bram reached out and gave his sister's arm a savage pinch. 'Mind your own business, Sister,' he mouthed. Aloud he said, 'What else indeed?'

* * *

It was now late April and spring was on its way at last. The hawthorns were blossoming

116

in the hedges and Dorothea had been drying primroses. They made a good mild tisane against insomnia and anxiety and Dorothea often used it. Fanny, in particular, liked it. Earlier that afternoon, Dorothea had watched from the window of her herb garret as Veryan set off for Quilquin Hall. He had taken Sir Walter's chestnut and he had, she noted with a jolt of surprise, a good seat on a horse. He was, for once, sitting up straight, and without his spectacles he was a surprisingly well-looking man. As well as visiting the Gunthorpes regularly he had been out and about the estate ever since her father's death and the exercise seemed to be doing him good. There was a touch more colour in his lean cheeks and he had stopped picking at his food.

Dorothea frowned down at a new tray of seedlings, this time some purslane and some winter savory which needed her extra care. She had not expected her cousin to be taking his duties as a landlord so seriously, but Josh reported that, with Ozzie to guide him, he was gradually making himself known to all the tenant farmers and learning the lie of the land.

Indoors, he spent most of his time going over the accounts, and it was this that worried Dorothea most. The set of accounts he had were, as he was bound to discover, grossly inadequate. They correctly showed the rents and Sir Walter's share dividends as well as the outgoings of the estate. But these did not add up. Sir Walter's outgoings far exceeded his income. It would only make sense if Veryan had had access to the red leather ledger which contained the accounts of the *Maria*, a web of credits and debits whose tentacles reached to almost every family in east Cornwall.

Dorothea had removed it. The *Maria* was hers, she told herself firmly. It was no concern of Sir Veryan's.

Cornwall, as Dorothea well knew, was a desperately poor county and smuggling, for the Cornish, was a trade like any other. Fishing was seasonal and spasmodic at best. There were no mines on the Selwood estate to offset the fishing and provide jobs. The farming methods were fifty years behind the times.

For years, Dorothea had tried to persuade her father to invest in new methods: seed drills, some proper system of crop rotation or using seaweed, or even excess pilchards for manure, but he would never bother. A prudent long-term investment had never been his style. He liked the excitements of contraband and the quick profits.

118

Her cousin, she conceded reluctantly, was not unintelligent. Sooner or later he would come up against the discrepancy in the accounts. Porthgavern was poor, but nothing like so poor as it might have been without the smuggling. Only three years ago her father had paid for the building of a stone harbour wall. It was made of handsomely dressed stone and his munificence was commemorated by an engraved inscription. It was the kind of gesture Sir Walter liked to make. Sir Veryan might well wonder how Sir Walter had paid for it.

And what would he do about it when he found out?

She was so worried about this that she finished watering her seedlings and left the herb garret. Sir Veryan was safely at Quilquin Hall so she would not risk running into him. She would go and visit one of the tenant farmers, Michael Cross and his wife. Her cousin had mentioned seeing them only the previous evening. Michael, as she well knew, was involved in the smuggling, perhaps he would be able to tell her how Sir Veryan was reacting to what he found.

The Crosses' smallholding was only a mile away and comprised about twenty-five acres. Michael grew some barley and had a few cows and sheep. The cows were the small tough Cornish breed, well used to foraging on poor soil. All the same thought Dorothea, not for the first time, long-term investment could improve the soil and the farm could then support the red Devon cows, which were larger and more productive.

'It would benefit you in the long run,' Dorothea had told her father. 'If the tenant farms are more profitable, then you can reasonably raise the rents. Everybody gains.'

Her father had pushed the idea away impatiently. Improvements would mean a financial outlay and he preferred to spend his money in more exciting ways. He liked the acclaim and publicity the new harbour had brought him, but he had no interest in more mundane improvements. His daughter certainly ran things efficiently, but she was only a woman after all. What could she be expected to know about anything?

The Cross cottage was a long, low building made of cob and reed thatch. The Crosses lived at one end and the other end was used for pigs. A few hens were pecking about in the yard as Dorothea came up and a dog began barking.

Mrs Cross, a thin, wiry woman with faded brown hair drawn back tightly in a bun, came out of the house.

'Oh, Miss Thea! Do 'ee come in. Michael

be gone to Bodmin market. 'E'm be sorry to miss 'ee.'

Mrs Cross was a slight, tetchy woman who suffered from a nervous complaint Dorothea could never quite pin down. Dorothea had heard it said that she was somewhat resentful of Michael's half-brother Abel Watson who, she felt, had been given help by Sir Walter when they, who were respectable folk, had not.

However, Mrs Cross liked a visitor and in no time she had poured Dorothea a cup of (contraband) tea and settled down for a gossip.

'Sir Veryan called yesterday,' she began. She was obviously dying to talk, but not sure how far she might go.

'I know,' said Dorothea, thinking it best to be open. 'But I confess I am worried, Mrs Cross. He knows nothing of the free-trading and . . . ' She got no further.

'Oh, Miss Thea, my Michael be that worried. The first thing Sir Veryan said was that 'e'd 'eard turrible stories of smuggling hereabouts and 'e intended to deal with it very severely.'

Dorothea bit her lip. He would, she thought.

''E says 'e and that Mr Gunthorpe be acting together in this. I expected my Michael

121

to tell 'im straight that Mr Gunthorpe was up to no good and only after what 'e could make out of it, but the great *bobba* said naught about it. 'E said afterwards that it don't do to get on wrong side of Landlord, but I think this Sir Veryan be so green as grass. Pardon me, Miss Thea, for speaking my mind, and 'e don't know Mr Gunthorpe's reputation and somebody ought to have told 'n. 'E'm not so bad, for a foreigner, and 'is heart be in the right place.'

Dorothea reached over to pat Mrs Cross's hand soothingly. Unfortunately, she thought, he won't be told. He'd certainly taken against herself. Mr Fawley had told her that he'd urged Sir Veryan to ask her about estate matters, but so far he had refused to do so and Dorothea had too much pride to offer advice unwanted.

Having started Mrs Cross couldn't stop. Dabbing at her eyes with her apron she went on in a wail, 'Oh, Miss Thea, I be worried about my Michael. Ever since 'e were taken up for carrying a dark lantern, afore Christmas, 'e'm not the same.'

'But he was released without charge,' said Dorothea, puzzled. 'My father would have got him off anyway, but it wasn't necessary. I remember talking to him about it.' It was an occupational hazard of smuggling activities that they carried a penalty. A dark lantern, which was so made that the light shone only in one direction and was often used for signalling out to sea, was regarded by the authorities as particularly suspicious. 'No Cornish jury would convict a man on suspicion of smuggling, Mrs Cross.'

'I know, Miss Thea. But ever since 'e got off 'e'm been moody.'

'I will help all I can, Mrs Cross,' said Dorothea. 'But I don't have much influence any more. All I can offer you at the moment is a little something I know you like.' She handed over a small packet. She would send over some of her primrose tonic later, she decided.

'Oh, snuff!' cried Mrs Cross, her eyes lighting up. 'I don't care for tobacco, nasty, smelly stuff. But I do like my bit o' snuff.'

* * *

Dorothea dismissed Michael Cross from her mind as she walked back over the sheep-bitten turf. Mrs Cross had confirmed what she had suspected, that Bram was trying to urge Sir Veryan to stop the Selwood smuggling, doubtless planning to take over

123

himself. If he had a spy in the ranks it would be easy enough for him to know when a run was going to be made and summon the local militia. Her father had always made it clear that he wouldn't have the militia on his land, but Sir Veryan would doubtless welcome them. The *Maria* would be impounded, broken up and her cargo sold and the result would be desperation amongst the poor, particularly those in Porthgavern. Dorothea didn't like to think of who might be taken: Abel, Michael, Daniel even. It could be any of them.

There were wider implications, too. So far, her cousin seemed to be getting a wary welcome. But if he actually took steps to stamp out the smuggling, there would soon not be a more hated man in east Cornwall. There had been a high-minded vicar with a parish near Penzance, her father once told her, who had attempted something similar. His body was found up on the moor, his head stove in by a rock. The local opinion was that he deserved it.

Much though her cousin exasperated her, Dorothea did not want him killed. She doubted whether he would heed any warnings. He certainly seemed to be very thick with Bram Gunthorpe, visiting there twice a week or so. Or was it Isabel?

Dorothea made a face. That young lady had taken to wearing a fetching new bonnet in church and Dorothea doubted whether it was for general delectation. Was she the sort of woman to attract him? Dorothea didn't know, but she didn't relish the idea of Isabel as Lady Selwood.

There seemed to be no end to the problems her cousin's arrival had brought.

When she arrived back at the Priory she went round to the stables. Josh was in a loose-box rubbing down one of the horses. He put down the hank of straw and came out.

'He intends to stop the smuggling,' said Dorothea bluntly. 'And Mr Gunthorpe, our revered local Justice of the Peace, is to help him.'

'God help us.'

'He'll need to. But Josh, how can I order another run when we probably have a traitor amongst us and Sir Veryan on the other side? We'd have Riding Officers poking their noses into everything and dragoons swarming all over.'

'Forewarned be forearmed,' said Josh. 'The militia would most likely come from Launceston. We could be having several hundred men ready for 'n if need be.'

'Horace would love that!' said Dorothea

dryly. 'But people would get hurt, my cousin's name would be reviled and I don't know what else. No Josh, there must be another way. We must find the spy.'

'I don't see how. Sir Veryan do take Ozzie with 'im on 'is rides. If 'tis 'e, there be nothing us can do to stop 'n meeting Gunthorpe.'

'I can't believe it's Ozzie. Why, he's devoted to Horace. They've known each other since they were babies.'

'And warning be to get Master Horace out of the way.'

Dorothea closed her eyes for one agonized moment. 'I wonder whether we could find somebody with a friendly eye over at Quilquin?'

'An informer, 'ee mean?'

'Yes. If Gunthorpe can do it, I don't see why we shouldn't. What about Sukey? Unless she's sweet on Gunthorpe.'

'Sukey be Mary's cousin,' Josh reminded her. 'I can't think why 'er ma let 'er go to work there after what did happen to poor Mary.'

'Sukey is badly marked by smallpox and unlikely to tempt Mr Gunthorpe. Mrs Gunthorpe's careful about who she employs nowadays. She pays well too.' She'd have to,

126

thought Dorothea bitterly. In her opinion, Mrs Gunthorpe was not entirely blameless in Mary's tragedy.

'Sukey be a good girl, though,' said Josh. 'Shall I drop by and see 'er ma then, Miss Thea? 'Ave a quiet word about it?'

'Take her some tea,' said Dorothea. 'I'll pack you up some.' Sukey would be a good choice, she thought. Bram, as she well knew, ignored women whom he did not find attractive. He would simply not see her.

She left Josh and went back into the house through the kitchen door. Mrs Kellow was there with Lucy, who was arranging biscuits on a plate.

'Sir Veryan be just come in, Miss Thea,' said Mrs Kellow. 'Tea will be served in the prior's room very shortly. Miss Potter and Miss Sylvia be there already.'

'Thank you,' said Dorothea. 'Is Master Horace in?'

'Not yet, Miss Thea. He went rabbiting with some friends. Lucy, go into the larder and fetch the plum cake.' When Lucy had gone she added, in a low voice, 'Don't 'ee fret, Miss Thea. Master Horace be safe enough. He be with the Fawley lads.'

'Thank God for that. We may even get some rabbits,' said Dorothea smiling faintly.

And her cousin was happy to be having tea with Fanny, she thought. One bright spot in all of this was that he was tolerating Fanny's contaminating presence, though God knows what might be in his mind as to her future. Still, while it lasted she was spared having to entertain Mrs Gunthorpe and Isabel. For that she must be thankful.

Surely any sensible man must prefer Fanny's quiet and soothing company to Mrs Gunthorpe's? It began to seem that in this, if in nothing else, her cousin was a sensible man.

★ ★ ★

That evening, after dinner, Veryan sat with Fanny, Dorothea and the FitzWalters in the drawing-room. He had been out most of the day and he was feeling pleasantly tired. In Oxford he had rarely slept well, often reading into the small hours. Here, he fell asleep as soon as his head touched the pillow. Miss Potter had commented, with pleasure, on his improved appetite and Veryan had noticed that his clothes were getting tighter. He must be putting on weight. He said as much.

'I think, if I may say so, Sir Veryan,' said Fanny in her gentle way, 'you could do with putting on a little weight. All that riding is probably developing your muscles.'

Dorothea raised her head from where she was darning a pair of Horace's socks and looked across at her cousin. He was still very thin, but he looked less insubstantial. She was disconcerted to find that she was looking at him with pleasure. Veryan caught her look and Dorothea flushed slightly. He looked away.

He felt surprisingly content, considering how little he opened a book these days. And though he scarcely registered the change, women were beginning to seem less alien to him. His mother had been frightened of his father and spent most of her time on the sofa in her boudoir. Winchester and Oxford had been entirely masculine worlds. Yet here he was, surrounded by women. Miss Potter was kind and welcoming. She had swiftly learned just how he liked his tea or coffee and never forgot it. She had his favourite spiced ham there for him at luncheon. He had learned to enjoy Sylvia's outspoken remarks, even though she spoke with a frankness which at first had shocked him.

And Miss Selwood? Surreptitiously, Veryan surveyed her. Now he had become accustomed to the oddity of her colouring he decided that he rather liked it. It was certainly unusual. Then again, 'Miss Thea' was spoken of with affection everywhere on the estate. She was concerned about the tenants' welfare and did her best to remedy their problems. Sir Walter received the sort of tolerance they might extend to part of the natural order over which they had no control, but they recognized Miss Selwood as a friend.

It took some time for Veryan to come to terms with this; he himself found Miss Selwood so implacable in her antagonism to him that it was a shock to realize that elsewhere she was regarded quite otherwise.

'She be proper knowledgeable about 'er herbs, sir,' Mrs Abel Watson had told him. 'She do know what 'ee should have for your cough or cut. She did save my Diggory's life, that she did, when 'e had summer fever when 'e were two. She were 'ere for three days and nights, sir, and scarcely slept. She did pull 'im through, and me and Abel will never forget it.' Then she added casually, 'But we be kin, of course.'

Kin! thought Veryan. How absurd. But he was thoughtful on the way home.

There was something else that he had picked up on his visits, and that was an unspoken hostility about Bram Gunthorpe. No one was being explicit, but he could

130

sense it all the same. Probably resentful because he is a Justice of the Peace, he thought. They know he is an upholder of the law and maybe they get their duty-free brandy and don't like the thought that it might be taken away from them.

'How are you getting on with meeting your tenants, Sir Veryan?' asked Fanny. She was mending one of Veryan's shirts.

'Well, I think, thank you. I am, at least, beginning to understand the accent! It's all seeming less strange to me.'

'That's nice,' said Fanny placidly.

'I am amazed how many tales there are of the supernatural,' went on Veryan. 'Everywhere I go I hear stories of black dogs or spectres who haunt lonely roads.'

Dorothea looked up from her darning and exchanged a quick, amused glance with Horace. I bet you do, she thought. Black dogs and ghosts always haunt lonely places where one might chance upon a smuggler or come across some hidden cache of brandy. And very useful such apparitions were too!

Veryan caught the look and his more kindly sentiment towards Dorothea vanished. Again there was this feeling of unspoken knowledge to which he had no access. Just when he was beginning to think he might belong here, there would come a look or half a sentence which showed him that he was still an outsider.

* * *

The following day Veryan came down to breakfast to find only Sylvia there. Sylvia had a healthy appetite and was happily tucking into toast, ham and eggs. She looked up apprehensively as Veryan entered. She had been about to pour herself a second cup of coffee, but stayed her hand. She glared at him resentfully. Why was he able to go over to Quilquin Hall when she had never been invited to set foot in the place? It wasn't her fault that her parents weren't married. Miss Gunthorpe sometimes smiled at her in church, but Mrs Gunthorpe just stared right through her.

The only one who paid her any attention was Bram. He had offered her a ride on his new horse, too, but her mother had said no. It was all so unfair. Horace said that Bram was an ugly customer and Sylvia should watch out for him, but Sylvia didn't see it that way at all. Why should Horace be so censorious? Mr Gunthorpe was a gentleman and, besides, he teased her and made her laugh. Where was the harm?

This horrid new cousin was just like a

schoolmaster with his preachy ways. Sylvia enjoyed making outrageous remarks and seeing him blink his eyes as he did when he was shocked. She had seriously thought of putting a slug or two in his bed, but in the end she didn't have the nerve.

'Good morning, Miss Sylvia.'

Sylvia inclined her need. She hated calling him 'Sir Veryan' and avoided it wherever possible. A silly name anyway; everybody knew it was the name of a village and, besides, he didn't deserve to be *Sir* anybody.

Veryan was peering short-sightedly at the food on the hot plate — warmed underneath by a couple of oil lamps. He looked around in a puzzled way.

Sylvia stifled a giggle. His hair was untidy and he looked like a startled owl.

'Do you need any help?' she asked politely.

'The coffee?'

'It's here. I have it.'

'Could you pour me some please, Miss Sylvia? I should be sure to spill it if I tried.' Veryan appeared to be resigned to his myopic state.

Sylvia did so and put it beside him and then moved the milk and sugar within reach. Veryan helped himself to ham and eggs and sat down.

'Are you by any chance free this morning, Miss Sylvia?'

Sylvia goggled at him. 'Free?'

'I want to go to Porthgavern. I'm particularly anxious to meet this Tamsin Bright, is it? — and see the state of her roof. You could introduce me to people and tell me what I ought to know.'

'Tamsin Wright,' corrected Sylvia. 'But why me?'

'Because I hope I can rely on you to tell me the truth about what's important.' Veryan put down his knife and fork and looked at her. It was a surprisingly direct gaze.

'Do the others lie then?'

'Not exactly,' said Veryan scrupulously. 'But I'm not convinced that I'm getting the whole truth either.'

Sylvia digested this. 'I daresay they think you'll disapprove,' she said candidly. Veryan was still looking intently at her, but it was not, she felt, an unfriendly look.

'You don't strike me as the sort of girl to worry about what I'll think,' he said, smiling suddenly, and added, 'I am aware that you find me fuddy-duddy, Sylvia. I had no brothers or sisters to show me otherwise. I shall, if I may, rely on you to teach me better.' Veryan was not used to apologizing to schoolgirls and it was the best he could manage.

'I'll try, Cousin Veryan,' said Sylvia gruffly, embarrassed in her turn.

* * *

Considering that Veryan and Dorothea rarely spoke directly to each other it was surprising how much they occupied each other's thoughts. Dorothea often found herself thinking about her cousin while she was making up her potions and mulling over what she had heard him saying to the others.

Something was changing and she wasn't sure she liked it. Whilst her father was alive the house seemed to be divided into male and female sides. Sir Walter kept to the library or pursued his amours outside; when Horace was at home he was out on his own pursuits; sailing, fishing or riding about the countryside.

Dorothea had her work on the estate, but usually she was in the garden or in her herb garret and the evenings she spent with Fanny and Sylvia.

Now they were far more together. Both Veryan and Horace sat with them of an

135

evening. Her cousin seemed to enjoy chatting to Fanny and recently he'd taken to teasing Sylvia and discussing things with Horace. Sometimes he would play speculation with the FitzWalters.

The new relationship was demonstrated when one evening Veryan's front lock of hair fell down for the third time and Sylvia expostulated, 'Why don't you get your hair cut, Cousin Veryan? You can't see anything!'

'Sylvia!' cried Fanny. 'Pray excuse her, Sir Veryan.'

Veryan only laughed.

'You'd look much more handsome with it cut, wouldn't he, Thea? At the moment you look like a Goonhilly pony. Josh would cut it for you, Cousin. He always cut Father's.'

Dorothea was speechless.

'I know I'm not handsome,' said Veryan. 'The most I can hope for is to pass unnoticed.'

He spoke without bitterness, but there was a wistful note in his voice that Dorothea had never heard before. What has happened to him, she wondered? There was some sadness there that touched her suddenly. She wasn't sure she liked it.

The improvement with Sylvia spilled over to Horace who renewed his offer to show his cousin some good rides and they went fishing together.

Veryan took to reading to them of an evening — using Lady Selwood's lorgnette, which made Sylvia giggle. At first Horace and Sylvia scarcely listened, but when Veryan started on Scott's *The Lay of the Last Minstrel* they both stopped what they were doing.

' *'Why watch these warriors, arm'd, by night?*
They watch to hear the blood hound baying:
They watch to hear the war-horn braying; . . . ' '

'I say, Cousin,' exclaimed Horace, 'this is something like!'

Veryan read well, Dorothea noted half-resentfully. His deep voice was expressive without being affected and he had a good ear for the poetry. It was a tale of border battles, love and revenge. There were ancient curses, wizards, malignant dwarfs and thwarted lovers: to hear him reading of love and passion in that deep clear voice made her feel . . . what? Dorothea did not know, but she was aware that it stirred depths she would have preferred left undisturbed.

137

She wrenched her mind away. When she was little her mother had read to her, Bible stories mainly, but also bits of Shakespeare. She had often wondered if her own love of gardening was because of that early reading.

Hot lavender, mints, savory, marjoram,
The marigold, that goes to bed wi' th'
    sun
And with him rises, weeping: these are
    flowers
Of middle summer, and I think they
    are given
To men of middle age. Y'are very
    welcome.

Now why did Sir Veryan make her think of that?

The following morning, Fanny said, 'Dear Cousin Veryan. I don't know what it is, Thea, but he seems to be making us into a family.'

'It's 'Cousin Veryan' now, is it?' said Dorothea, pulling at her sewing with sharp little tugs.

'He said I might. And he's such a good influence on Horace and Sylvia.'

'A paragon, in fact.'

'But?'

'I just wish he'd behave well to *me*.'

138

'But Thea . . . He treats you with the greatest civility.'

'He treats me . . . He resents me. I don't know why.'

'He isn't used to clever females, dearest.'

'I, clever? I'm nothing out of the ordinary.'

'You know all about the estate, though.'

'Which he never asks me about,' retorted Dorothea acidly. They had been sowing barley recently. Sir Veryan had not asked her about it, or what price calves would fetch, or anything else. He enjoyed Fanny's cosy femininity, was amused by Sylvia and got on with Horace, but as far as she was concerned, he seemed only to want to push her out.

'You are rather prickly sometimes, Thea,' said Fanny gently. 'You did snub him about the Milletts.'

'He was being so censorious,' said Dorothea stung.

'I'm sure it was only because he didn't understand,' urged Fanny. 'You might have explained about Jack's accident.'

'He could have asked instead of just assuming that Jack was lazy.'

Fanny gave up.

★ ★ ★

139

Matters came to a head a few days later. Dorothea had spent most of the morning in the herb garret and then went into the garden to check on her chervil. When she got there she found Veryan standing in the garden in earnest discussion with Bill Kellow, the gardener.

'Well, I don't rightly know . . . ' Bill was saying. 'Miss Thea 'ud be that upset . . . '

Dorothea stepped forward. 'What would I be upset about?' she asked, trying to quell a sudden surge of anxiety. Bill tugged his forelock and left. Plainly, he did not want to be involved. Veryan turned reluctantly.

'I thought of expanding the vegetables,' he began. 'There's a market for early broccoli, I understand. Kellow has explained that it would need a sunny spot which would entail grubbing up your bits and pieces.' He gestured vaguely towards the herbs. Something snapped in Dorothea.

'You really dislike me, don't you? Anything, but anything that I have done you want to destroy. I've been dealing with the cattle going to Bodmin market for years. You know that. But have you ever asked me anything? You'd rather die! Indeed, you're happy to be swindled by Farmer Wynn into letting him have a cow for three guineas. It's all over the county!' Veryan, she saw with satisfaction was looking furious.

'And now it's my herbs. Does it ever occur to you that I haven't been involved with the estate for my own selfish reasons? Father gambled. Hugely. Some years there was a shortfall of over two thousand pounds. He never cared about the estate except for what it would bring in.

'I was the one who was left to pick up the pieces. Mr Fawley could never stand up to Father. I could. In the end, Father would give in because it was easier. You may see me as a nagging, unwomanly female, Sir Veryan, but without my efforts you wouldn't *have* an estate.

'I'm sorry I don't conform to your starchy notions. I'm sure Miss Gunthorpe will do much better. But you'll keep your hands off my herbs or I won't answer for the consequences.' Dorothea brushed angrily at the tears of pure rage that were coursing down her cheeks. She spun on her heel and was about to storm off.

'Miss Selwood! Cousin Dorothea! Please don't go.'

Dorothea hesitated.

'Couldn't we discuss this? I shan't touch your herb garden. I didn't realize . . . '

Dorothea's anger began to subside. Veryan, for once, was looking straight at her. His

141

blue-grey eyes had very small hazel flecks in them she noticed. Unconsciously, she pushed a stray wisp of hair back into place. She then took out her handkerchief, mopped her eyes and blew her nose.

'What do you want to discuss?' she asked suspiciously.

'We might start with the garden,' suggested Veryan. She looks much better when she is animated, he thought. Almost pretty — in spite of her red nose from all that crying.

5

Bram was cautiously optimistic, at least as far as getting his fingers in the Selwood smuggling pie was concerned. Selwood now visited them regularly and Bram had been bored by Veryan's earnestly expressed desire to be of benefit to those on his estate. He had put up with such mawkish sentiments in the hope of influencing Selwood in other directions; for example, between Selwood and Dorothea. He had swiftly discovered that Veryan disliked and mistrusted his cousin and this suited Bram's book very well. Accordingly, he had pooh-poohed Dorothea's assertion that Veryan had sold a cow too cheaply at Bodmin market.

In fact, Bram's sole interest in his estate was to squeeze his tenants for as high a rent as possible. Unlike Dorothea, he had never been to Bodmin market in his life — it would be beneath him as a gentleman — and in this he agreed with his mother that it was a most unsuitable place for a lady.

'Mr Fawley remarked on her ability,' said Veryan, frowning.

'He would though, wouldn't he?' responded

Bram. 'I daresay it lets him off the hook. I cannot credit that Farmer Wynn, a most respectable man by all accounts, would cheat you, Selwood. The idea is ridiculous.' Nobody knew better than Bram how to set one person against another.

'I have a kindness for young Horace,' he said next. 'May I ask if you have made any decision about his future?'

'I have agreed to allow him to finish the school year, at least. I cannot say that Horace himself was best pleased. Term starts next week.'

'Next week? Poor Miss Potter will be devastated to lose him so soon after Sir Walter's death.'

'You think I shouldn't?'

Bram shrugged. 'A week or so wouldn't make much difference to the school and it would cushion the blow for his mother.' Bram changed the subject. There was no point in pushing it. His mother had done more harm than good, he thought, by her tactless insistence on Miss Potter and the FitzWalters going: he could see that it had served no purpose other than to put up Sir Veryan's back. He certainly showed no signs of booting them out.

Bram had several grudges against Horace that he wanted to satisfy: he had been one of those in the fishing-boat that had decoyed and duped the Revenue cutter. Secondly, Horace had refused to gamble and had not been too tactful about it. 'No thank you,' he'd said and then muttered, 'You win too damn often for my liking.' Bram had affected not to hear, but he'd been furious. Finally, Horace had more than once removed Sylvia from his vicinity. Horace should be taught a lesson. And soon.

At dinner in Selwood Priory that evening, Veryan announced that he had decided that Horace should have another fortnight at home to be a comfort to his mother. He would write to the school in Exeter and tell them.

'Oh I say, Cousin Veryan, thanks!' cried Horace. 'The Fawleys have asked me to go mackerel fishing with them one evening and I really want to go. Capital sport.'

Dorothea looked up, her eyes wide with dismay. It had been a comfort to know that by next week Horace would be safe. 'Why?' she asked suspiciously.

'I've just said.' Veryan's hackles rose, as they always did, when she questioned his decisions. 'So that he may support his mother.'

Dorothea brushed this aside. 'It was only

yesterday you were talking of him going back to school.'

'As it happens I was talking to Mr Gunthorpe today. He suggested it.'

Yes, he would, thought Dorothea.

'I think it's very kind of Mr Gunthorpe,' said Sylvia eagerly.

'He also mentioned giving you a ride on Brandy,' said Veryan, smiling. 'We'll have to see what can be arranged.'

Dorothea and Fanny looked at each other in dismay. Horace put down his knife and fork. 'I say, Cousin, is that wise?'

'Why shouldn't I have a treat too?' flashed Sylvia. 'Are boys the only ones allowed to?'

'What's wrong with Mr Gunthorpe, then?' asked Veryan indulgently. 'He seems a gentleman to me.'

'He is,' affirmed Sylvia hotly.

'No, he ain't,' interrupted Horace. 'We all know what happened to Mary Pengelly . . . '

'That's not fair,' cried Sylvia. 'Father's had babies all over the place and nobody ever suggested that he wasn't a gentleman.'

Fanny, after an agonized look at Dorothea, rose from the table and, with a muttered excuse, left the room.

'Sylvia!' cried Dorothea. 'You've distressed your mother.'

'Oh well!' Sylvia subsided. 'All the same,

146

I don't see what Mary Pengelly has to do with my going riding with Mr Gunthorpe.'

'Nothing at all,' said Veryan firmly. If this Mary had been an unchaste maid up at Quilquin Hall, as he gathered she had, Gunthorpe was quite right to dismiss her.

Sylvia stuck her tongue out at her brother. The rest of the meal was eaten in silence. Dorothea did not know how to reopen the subject. Veryan, she had begun to realize, had a streak of obstinacy that led him to dig in his toes at the first sign of opposition. Sylvia, she was sure, did not know the whole of poor Mary's story and it was not a fit subject for the dining-room in any case. She would have a word with Fanny who seemed to be able to manage Sir Veryan without driving him into a corner. She herself would have enough to do keeping an eye on Horace.

★ ★ ★

The following morning Dorothea was in the herb garret. She was preparing an infusion for Tamsin Wright's cough and bunches of dried cowslip, marshmallow, soapwort, mullein and balm of Gilead were lying on her table waiting to be weighed out. As usual, she found herself thinking about

Veryan. Fanny had obviously explained about Mary Pengelly, for Veryan had been in a conciliatory mood at breakfast that morning.

'You should have explained, Cousin,' he said, reproachfully.

'I did not wish to discuss so unsavoury a subject in front of Sylvia.'

'Of course; I do not believe that Mr Gunthorpe, however reprehensible his behaviour might have been, meant so dreadful a tragedy to occur.'

Dorothea did not wish to antagonize her cousin again so she confined herself to shaking her head sadly.

'Nor do I think that he has any improper designs on Sylvia. Why, she is only a child.'

'Mary was only fourteen,' retorted Dorothea, before she could stop herself. She saw Veryan's lips tighten and added hastily, 'It would save Miss Potter a great deal of anxiety if she knew that Sylvia was properly chaperoned. She feels her daughter's position to be particularly awkward and whereas Mr Gunthorpe's intentions may be of the purest,' — she tried to stop a note of irony creeping in — 'nevertheless, riding alone with him might give rise to gossip which would be very detrimental to Sylvia's chances in life.'

'Hm,' said Veryan thoughtfully.

Thinking over this conversation Dorothea

felt mildly encouraged. She had learned that her cousin could not bear a flat contradiction. But this time she had managed to convey her worries about Sylvia without betraying too much scepticism about his view of Bram Gunthorpe. She could not help wondering whether Bram himself had used a similar technique to get Veryan to agree to the riding expedition in the first place.

Dorothea was not used to dealing in subtleties. Her father had always demanded that she be straightforward. 'Can't bear missishness,' he said. 'Say what you mean, girl.' She had always been straightforward with Josh or Horace. It was true that she softened things with Fanny: she had not told her of the threat to Horace, for example, and they had never spoken directly of the smuggling. She hadn't realized that she would have to do it with Veryan.

She stripped off some dried mullein leaves and then began to crumble the flowers into a small bowl. She did not, at first, hear the knock downstairs. It came louder. She stopped crumbling the flowers, wiped her hands on her apron and went downstairs. It was Diggory.

'Please, Miss Thea, my dad do say that 'e and Dan'l 'ud like a word if convenient.'

'When?'

'So soon as may be, Miss Thea.'

'I'm here all morning.' Sir Veryan had gone over to Quilquin Hall again — doubtless to bask in Isabel's smiles and to lap up Bram's insincerities. She smiled at Diggory and handed him a couple of aniseed twists. He bobbed his head and left.

It could only be about the *Maria*, she thought. She knew that the repairs were completed and she would be ready to sail. The moment Diggory had gone, Dorothea locked the door, went to the hidden safe and took out the money. Four hundred guineas. She sorted it into eight leather bags. Some rent money had come in she knew and she toyed with the idea of borrowing some — she had a spare set of keys to the library safe — but decided it was not worth the risk.

She had had some conversations with Veryan about expanding the garden produce to take advantage of the navy garrisons now stationed in Plymouth and she was aware that he was keeping careful accounts in a meticulous Italianate hand. Any 'borrowing' would almost certainly be discovered.

An hour or so later, Abel and Daniel arrived. Dorothea let them in, locked the door behind them, offered them some brandy and they sat down on a wooden bench by the window. Daniel liked to keep an eye out for who might be coming or going.

They talked for some time about the threat to Horace, the problems of Sir Veryan's new drive against free-trading and Dorothea's only having 400 guineas to invest. Daniel was philosophical.

'I do know a gentleman who'd be glad to rent some space in the *Maria* for this voyage,' he said. 'He'll offer 'ee a hundred guineas, Miss Thea.'

'Is he safe?'

'Aye. He be a retired admiral in Plymouth. He can sell as much tobacco and brandy as I can bring him, he do say. He'll pay 'ee a hundred guineas and me ten per cent.' He saw she was looking worried and added, 'He be sound, Miss Thea. I've known'n for some years.'

Dorothea looked at Abel who nodded. 'Do it,' she said. 'My share can go into the stock.' She handed Daniel the bags of guineas. He signed for them and pushed them into a satchel by his side.

'What do 'ee want this time, Miss Thea?'

'As much lace as you can manage. Top quality, Daniel.' The London season was nearly upon them. Debutantes all over the West Country and their mamas would pay good prices for lace just now. 'Otherwise, whatever you think best.' She watched as

Daniel noted down her requirements.

'Take particular care this time, Dan,' she finished. 'Gunthorpe has no money owing and I daresay he'd like to get his hands on some. He will almost certainly try something with the militia.'

'I did hear tell he be gambling in Plymouth. I did meet some men in Mayoralty House.'

'Winning or losing?' asked Dorothea sharply. This was most unwelcome news. What was he doing there? That was where they held auctions of ship's goods either taken from the French or else smugglers' ships' goods captured by excisemen.

'Winning. He did make sure o' that, I daresay.'

'Don't 'ee worry, Miss Thea,' put in Abel. 'The word be out. We'll keep a watch on what Gunthorpe be doing.'

'You be careful too, Abel. I don't want trouble. Oh I wish my cousin hadn't taken this maggot into his head.'

''E be doing good things, Miss Thea. Tamsin's roof be near finished and I heard 'e be looking to improve they fish cellars.'

'That's the problem,' said Dorothea wryly. 'He means well.'

★ ★ ★

That evening the family were assembled for dinner. The gong would sound in five minutes. Sylvia, in a high-necked white dress with a black sash, was leafing through a back number of *The Elegancies of Fashion*. Fanny was occupied with some sewing and Dorothea was trying not to worry. Where was Horace? From his school reports she knew that he was frequently late with handing in essays, but he was never, ever, late for meals.

Veryan was absorbed in the *Odes* of Pindar.

The gong went. Fanny looked up. 'No Horace?'

'We shan't wait,' said Veryan, snapping shut the Pindar. He disliked unpunctuality and was determined that Horace should learn the manners of a gentleman. He rose. 'Mrs FitzWalter.' He offered Fanny his arm.

Fanny, slightly pink, rose in her turn and placed her fingers on his sleeve. Sylvia looked at Dorothea and grinned. Thank goodness for that, thought Dorothea. Her cousin had decided to bestow his own measure of respectability on Fanny's position. Perhaps he'd eventually come round in other areas. She was guiltily aware that that very morning she had set in motion a course of action of which

153

he'd thoroughly disapprove. But where was Horace?

There was the sound of running feet and Mrs Kellow rushed in, not waiting to knock. 'Miss Thea!' she gasped, one hand at her heaving bosom. 'There been an accident. Ozzie just brought Master Horace back. There been a rock fall.'

'Horace!' gasped Fanny. She swayed and fell. Sylvia ran to her mother.

'Is he much hurt?'

'His arm, Miss Thea. You'm better have a look. He was hit on the head too, but he be conscious.'

'Cousin.' Dorothea turned to Veryan. 'Please look after Fanny. Sylvia, your mother's hartshorn should be in her reticule.' She left the room before Veryan could expostulate.

Horace was lying on the kitchen floor. Somebody, Mrs Kellow probably, had cut him out of his jacket and shirt. His eyes were shut and blood seeped from a jagged cut on his head. One arm lay bruised and swollen by his side. Lucy was gently mopping at the head wound.

Dorothea made a quick survey. 'Cut off his hair please, Mrs Kellow. That wound will need stitching. Where's Molly?'

'Here, miss.' Molly, white-faced and

trembling, was standing by the door, her hands twisting in her apron.

'Molly, get my medicine bag. It's up in my room. Lucy, put the kettle on, please.'

Dorothea turned her attention to Horace's arm. The bruise was spreading right up to the shoulder. It looked bad, but it might have been worse. Mrs Kellow had finished cutting Horace's hair and revealed a jagged cut about an inch and a half long. 'Brandy, please, Mrs Kellow.'

Mrs Kellow handed her a glass and Dorothea, putting one arm under Horace's back to support him, ruthlessly tipped it down his throat. 'I want him out of it.' She held out the glass for a refill. This time she took the clean cloth Mrs Kellow had ready and cleaned the wound with the brandy. Horace winced. He was moving his head from side to side. 'Beauty,' he muttered.

'Broke her foreleg, she did,' whispered Mrs Kellow. 'Josh be gone out with Joe. She'll have to be shot.'

'And Ozzie?'

'Cuts and bruises, but he be in better shape than Master Horace. The cob she be all right. Ozzie brought Master Horace in slung over the horse.'

Dorothea nodded. Molly had come back with the bag and had once more retreated to the corner of the room, sniffing audibly. Dorothea nodded to Mrs Kellow who came and held the cut together. Dorothea put several stitches in with strong silk thread, wiped it with a measure of brandy and bandaged it.

'Not as bad as it looked,' she said tersely, 'We'll have to watch the concussion, though.'

The arm was different. Gently, she began to feel it. It had swollen horribly and turned black. She moved it in the socket. Horace groaned, but it seemed to be all right. The elbow, too, worked. 'It may not be broken after all,' she said. 'I don't want to make bad worse.'

'Ah, 'e do look mortal bad,' said Lucy. She had a soft spot for Master Horace, who was not above stealing a kiss or two.

'We must give it a chance to heal,' said Dorothea. 'The arnica will help with the bruising and I think a comfrey poultice, Mrs Kellow. That will help any internal bleeding.' She glanced across at Molly. 'Molly, go and tell Miss Potter that Master Horace is badly bruised and cut, but should be all right. She can see him in a little while. And then go and get his bed ready. Pull it back so that we can get him in.' She wondered briefly whether she should apologize to Sir Veryan for being bossy again, but decided that he'd have to put up with it. Molly bobbed a curtsey and left.

Half an hour later, Horace, thoroughly doped with laudanum, was put to bed and Dorothea went to the stables to see to Ozzie. He was lying on the straw mattress in the loft he shared with Joe, the gardener's boy. As Mrs Kellow said, Ozzie had got off lightly. Dorothea dealt with his cuts and bruises.

'How be Master Horace?' he asked groggily, when she'd finished.

Dorothea told him. 'What happened, Ozzie?'

'I'm not rightly sure, Miss Thea. We be trotting back along the sands when this fall of rock comes. 'Course, rocks do fall there sometimes, but it bain't raining, nor nothing.'

Dorothea was silent.

'Beauty be done for, Miss Thea.' Ozzie was nearly crying. 'Master Horace, he'm be proper upset. If only I'd gone in front.'

'Don't blame yourself, Ozzie. You brought Master Horace home safely. It wasn't your fault.' She saw that he was still unconvinced and added, 'Here, drink this. We'll see how you are in the morning.'

She waited while Ozzie took the laudanum and then left. It seemed to be one thing after another, she thought. Still, at least Horace would be confined to the house for a while.

She arrived back in the kitchen to find a grim-lipped Veryan. Oh God, she thought, he's on his high horse again. He turned round as Dorothea came in and said, 'I've been explaining to Mrs Kellow, who does not appear to understand me, that Horace should be seen by a proper doctor. These herbs of yours are all very well, but his injuries look serious to me and I want a professional to have a look at him.'

Dorothea opened her mouth and shut it again. Careful Dorothea, she thought. She could see that he was seriously upset, probably as much by her high-handedness as by concern for Horace.

'I should have consulted you before treating Horace, Cousin,' she said carefully. 'Please forgive me.' He cannot have enjoyed being left with an unconscious Fanny, she thought. She wasn't sure how to continue. After a moment or two she added, 'The nearest doctor is Doctor Tripp in Launceston, but he's usually to be found propping up the bar in the White Hart, I fear.' Veryan, she saw, had come out of his mood and was looking thoughtful.

'I didn't mean to impugn your abilities, Cousin,' he said.

Dorothea laughed and after a minute or

so Veryan smiled reluctantly. 'Would you be willing to wait until the morning and see how he goes on?' she asked. 'I think it would be best for him not to be disturbed again tonight.'

'I do believe you are trying to manage me, Cousin,' said Veryan. There was a touch of mischief in his voice she had never heard before.

'I am all too aware of how much I antagonize you,' said Dorothea ruefully. 'I really do not mean to. My father always told me to speak my mind and not be missish, but Fanny has explained to me how bossy I sound. I have been trying to be more conciliatory.'

'Hm,' said Veryan, slightly nonplussed by her straightforwardness. To cover up his embarrassment he said, 'Mrs Kellow, if everything is now returned to normal, I believe we could do with some dinner.'

★ ★ ★

With extreme reluctance, Veryan wrote to the Warden of New College, Oxford and resigned his fellowship. It was like cutting a lifeline, but there was no help for it. Whether he liked it or not — and he didn't, Selwood Priory was going to have to be his home for the immediate future.

He then wrote to Toby Marcham and asked him to organize the packing up and carriage of his books to the Priory. They would have to go by sea and it would be an expensive business, but Veryan couldn't bear to sell them as would have been sensible.

Toby responded by inviting himself to stay. He'd borrow the family travelling coach as far as Plymouth and, if Veryan could arrange transport by sea from Plymouth to Porthgavern, bring the books himself.

Toby was curious to see how Veryan was settling in: he simply couldn't imagine so reclusive a person striding over his acres and hobnobbing with the local farmers. Veryan's knowledge of things agricultural was confined to Virgil's *Georgics*; how on earth would he cope with the muddy reality?

There was another reason. Usually, April saw Toby in London for the season. He took a couple of rooms in Half Moon Street and set out to enjoy himself. Unfortunately, a number of mamas over the years had done their homework on him: he was a personable young man, his income was modest, but he was an only son and in due course would inherit a very pretty little estate and, in short, should be put on their list of acceptable sons-in-law.

He decided that a month or so in Cornwall was preferable. It would leave him enough time to go to London in June should he wish to do so.

Are you sure you wish to come to such a savage place? wrote Veryan. *Of course, I should be delighted to see you, but I must warn you that there is nothing whatever to do — no civilized pleasures, that is.*

Toby had none of Veryan's problems travelling. He took the journey by easy stages and no landlord fobbed him off with an inferior room. Most of the chambermaids, confronted with a handsome and generous man, were happy to oblige him in ways Veryan would certainly not have approved of.

When he arrived at the Royal Hotel in Plymouth, there was a message awaiting him: he was to ask for Abel Watson, whose lugger was currently lying in Sutton Pool. The books were manoeuvred onto the deck with surprisingly little trouble — to a man who had been shifting ankers of brandy all his life in darkness and under difficult conditions, to move books, however unwieldy, was no problem. Toby accompanied Abel on the lugger and the coachman and postilion returned with the travelling coach to Toby's father.

Veryan had been wary of explaining the situation at Selwood Priory and Toby was astounded to find the reality. Here was the Reverend Sir Veryan Selwood, Fellow of New College, Oxford and author of a number of erudite monographs on Greek literature, not only condoning, but seeming perfectly content with a situation which a month or so ago would have had him sending for the officers of the nearest magdalen.

Toby was very much amused. He at once followed Veryan's example and called Fanny 'Mrs FitzWalter' and treated her as he would his hostess; Horace, interestingly pale and with his arm in a sling, was just like any other adolescent; and he gently teased Sylvia.

And, to Veryan's consternation, he got on well with Dorothea.

'She's refreshingly direct,' he said to Veryan the evening after his arrival. They were sitting in the library over a glass of brandy.

'Scarcely ladylike,' retorted Veryan.

'Nonsense,' said Toby laughing. 'She's straightforward. You can trust what she says.'

'You cannot trust her at all,' replied Veryan. 'I constantly feel that she gives me only half the information. She may be direct, but she's not open.'

Interesting, thought Toby. Miss Selwood

somehow seems to have got under his skin. Aloud he said, 'And that wonderful colouring. She's appallingly dressed, of course, but properly togged out, she'd be a sensation in London.'

'Miss Selwood?' said Veryan incredulously. 'Why the locals half-think she's a witch with that mismatched colouring. Wait until you see Miss Gunthorpe. Now she really is pretty.'

Gunthorpe, thought Toby, the name rings a bell. Then he thought, Veryan has changed. He'd never known him offer a personal remark on any woman before. He looked better too. He'd filled out a bit and lost some of that scholarly pallor.

'Excellent brandy,' he said. 'Do you get much smuggling round here?'

Veryan closed his eyes for a moment. 'I'm rapidly coming to the conclusion that there's nothing else. I'm endeavouring to put a stop to it.'

Toby looked at him in consternation. He hoped Veryan hadn't bitten off more than he could chew.

★ ★ ★

In the drawing-room, Dorothea and Fanny were gossiping about their new guest.

Dorothea had not wanted him to come at all. God save them from another starchy recluse! But the moment they met she felt that, at last, she had an ally. It was perfectly obvious from Molly's and Lucy's smirks that Mr Marcham's charms were not lost on them. She said as much.

'I do hope we don't have that sort of trouble,' said Fanny anxiously.

'Oh, I think not. Mrs Kellow will keep an eye on Lucy and Molly. And he behaves just as he ought to Sylvia.'

'But she might fall in love with him. He is very good-looking.'

'She'll be safer with Mr Marcham than with Bram Gunthorpe,' replied Dorothea. 'Don't you like him, Fanny?'

'Oh yes, his manners are most gentleman-like. But . . . I feel such a fraud being called Mrs FitzWalter.' Fanny's lip began to tremble.

'Why should you not be Mrs FitzWalter?' said Dorothea bracingly. 'It's an excellent idea. I cannot imagine why Father didn't think of it years ago.' Things, she felt, were looking up. Horace was improving steadily. He was still very upset about Beauty (far more so than about his father) but her cousin had promised him another horse in due course. Then Mr Marcham looked as though he would make an agreeable addition to their circle; he would certainly provide Sylvia with a more acceptable sample of masculine attention.

The only thing that did surprise her was that Sir Veryan had a friend like Mr Marcham in the first place. Perhaps her cousin had unexpected depths.

★ ★ ★

Shortly after his arrival, Veryan took his guest over to Quilquin Hall. He himself found Miss Gunthorpe's contrived expressions of admiration tedious, but he guessed that she would appreciate making the acquaintance of the eligible Mr Marcham. He had no doubt that Toby would be able to fend her off far better than he managed to do.

The moment Toby met Bram Gunthorpe he knew where he'd come across the name before. For a while, Gunthorpe had patronized a gaming-hell in King Street, an establishment notorious for its card sharps and carefully concealed mirrors to entrap greenhorns from the country and fleece them. Gunthorpe was too skilful to have been caught cheating; on the other hand, there were several men Toby knew who would no longer play with him.

Toby listened, therefore, to Bram's strictures on the evils of smuggling with some incredulity.

'I am a Justice of the Peace,' he told Toby. 'You must know, Mr Marcham, that is a thankless task hereabouts. Smuggling is rife as Selwood here can confirm.'

'Shocking,' said Toby dryly. The man's a hypocrite, he thought. Any *habitué* of a King Street gaming-hell was scarcely likely to be concerned about smuggling.

The door opened and Mrs Gunthorpe and Isabel entered. Introductions were made. Mrs Gunthorpe with the ease of long practice, extracted from Toby his status — 'Only son and no sisters' she could be heard muttering; his estate and political opinions — 'Whig', she shook her head disapprovingly — and his age. She then introduced him to Isabel.

Isabel was delighted to meet Toby. She had found Veryan very uphill work: he could not even frame a compliment, although she threw several cues his way. Mr Marcham knew his duty.

'Miss Gunthorpe. Now I see what has kept my friend so long in Cornwall.'

Mrs Gunthorpe had taken Veryan by the arm and moved him firmly to one side. 'Sir Veryan,' she began, 'it will not do. You must remove Miss Potter and those children.'

Veryan drew himself up. For a moment he looked like Sir Walter. 'Must, madam? I must?'

'People are beginning to talk. All this procrastination is most inconvenient.'

Bram had been listening and said impatiently, 'Come, Mama, Sir Veryan has weightier matters on his mind than his domestic arrangements. Selwood, would your friend enjoy a convivial evening at the White Horse in Liskeard, do you think? I know you, in holy orders, don't gamble, but Marcham might enjoy it and I could introduce him to some good fellows. Tripp, for example, our local doctor.'

Mrs Gunthorpe sniffed. 'Drunkard.'

'He enjoys good company, that's all.' Bram flashed his mother a warning look.

'You'll have to ask Marcham,' said Veryan. 'I have no objection.'

Toby, however, refused. On the way home he said, 'I came across Gunthorpe in London a couple of years ago. He didn't recognize me and I didn't remind him.'

'Why not? He's a pleasant companion.' Veryan was frowning.

If you like gamblers with dubious reputations, thought Toby. But he'd learned to be careful with Veryan and said only, 'I know nothing against him, but he keeps some pretty queer company.'

Veryan said nothing.

After a moment, Toby laughed and said, 'I can quite see why Mrs FitzWalter stays. The thought of Mrs Gunthorpe having *carte blanche* to visit is singularly unnerving!'

Veryan smiled reluctantly.

'I can think of many ladies in Society with far worse reputations than Mrs FitzWalter. And I like Miss Selwood, too.'

'Ah, Miss Selwood,' said Veryan dryly.

'You don't like her?'

'I find her self-opinionated, bossy and her conversation does not have that modest reserve which is becoming to females,' said Veryan stiffly.

'You prefer Miss Gunthorpe, then?' said Toby, intrigued. He couldn't remember ever having discussed women with Veryan before.

'Miss Gunthorpe?' Veryan looked taken aback. 'No. Though she is, of course, a lady. And pretty, too.'

'If you like china dolls,' said Toby. 'Personally, I prefer Miss Selwood's fire and ice.'

'She's skinny,' said Veryan.

'Slender,' corrected Toby.

Veryan was silent.

168

★ ★ ★

In spite of Veryan's sour words to Toby Marcham, the cousins had managed to achieve a cautious truce. 'You must explain things, Thea,' Fanny had said, and Dorothea made a conscious effort to do so.

For his part, Veryan took care to ask Dorothea about estate affairs and Dorothea told him what prices could be asked for cows or sheep and what prices he could expect to pay. Mrs Gunthorpe had unwittingly confirmed Dr Tripp's drunkenness and Veryan could see for himself that Horace's wounds were healing as they ought.

They even found themselves discussing seed drills and improved stock breeding.

'You know an awful lot,' said Veryan, just stopping himself from adding, 'for a woman'. She's a bit like Matty, he thought suddenly. Matty would say what she thought, too. And she was always encouraging. He was so surprised at this revelation that he missed what Dorothea replied and had to ask her to repeat it.

Dorothea made a face. 'I was saying that my knowledge has not been of much use up to now. Father could never be bothered.'

'I am surprised. It could have improved the income from the land, if your calculations are right, by several hundred per cent.'

'Father preferred gambling,' said Dorothea shortly.

No lady should criticize her father, thought Veryan. But he was learning, so, after a moment he said, 'With Gunthorpe?'

'Oh yes, and with anybody else who would play.'

'Marcham says that Gunthorpe gambled in London. Had you heard this?'

Dorothea nodded. And up to his neck in smuggling she wanted to add. Instead she said carefully, 'I know Mrs Gunthorpe is seriously worried. Mr Gunthorpe 'borrows' money from her.'

'Impossible. No gentleman would do such a thing.'

'Quite.' Dorothea attempted to remove all trace of irony from her voice.

Veryan opened his mouth and then shut it again.

But there were other things on Dorothea's mind, apart from her relationship with her cousin. Mrs Kellow had asked for a word with her.

'Sorry to bother 'ee, Miss Thea. 'Tis Molly. I don't rightly know what be the matter with her. She be off her food. Just picks at it. She won't say anything. Just bursts into tears.'

Oh God, thought Dorothea, now what? Mr Marcham? Surely not. Molly was a pretty girl, rather buxom, with glossy brown hair and ringlets she liked to toss about. She had a habit of falling in love with unsuitable men. The last one had been a ne're-do-well from Cawsand way who, fortunately, had been pressed and was now, Dorothea hoped, serving his country in His Majesty's Navy.

Ozzie was rather smitten with Molly's charms, but it was unlikely that Molly would be so sensible as to return his affection.

'She's not . . . ?'

'No, God be praised.' Mrs Kellow kept a firm eye on the maids.

'I'll have a word with her,' said Dorothea. 'I daresay she's in love again.' She remembered Molly cowering by the door the night Horace was brought in. Oh God, surely Horace wasn't starting to follow in his father's footsteps? Then she remembered the note. Could it have been from Molly and that was why she was so upset? But no. Molly couldn't write.

Molly, when summoned to the herb garret would say nothing. She burst into hysterical tears and cried, 'I done nothing wrong, Miss Thea.'

'Nobody is suggesting that you have, Molly.'

Dorothea checked her pulse — tumultuous — her tongue, eyes and throat and asked a number of questions. The girl seemed all right. There was nothing physical at any rate. All the same, there now seemed a distinct possibility that Molly had put the note in the saddle-room, on behalf of an unknown person.

'Thank you for your help with Master Horace last week,' she said casually, as she turned to make up a tonic. There was a small looking-glass on the wall in front of her and she managed to keep an eye on the maid as she spoke.

Was it the light or had Molly turned pale?

'It would be dreadful if anything had happened to him,' Dorothea went on, and watched Molly's fingers twist in her apron. 'Would you like this flavoured with elderflower or peppermint, Molly?'

'Peppermint.' Molly's voice was barely above a whisper.

Dorothea turned. Molly was staring rigidly in front of her. 'I can't tell 'ee nothings, Miss Thea. It be an accident.'

'I wish I could be sure of that,' said Dorothea. Molly seized the bottle Dorothea held out to her and fled.

Dorothea washed her hands and put away

the measuring spoons and jugs. It now looked as though the person they were looking for was not anyone from the house but another person, probably male, with whom Molly was in love.

Who could she ask? Lucy, she suspected would instantly close ranks to be loyal. Molly was as close as an oyster and Mrs Kellow certainly did not know. Would Ozzie? But it seemed cruel to ask him.

★ ★ ★

It was ebb-water in Bram's financial affairs. Quarter-day had brought in £400, but most of that was swallowed up in debts. Several tradesmen with whom he dealt had become tiresomely insistent on being paid and his little gambling group in Liskeard was not so welcoming as it had once been.

There was, however, a £300 reward out for the capture of the *Maria* and her crew. He knew the *Maria* had left for Roscoff once more but, as yet, there was no word of her return. Unless his contact had betrayed him.

He went to his desk and penned a swift note, sealed it and rang the bell. Sukey appeared.

'Here, girl, I want this delivered at once.

Tell Collins to do it now.'

'Yes, sir.' Sukey curtseyed, took the note and left the room hastily. Mr Gunthorpe was not above kicking any servant who was not fast enough. And he looked in a rare temper.

She dropped the letter in her pocket and went down to the kitchen. Cook was busy in the larder. Sukey took one of the kitchen knives and crept upstairs to the attic room she shared with two of the maids and locked the door. There was a candle with a tinder-box on the mantelpiece. She lit it and then held the knife to the flame. When she judged it hot enough she slid the knife under the seal and inched open the letter.

Sukey had learned to read from the family Bible and though this writing was something of a scrawl she managed to make it out.

Meet me at ten o'clock Sunday night. Usual place.

She reheated the knife, warmed the wax and resealed the letter. Mrs Kellow should hear of this.

6

'Michael!' exclaimed Dorothea. 'It's Michael Cross? Why . . . I . . . Oh, my God.' She sank down on a chair.

She and Mrs Kellow were sitting in Mrs Kellow's parlour, a snug room just off the kitchen with a cosy fire in the grate, two Windsor armchairs with comfortable cushions on either side and a pair of Staffordshire dogs on the mantelpiece.

'That be what Sukey told me after church, Miss Thea. I suppose it could be about something else entirely . . . ' she added doubtfully.

'Michael Cross,' repeated Josh, who was standing by the window. ' 'E'm not been hisself recently by all accounts. Moody, Abel says. I didn't take no notice as they never got on. But I do know from what Abel be saying after the *Maria*'s last trip that 'e did think somebody be a blabbermouth at the very least.'

'Mrs Cross was complaining, too. No wonder Michael was not himself, with this on his mind.' Dorothea thought back to the day of the last run. She had thought something was wrong then, but could not pin it down. Michael, she now realized, had been too eager to reassure. His voice had been odd, too. Dorothea was experienced enough in dealing with people in all sorts of trouble; she knew the signs of distress or evasion. Had she been more aware she would have picked them up, she was sure, and they would all have been saved a lot of trouble.

'Poor chap,' said Mrs Kellow.

'Poor chap!' echoed Dorothea scornfully. 'To be willing to betray his fellows, his half-brother even.'

'He be hardly willing, Miss Thea,' said Mrs Kellow firmly. 'Mr Gunthorpe will have some hold over 'm and I wouldn't care to be in Michael's shoes.'

'Nor I,' said Dorothea with a shudder. 'You are right, of course. We cannot tell what pressure he was under.'

'We need to know what Mr Gunthorpe do mean to do,' Josh put in. 'I'd best follow Michael this evening and see where 'e do go.'

Later, when Josh had left, Mrs Kellow drew her chair closer to the fire and said, 'If Molly be entangled with Michael Cross, she'm a very silly girl — and Ozzie be so devoted. She don't deserve him, really she don't.'

Dorothea sighed. Something would have to be done. She could not have a maid who was involved with a married man, one moreover, who was a tenant on the estate. But then Molly had never shown much sense where men were concerned. However, she didn't know how far it had gone. It was possible that it was more in Molly's head than anything more serious. Dorothea liked Michael well enough, but, as he was nearing forty, balding and had lost a number of teeth, he was hardly love's young dream.

Mrs Kellow leaned over and patted Dorothea's hand. ''Ee look tired, Miss Thea.'

Dorothea smiled wearily. 'It's one thing after another. As well as all this I am worried about Master Horace. He is all right at the moment, but when his arm heals? He's badgering Sir Veryan to let him leave school now and go into the army. His poor mother, of course, doesn't like it.'

'You can't rightly blame her, Miss Thea. With that nasty Bonaparty or whatever he do call hisself now, stirring up trouble again. She'm right to be worried.'

'I suppose so. But Master Horace must do something. He is not cut out for university and I cannot see him being a clerk in some office. What else is there for him?'

'Poor lad,' said Mrs Kellow sympathetically. She had a soft spot for Horace. He's betwixt and between, she thought. Brought up a gentleman's son and yet without the privileges and support that usually accompanied that state. It was not an easy position.

Dorothea's mind was similarly engaged. If the smuggling could provide Horace with a few thousand pounds, the sort of money a younger son might expect to inherit, then that would make all the difference to his future. If her cousin could be persuaded to buy him a commission in the 32nd, Cornwall's regiment, perhaps, or maybe Horace would prefer another regiment, one where his background would not be known? 'Horace would do very well in the army, I think. The discipline would be good for him and he would enjoy the adventure.'

'You'll never persuade Miss Potter — Mrs FitzWalter I should say,' replied Mrs Kellow.

'Then there's Sir Veryan being so thick with Mr Gunthorpe,' cried Dorothea. 'Why can't he see what sort of man he is? I know he's trying to do his best on the estate, having roofs mended and so on, but I never know when he'll get some pig-headed idea into his head — from Mr Gunthorpe like as not — and he'll stick to it, no matter what.

'And now I'm worried about what Mr

Gunthorpe has in mind about the smuggling. It's clear to me that he wants to take over, or at least have a clear run for his Cawsand operation. If the Selwoods go then he can step in. Bigger profits for him and he takes over our customers.

'No, I dare not trust my cousin.' Dorothea looked suddenly sad.

'You would like to?' asked Mrs Kellow, trying to suppress a surge of feminine curiosity at this interesting development. It had crossed her mind more than once that, if they could only overcome their mutual antagonism, they might have much to offer each other.

'Yes, I would. Father was right. He is not a shirker and heaven knows he's been landed with an estate which is in need of serious attention. We must be fifty years behind the times here. But he's blinkered and at the moment he's under Mr Gunthorpe's thumb.'

'Perhaps Mr Marcham'll help,' observed Mrs Kellow. 'He do seem a very worldly gentleman.'

'Yes.' Dorothea smiled suddenly. 'Somehow I doubt whether Mr Marcham would be too horrified to find a half-anker of brandy outside the door!'

The following morning, Veryan was out on estate business and Toby, Dorothea, Sylvia and Fanny were in the drawing-room. Toby was wandering round looking at the tapestries. It amused him that the three women were so unconcerned about the really scandalous subject matter. Admittedly the colours were faded but there was no doubt at all as to what the various gods, nymphs and shepherd boys were up to.

'I believe they are from Prior Gilbert's time,' remarked Dorothea, glancing up from her sewing. She and Fanny were trying to repair the brocade curtains that had been in Sir Walter's room.

'No wonder the priory was dissolved,' replied Toby, admiring the nubile figure of the fleeing Ariadne as doubtless Prior Gilbert had done before him.

'If you think those are indecent you should see the wall paintings in the prior's room,' observed Sylvia naughtily. 'They're of Fat Mab.'

'Who was Fat Mab?'

'The last prior, Prior Gilbert's mistress,' said Sylvia with complete unconcern. 'I always rather liked Sloth. Mab is lying on a sort of bench with nothing on and she has her eyes closed. There's a great pile of sewing, or perhaps it's washing beside her that hasn't been done. I feel a great deal of sympathy for Mab. Horrid sewing!'

'Sylvia!' cried Fanny. 'Pray excuse her, Mr Marcham.'

Sylvia raised her eyes to the ceiling impatiently.

Toby looked across at Sylvia. She is delightfully unspoilt, he thought, but she really should not say such things. Her innocence could be woefully misinterpreted. He turned to Dorothea. 'I must see the prior's room. Has Selwood seen it?'

'I suppose he must have.' Dorothea looked up briefly from her sewing. 'Mrs Kellow took him all over. I'm surprised he hasn't ordered the walls to be whitewashed in case the paintings corrupted our morals,' she added dryly.

'I think it's more likely he couldn't see them,' Toby replied. 'What happened to his spectacles?'

'He trod on them.'

'He looks much better without them,' observed Sylvia. 'I think he's really quite handsome, but Thea doesn't agree with me.'

Dorothea's colour rose. 'Sylvia! I never said anything about Sir Veryan's looks.'

'Oh well,' Sylvia shrugged and turned to look out of the window. 'Oh!' She gave a squeak. 'It's Mr Gunthorpe! And he's brought Brandy with him. I'll go and change.' Before anybody could stop her she had run out of the room.

Fanny looked at Dorothea in consternation. 'She must not go with him,' she whispered.

'No,' said Dorothea firmly. 'But I'll wager that Bram will say that he has Sir Veryan's permission. Now what? I suppose I shall just have to make myself unpleasant.'

Toby had been listening intently. 'Ladies, do not distress yourselves. If Gunthorpe has indeed come to take Miss Sylvia out riding then, with your permission. I shall go with them.'

'It's just that . . . ' floundered Fanny. 'Mr Gunthorpe is very kind, but Sylvia . . . '

'I understand perfectly, believe me,' said Toby. He'd seen the way Bram had eyed Sylvia during church and not liked it at all. 'Leave it to me. I'll go and change.'

When Bram was announced by a flushed Lucy some fifteen minutes later he greeted both ladies and began, 'I am come with Sir Veryan's permission to give Miss Sylvia a ride on Brandy . . . ' He got no further.

'I'm so sorry, Mr Gunthorpe,' exclaimed Dorothea, 'but my sister and Mr Marcham are at this very moment about to go out riding. Perhaps you would care to accompany them? I am sure they would be delighted.'

Whatever Bram's intentions had been there was nothing he could do but express himself happy to accompany Mr Marcham and Miss Sylvia. He was plainly put out, though, and managed to plant a number of barbs in Fanny's sensitive skin. If there had been a cat around, thought Dorothea, he'd have kicked it.

Sylvia, when she heard, looked mutinous. She'd done a quiet bit of scheming for this moment, involving a few words after church with Jane, Miss Gunthorpe's maid, who was very sympathetic and had promised to hint to Mr Gunthorpe that Sir Veryan was out on estate business most mornings. Trust Thea to put her oar in, she thought. Just because she was a spinster, did that mean that everybody else had to be as well?

Dorothea exclaimed brightly, 'Are not you fortunate, Sylvia? Two beaux! I declare I am green with envy.' It was the best she could do.

Sylvia managed a not-very-gracious smile at Toby.

Dorothea and Fanny watched them go from the drawingroom window. 'Thank goodness for Mr Marcham,' said Dorothea.

'Do you know, Fanny, I believe Mr Gunthorpe was lying when he said that he had my cousin's permission. He probably knew that Cousin Veryan was out and thought he would try his luck.'

* * *

'But this is charming,' said Toby. The three riders had turned along the coast and were now travelling eastwards along the clifftops. The turf sloped gently down to the cliff edge some twenty yards away and on either side were hedges of hawthorn and stands of Scots pines, their trunks gleaming pinkly in the sun. There was a chatter above them and a red squirrel darted up a tree and away into the canopy. Little flocks of chaffinches flew about.

Bram glanced out to sea. There was a good vantage point here and any smuggler's ship would be plainly visible. But so would any Revenue Officers coming from inland, unless they managed to get amongst the Scots pines without being seen.

'Charming indeed,' he agreed. 'And especially with so fair a companion.' He bowed towards Sylvia, who giggled.

That young lady was pointedly ignoring Toby. She'd seen the look he had exchanged with Dorothea and her mother and she resented this surveillance.

'Is it possible to get down to the shore from here?' asked Toby.

'There's a path down about half a mile further on,' said Sylvia. They had passed Morvoren Cove without comment. It was not visible from the top of the cliffs and Sylvia knew better than to draw attention to its whereabouts. Sylvia had never been anywhere near the cove during one of the smuggling operations, but secrecy had been impressed upon her from her earliest youth, and she had learnt the lesson well.

'Are you sure it's safe, Miss Sylvia?' asked Bram, as they approached what looked like a very precipitous slope. 'You are riding side-saddle and my horses do not know the route.'

'We can leave the horses here,' said Sylvia. It occurred to her that if they walked down then Bram would — delirious thought — lift her on and off her mount and maybe even hold her hand going down the cliff.

'What do you think, Marcham?' said Bram. 'Shall we do as this child suggests?'

'Child! I am thirteen!' expostulated Sylvia.

Bram laughed. 'A mere infant.' But, as Sylvia had hoped, he lifted her down and gave her waist a little squeeze which sent the colour flying to her cheeks. He made sure that he went down first and held her hand where necessary — and a number of times where it was not.

In fact, Sylvia had been running wild up and down the cliffs since she was a child and could perfectly well manage far more precipitous routes on her own had she chosen to do so. But the warmth and strength of Bram's hand, even through her gloves, was tantalizingly thrilling, and the way he looked at her made her feel a sort of delicious alarm.

Toby had been left to tie up the horses and loosen girths. He followed in silence. Sylvia's feelings were all too evident, he thought. Her lips were gently parted, her cheeks flushed and her eyes shone. She was also, as he had already discovered, dangerously naïve.

All this would not have mattered with an honourable man, but Gunthorpe, Toby could see, was discreetly fanning the flames. Toby had no doubt that there would be little squeezes and secret smiles.

At the bottom of the cliff was a sandy bay which stretched along for about half a mile. The tide was going out and had left small rock pools and lines of bladder-wrack and driftwood. It smelled pleasantly seaweedy and salty.

'This would be a good place to eat *al fresco*,' observed Bram. It was suitable for other purposes too: it was secluded and had a long beach. You could land a very sizeable cargo here. 'What did you say it was called?' he asked.

'Runrock Bay,' replied Sylvia. 'Horace and I used to come here often as children. We made fires and cooked fish. Mackerel usually. Then we'd leave our clothes by that rock there and swim.'

Both gentlemen had an instant picture of a naked Sylvia playing in the sea. She really should not say such things, thought Toby, turning away and pretending to study the distant horizon. She just does not know . . . Bram moved closer to Sylvia and said in a low voice, 'You'd make a very pretty little mermaid. I'd have liked to have joined you.'

Sylvia blushed scarlet and murmured something inaudible. For the first time she was glad of Toby's presence. She moved away and cried, 'Can you see any dolphins, Mr Marcham?'

Toby turned and came towards her. 'Dolphins? No. But they must be a splendid sight.' He could see her heightened colour. Poor child, he thought. But she'd have to learn. Perhaps she'd be more careful next time.

187

Bram bit his lip and pushed impatiently at a dead crab with his foot. Little tease. He would like to teach her a lesson. Damn Marcham. If he hadn't been here Sylvia could have been shown how to be more co-operative.

Toby picked up an urchin's shell and handed it to Sylvia. 'Pretty,' he said and smiled.

'Thank you,' said Sylvia gruffly. She stood for a moment looking down at the shell.

'Come Gunthorpe,' called Toby. 'We had better be getting back. We promised we'd be no more than an hour or so. We don't want a search party.'

On the way back, Bram treated Sylvia as he might a child. He contrived to give the impression that she had disappointed him. If she wished to be taken seriously as a woman, he seemed to be hinting, then she should be able to respond to his overtures with more grace.

Sylvia held her head high, but he could see a trace of tears. Good, he thought. Next time she would be more eager to show him how mistaken he had been.

Toby, following behind, watched with a growing sense of unease.

★ ★ ★

The following afternoon, Dorothea decided to go and visit Mrs Tregair, Ozzie's mother, who lived in Egloscolom. Mrs Tregair was a widow who had two other children besides Ozzie. Peter, a lively little boy of nine, was employed as a bird scarer on the home farm at a penny a day, and Jenny who was six. Poor Jenny had had infantile paralysis as a child and was now barely able to walk, save with the aid of crutches. She was a thin, wizened little creature, with wispy fair hair and large grey eyes. Every winter she had frightening attacks of bronchitis, during which she was devotedly nursed by her mother.

Mrs Tregair was allowed one shilling and sevenpence a week by the parish and, in her spare time, she knitted heavy-duty fisherman's socks and fingerless mittens, which she sold for a few pennies each at Abel's chandler's shop in Porthgavern.

Dorothea liked Mrs Tregair and admired her uncomplaining and cheerful ways and she did what she could to help. This afternoon she was going to take a tonic for Jenny, some apples and a pound of (illegal) tea for Mrs Tregair. She was just about to set off, basket over her arm, when she met Veryan in the hall.

'Mrs Kellow tells me you are going to visit

Mrs Tregair,' he said. 'Will you allow me to accompany you? I do not believe I have yet met her.'

'Of course, Cousin,' said Dorothea with some reluctance. Would they be able to take a walk together without an argument? She handed him the basket and hoped that he would not see fit to ask her what was inside it.

They skirted round the back of the stables and headed towards the stile at the end of the paddock which gave onto the Egloscolom road. 'I see you've been having the fencing repaired,' said Dorothea, gesturing towards a new stretch between two ragged lines of hawthorn hedging. Surely they might discuss fencing safely?

'I'm employing a couple of men from Egloscolom to go round the estate and repair what needs doing; fencing, clearing ditches and the like.'

Dorothea digested this. Part of her felt pleased that the long-awaited repairs were at last being tackled, but another, less generous, part felt resentful that Veryan, who after all was a total stranger, had the power to come in and make a difference whereas she, who was born and bred here, could not.

She must not be mean, she told herself. 'That is good news, Cousin. And the men will be glad of the work, I know.'

Veryan stopped to watch a pair of crows. 'Fawley tells me that crows attack new-born lambs,' he said. 'Perhaps I should ask Marcham to go out and shoot them. Or would Horace like to if his arm will stand it? He enjoys sport and I don't think he has yet forgiven me for selling the game-cocks.'

'They could both go. There is not a lot we can offer Mr Marcham in the way of sport. And I do know that men seem to like killing things. My father did at any rate.'

Veryan was silent.

Dorothea peered cautiously at him. 'I did not mean to imply that you should be like my father in this. God forbid.'

The last two words were so emphatic that Veryan smiled. 'My father thought I was a milksop,' he said, turning to look at the crows again.

'What nonsense,' said Dorothea roundly. 'I am sorry to speak so of your papa, Cousin Veryan, but from everything I've heard, he sounded a veritable brute.'

'He was.' Veryan transferred his gaze from the crows to some baby lambs, gambolling in the next field. He didn't look at Dorothea. And I loathed him and everything he stood for, he thought suddenly. Was that why I shut myself away in Oxford? There seemed to be no alternative: it was either an academic life or following in my father's footsteps. But there is a third way, and that is what I am doing now.

Dorothea had listened over the years to a good many people. One of the reasons she was trusted was that she understood that sometimes silences need to be respected. Veryan's silence did not feel antagonistic, but rather thoughtful.

She walked along quietly by his side with a curious sense of increased intimacy.

They had now reached Egloscolom and Mrs Tregair's cottage was behind the church.

'What do you think of our vicar?' asked Veryan suddenly.

'Mr Normanton? He was a friend of my grandfather's,' Dorothea said carefully. She recalled that her cousin was a man of the cloth.

'That does not answer my question. I suspect you are trying to have a care for any clerical sensibilities I might have!'

Dorothea laughed. 'Perhaps. Very well. I am sure that you can see for yourself that he is frequently drunk and is quite incapable of fulfilling any pastoral duties. However, I think you should know that the living is very small, only ninety pounds a year, and that my father promised many times that the endowment would be increased. You will not be surprised to learn that that did not happen. Mr Normanton is a disappointed man. Rightly so, in my opinion. On the other hand that scarcely excuses his behaviour.'

'Hm. Very succinctly put, if I might say so, Miss Selwood. What do you suggest I should do . . . '

He stopped. They had reached the Tregairs' cottage and a small girl with a crutch had hobbled out and was waving at Dorothea, her little face wreathed in smiles.

Dorothea went to her and picked her up. Jenny dropped the crutch and crooked one thin arm round Dorothea's neck and kissed her. 'I did know 'ee'd come soon, Miss Thea. Me ma did say 'ee wouldn't forget.'

Dorothea returned the kiss and stroked one pale cheek. 'I've brought you some of my special tonic. And some barley sugars. I know how much you like them. But come, Jenny.' She turned round. 'You must meet Sir Veryan Selwood. I'm sure your mother has told you about him.'

Jenny nodded, her face suddenly solemn.

'Cousin, this is Jenny Tregair.' Jenny hid her face in Dorothea's shoulder. 'She's very shy,' said Dorothea apologetically. 'She'll be all right in a minute or so. Let us go in and meet Mrs Tregair.' She turned as she spoke and, ducking her head under the lintel, entered the cottage.

Veryan stood looking after her. Seeing her standing there, the child in her arms, gave him a feeling almost of pain. It was as if some lost, almost unknown part of himself were cracking, or melting, he didn't know which.

He suddenly remembered Matty, all those years ago, showing him how to care for an injured baby rabbit he had found.

'It's frightened of you,' she'd said in a low voice, 'but if you move slowly and quietly it will see that you don't mean no harm.'

Veryan had been very fond of that rabbit and had kept it in a hutch at the bottom of the garden until his father had found and killed it. How strange that this prickly cousin of his should keep reminding him of Matty. He picked up Jenny's discarded crutch and followed his cousin into the cottage.

★ ★ ★

Josh had decided to follow Michael rather than Gunthorpe to their destination. If anything went wrong, and he was detected, he reckoned he could cope with Michael, whereas Gunthorpe was known to be dangerous when crossed. Accordingly, he set out that

194

evening for Michael's cottage a mile or so out of Porthgavern. The village street gradually petered out and ended as a mule track which led to Egloscolom.

It was a night of intermittent cloud and a half moon. Once his eyes were accustomed he could see well enough. There were few people about, but folks in this part of the world knew better than to ask where you were going. Josh pulled his hat well down and turned up his coat collar.

The track led past Michael's cottage. Egloscolom lay between the Selwood estate and Gunthorpe land and Josh guessed that it would be more likely that Bram would seek a meeting on his own land. He decided to find a hiding-place near Michael's cottage and await events.

The path passed to within ten yards of the Cross cottage. He could see candlelight flickering in one of the windows and hear voices. Good, Michael had not yet set out.

A short distance further on there was an old oak bent over the road by the prevailing wind. Josh climbed the bank and hid himself behind it. Whenever the moon came out from behind the clouds he could see the road in both directions with the village of Egloscolom in the distance and its squat church tower just visible above the trees.

It was a good twenty minutes before he heard a sound. Peering round the tree trunk he saw Michael, a heavy stick in one hand and his head and shoulders well muffled by an old piece of sacking. The old fool, skulking along like that, Josh said to himself. Anybody could see he was up to something.

Michael was plainly nervous. He walked along furtively, stopping whenever he heard a cow low or a rustle in the hedge. Poor sod, thought Josh. He's not cut out for this caper.

However, Michael did not go through the village. He struck off to the right by St Petroc's well and into a small wood. The woodland path led out onto the moor and for a while Josh was puzzled. Surely so open a place was dangerous? Then he remembered the bothy. Yes, he must be heading for the bothy. Gunthorpe could get there easily enough. Most of the way from Quilquin Hall would be on his own land and through his home wood. The bothy was on Selwood land, but deserted except during shearing when the sheep were up on their summer pastures. It was ideal: accessible yet secluded.

The problem from Josh's point of view was that the last field offered no cover. Michael was well hidden from the village, but once he got to the bothy he could easily spot anybody coming after him.

Gunthorpe, on the other hand, would be coming from higher ground. He would have the advantage. And, as far as Josh could recall, there was more cover to the north, furze and broom mostly, but better than an open field.

He retraced his footsteps. He'd go through the village and wait for Gunthorpe at the edge of the home wood and then follow him. He'd have to be quick though. He certainly didn't want to meet him unexpectedly.

Bram set out at about a quarter to ten. It would take him a good half an hour, but he had no objection to keeping his victim waiting. He walked at an unhurried pace, swishing at the hedgerow with his cane. He carried an unlit lantern and plainly had no objection to being recognized, for he wore his hat at its usual recognizable angle.

He passed old Mrs Pendean and her husband, furze cutters who lived near the home wood, and nodded curtly as he passed.

'Out wenching belike,' muttered old Mr Pendean.

Bram heard and smiled grimly. He did not notice Josh hidden in the shadows as he emerged from the wood and set off across the moor. There was scarcely a quarter of a mile to go and Josh could see the dim outline of the bothy. Bram was obviously unconcerned about secrecy, for he walked swiftly in a straight line. Just before he got there he stopped, put his hands to his mouth and called '*cu-ic, cu-ic*'. In a moment came the answering call. Satisfied, he went on, ducked his head under the lintel and vanished. A few moments later a dim light showed that the lantern had been lit and then a click as the shutter over the one small window closed.

Josh darted from furze bush to furze bush and hid himself behind the bothy. To his right there was a small chink of light low down. Josh flattened himself and lay as close as he could. All he could see were boots, Gunthorpe's probably, but if he pressed his ear to the spot he could hear well enough.

'As soon as you hear about the *Maria* you let me know, where and when, understand?'

'Yes, sir.'

'And then you go to Polperro and put in for that reward.'

Michael whispered something. There was a cry and a crash and then Bram's voice again. 'You'll do as you're told, or else I shall see to it that Selwood throws you out. Understood?'

'They'll kill me.'

'Pooh! They'll be in gaol or dancing on air. If it worries you, think of the three hundred pounds. You could buy your own land with that.'

Michael whispered something else. Bram laughed. 'You'll survive. Rats always do. Now get out.' There was another crash as the door was flung open and Michael staggered out. Bram threw his stick after him. Josh raised his head slightly and could just see Michael lumbering off over the field, swaying from side to side.

Too late Josh realized that he would be visible if Bram came out and glanced in his direction. He began to edge around the corner. As he did so he saw the chink of light go out. He froze. The moon had sailed out from behind the clouds and Josh could see the moonlight shadows of Bram's boots. They were frighteningly close. His nose began to tickle.

Just when he thought he must be discovered there was a noise and a scuffle. Bram swung round. A couple of Dartmoor ponies had come down and were cropping the grass. Josh heard the swish of a cane followed by a scream of pain and hoofbeats, then a laugh. Bram left the bothy without noticing Josh.

Later, when Josh reached Porthgavern once again, he spotted the torn poster nailed to the door of the fish cellar.

A CUTTER HAS BEEN SIGHTED
~ *hereabouts* ~
ENGAGED IN THE UNLAWFUL ACT OF

SMUGGLING

whosoever can lay information
leading to the capture of this ship
or its crew
will receive a reward of
~ *£300* ~
From His Majesty's Government
Polperro: 18th February, 1808
GOD SAVE THE KING

It had been there over two months and so far nobody had claimed it. Until now.

★ ★ ★

Dorothea found herself touched by the way Veryan had behaved during his visit to Mrs Tregair. He had treated her as he would any other woman: that is, he had removed his hat and remained standing until she had seated herself. He listened courteously to what she had to say about the state of the house and made his usual notes. He enquired after Peter and talked about Jenny's problems and he had gladdened Mrs Tregair's heart by telling her how well Ozzie was doing.

Her father had never done any of those things, she realized with shame. He had simply assumed his tenants were contented. Why should they not be? They were well supplied with cheap brandy and tobacco and their rents were not extortionate. Anything else was not his concern.

' 'E be a good man,' whispered Mrs Tregair to Dorothea as they left. 'Good-looking too,' she added with a smile.

Good-looking? Sylvia had thought so as well. Dorothea surveyed him surreptitiously on the way back. Yes, she supposed he was, though it was not in the flamboyant style of Mr Marcham's good looks. Her cousin's attractions lay in a certain quiet charm. But his looks had improved certainly. He walked with purpose and stood up straighter. His blue-grey eyes frequently held a look of laughter which was, she must admit, most attractive. And, yes, she liked his smile.

Dorothea was somewhat disconcerted to find herself thinking along these lines. They were not thoughts she was used to and she wasn't sure how to deal with them.

They made her more aware of her cousin's proximity than she found comfortable and she found herself half-wishing for a return to the previous fullscale animosity.

It was a relief to return to her herb garret and confer with Josh on what had happened the previous evening with regard to Michael. At least that topic was free of emotional undercurrents. Dorothea had arrived straight after breakfast and spent an hour or so stripping the leaves off some dried sage and by the time Josh came the whole room smelled pleasantly herby.

'The trouble is,' she said, having listened to his account, 'there are so many factors to be considered. The *Maria* is due back soon and Abel and I must make some arrangements for the landing. Michael will naturally be told and we know he will go to Polperro and Gunthorpe with the information.'

''Ee can't tell Abel the truth of the matter?'

'There's always been bad blood between him and Michael. Abel's a loyal friend but a dangerous enemy. I don't want Michael's death on my conscience. I could tell Daniel — he'd understand — but not Abel.'

'So plans do have to change at the last minute in time for Abel to tell everybody, but not in enough time to allow Michael to rouse up the Revenue men or Mr Gunthorpe?'

'Exactly.'

' 'Tis hard.'

'And somehow I have to prevent Sir Veryan from throwing in his lot openly with the Revenue men. I don't want his death on my conscience either. I think the first arrangement for the landing will have to be as far away as possible. Runrock would be suitable. The militia could go there direct from Launceston.'

'And the real landing?'

'Porthgavern?' suggested Dorothea with a grin.

★ ★ ★

On Tuesday evening, Veryan came into dinner looking stern but resolved. He had been over to Quilquin Hall and was obviously big with news. He waited until dinner was over and the fruit and nuts put on the table and then said, 'Thank you, Mrs Kellow. That will be all.' Mrs Kellow curtseyed and left the room, but not before exchanging a tiny nod with Dorothea.

'I have heard from Gunthorpe that there may be trouble on Friday night,' he began.

Horace looked up swiftly and glanced at

Dorothea. She gave her head an infinitesimal shake. Interesting, she thought, Cousin Veryan is always at his most portentous when he's been visiting Gunthorpe. She could not imagine her cousin being naturally susceptible to flattery, so what exactly was the hold that Bram had over him?

'Pray, what sort of trouble, Cousin?' she asked innocently.

'I am sorry to say it is smuggling, and on Selwood land too.'

'How dreadful!' exclaimed Dorothea. 'Are you sure?'

Sylvia had opened her mouth only to be silenced by a kick under the table from her brother.

'Naturally. The Polperro excisemen have received information which cannot be doubted. At least somebody knows their Christian duty.'

God, he's really making a mull of this, thought Toby. He'd seen the exchanges between Dorothea, Mrs Kellow and Horace and had arrived at a reasonably accurate conclusion: he doubted very much whether any of this was a surprise to Miss Selwood. But what the devil was Gunthorpe doing getting Veryan involved in stamping out smuggling? He could understand why Veryan himself was supporting the idea: he had always been one to take some high moral stance, usually about something of which he knew nothing. But Gunthorpe?

'Whereabouts exactly?' asked Dorothea. 'Not near here, I hope?' She hoped she sounded suitably alarmed.

'Runrock.'

'Gracious!' exclaimed Sylvia. 'That's where we went for our ride, Mr Marcham.'

'I have asked Gunthorpe to let the Launceston militia know that they will be welcome to use this house as their base. In fact, I hope they do: it will demonstrate my determination to be seen as a force for law and order. And on Friday night I want everybody in. Mr Gunthorpe will be coming over to dinner and after that we shall set out.'

Dorothea had been feeling mildly amused at the part she was playing, but then reality struck her. Sir Veryan was being quite as stupid as she had feared. Inviting the militia and Bram Gunthorpe and then planning to go with them himself! Was he mad or just suicidal? Did he really not understand that, if this mad venture succeeded, which fortunately it would not, he would be condemning to impressment or even possible death, dozens of men who lived on his own land and whose acquaintance he had been carefully cultivating over the last month?

Had he learned nothing?

Sylvia suddenly burst into tears. 'But they'll be our own people,' she sobbed. 'We'll know them! They'll be hanged, like Zeb Coates!'

'Mr Gunthorpe is a Justice of the Peace,' explained Veryan kindly. 'He has promised that there will be no hanging.' What did she mean, she would know them? They were smugglers.

'I daresay it will be impressment,' said Toby thoughtfully. 'The navy must be wanting men, especially now that we're at war with the French.'

'But if the prisoners go to the Quarter Sessions in Bodmin, Cousin,' put in Horace, 'then Mr Gunthorpe will have nothing to do with it, will he?'

'Oh, I'm sure he has influence,' said Veryan uneasily. Gunthorpe had been most insistent that the punishment would be minimal; a fine possibly, he'd said. Sylvia's wild words of hanging he could dismiss, but Toby's talk of impressment worried him.

The clock struck nine. 'Sylvia, it's time for bed,' said Dorothea. 'I'll come up with you if Cousin Veryan and Mr Marcham will excuse me. I want to check on that cough of yours.' She ignored Sylvia's look of surprise and continued, 'Horace too. I'd like to look at your arm.'

The gentlemen rose. Sylvia kissed her mother, Horace held open the door and they left the room.

'Shh,' said Dorothea, the moment the door closed behind them. 'Come up to the prior's room. I have something very important to tell you.'

7

The stable block at Selwood Priory had been built on the site of part of the old cloisters, but next to it a small stretch of original cloister remained, a right angle, and it had been turned into a triangular knot garden with box hedges, gravel paths and with a sweetly scented rose bush in the centre that had been much loved by Dorothea's mother. There was also a stone bench, and it was here that Dorothea was sitting quietly on the Thursday afternoon.

It had been a warm spring day and there were even a few rosebuds beginning to show pinkly through their fat buds. It was a peaceful place and Dorothea often came here to be quiet.

Today she had need of its calm, for she was worried. There were some aspects of Bram's arrangements that did not make sense and they made her feel uneasy. He was almost certainly planning something. But what?

First of all, why allow Michael Cross to claim the reward for the capture of the ship and crew? Once he'd learned of the arrangements, Bram could easily have claimed it himself without involving Michael. Secondly, why allow the militia to come to Selwood Priory before going to Runrock? It was several miles out of their way and there was always the possibility that somebody from the Priory could raise the alert: the house was scarcely a quarter of a mile from Porthgavern after all.

As she was sitting there trying to work out what she would do were she Bram, a shadow fell across her. She looked up. It was Toby.

'I hope I am not disturbing you, Miss Selwood?'

'Not at all. I was enjoying the warmth.' Dorothea moved along the bench and Toby sat down.

Mr Marcham, thought Dorothea, had been surprisingly quiet about the smuggling, asking no questions and making no comments. She more than half suspected that he had arrived at a very good idea of what was going on, but as long as he was content to keep quiet, she wouldn't probe.

Toby, it seemed, had other ideas.

'I've been wanting to talk to you, Miss Selwood.'

'Oh?' said Dorothea warily.

'Yes. I hope you agree with me that

it would be disastrous for Sir Veryan to go with the militia and Mr Gunthorpe tomorrow evening. It's quite bad enough that they should set out from here.'

Dorothea looked at him steadily for a moment and then said quietly, 'I know.'

'Shall I hit him over the head for you?'

Dorothea smiled. 'I trust it won't come to that. I've been thinking in terms of a little emetic in the pigeon pie at luncheon tomorrow.'

'Probably safer,' agreed Toby.

It was a relief for Dorothea to talk to somebody. 'He must not go,' she said. 'He's been a plague and a nuisance ever since he came, but he means well. And he is learning. But people won't stand for him betraying them as they will see it. He's a foreigner and just tolerated as a Selwood. But he won't be any longer if he's seen on Friday night at Runrock and it ends with several dozen local men in chains.'

'You surprise me, Miss Selwood,' said Toby. 'I had imagined that the militia would arrive at Runrock and find — what? — a couple of innocent fisherfolk with their lobster pots.'

Dorothea laughed. 'Perhaps.'

'Gunthorpe is very like Sir Veryan's father in some ways,' said Toby thoughtfully. 'The same underlying brutality. And Sir Veryan seems to want his approval, have you noticed?'

Dorothea looked thoughtful. Was that why her cousin was so under Bram's thumb? 'That explains a lot,' she said at last. 'I have been wondering why he cannot see through him.'

'It worries me seeing my friend so caught up in Gunthorpe's toils', said Toby. Gunthorpe, in his opinion, was an extremely dangerous man. It was the most curst luck that made him Veryan's nearest neighbour. 'If there is anything I can do, Miss Selwood, you have only to command me.'

How kind he is, thought Dorothea. She rarely received genuine offers of help — she had certainly never had any from her father. She found herself wishing, rather wistfully, that it had been Veryan who had wanted to make things easier for her, rather than Mr Marcham, pleasant though he was.

'The most useful thing at the moment, Mr Marcham, would be to take Horace and Sylvia riding tomorrow afternoon, somewhere away from the coast. Try Trespyrion Quoit. Oh, and avoid the pigeon pie.'

★ ★ ★

On Friday morning Veryan announced at breakfast that he was going over to Quilquin Hall to make final arrangements. 'I daresay Gunthorpe will ask me to take a nuncheon there,' he said. 'But I shall be back before dark. You will be all right, won't you, Toby? Cousin Dorothea, pray tell Mrs Kellow that there will be two extra for dinner; Mr Gunthorpe and the captain of the militia. He will be bringing two dozen men, but I am sure they will be happy with bread and cheese.'

'Certainly, Cousin.' Damnation, thought Dorothea. She had reckoned on Veryan being in for a meal. Now what? Perhaps she would have to ask Mr Marcham to hit him over the head after all.

After a quiet luncheon, Toby fulfilled his promise to remove Horace and Sylvia and they set out for Trespyrion Quoit. He could quite see that Miss Selwood would have her hands full. Why on earth had Gunthorpe agreed to this dinner arrangement, he wondered? It was out of their way and what could he possibly have to gain by getting Veryan involved? Or indeed getting involved himself? Surely he would be better off informing the militia and staying in the background? And what could Miss Selwood do to prevent the dinner from taking place?

Sylvia was in particular high-spirits: she seemed to have forgotten her annoyance at Toby's interference in her ride with Bram. She chattered away to him quite happily and told him all about the quoit.

'A wizard is supposed to be buried underneath,' she said. 'Only think, Mr Marcham, he could be buried with a *Book of Might* just like the wizard in *The Lay of the Last Minstrel*. I wish we could dig there and see.'

They had now arrived at the quoit, which consisted of three megaliths with a large flat stone balanced on top. It looked like some giant's table, or a three-legged stool perhaps.

They dismounted and Toby tied their mounts to a nearby tree. Then he walked all round. It was certainly impressive and local legends of a wizard being buried underneath did not seem so far-fetched: the quoit did exude a feeling of power. The shadows seemed deeper here and the air heavier. It was not a feeling of evil, rather one of immense age. The quoit seemed to hold an older, alien knowledge.

'How old is it?' asked Toby, touching one of the stones carefully. It was surprisingly warm.

'I don't know', replied Horace. 'The

Druids or something.'

'I think it's terribly romantic', pronounced Sylvia. She promptly went inside the quoit. 'Come and sit in here, Mr Marcham,' she called. 'It's just like a bed.'

'No thank you,' said Toby. 'I can see it from here. And I dare-say the grass is damp.' But, he thought, she really should not say such things to me.

Sylvia crawled out. 'Are you against free-trading, Mr Marcham?'

'Shut up, Sylvia,' said Horace. 'You know you're not to talk of it.' Girls! he thought disgustedly.

'I only asked,' said Sylvia indignantly.

Toby looked at them both, Horace guarded and Sylvia defiant. He suddenly felt about eighty. 'No, I'm not against it,' he said. 'Bad laws make for such things in my view. All the same, Miss Sylvia, I think it's best if we don't talk of it. Least said, soonest mended, you know.'

Sylvia bit her lip in vexation. 'I was only asking in a general way.'

'You stupid little gabbler,' hissed Horace. 'Anybody can see you're big with it. God knows what a blabbermouth like you has let out.'

'I haven't!' Sylvia was crying now.

'Horace,' said Toby, seeing that Sylvia was

214

really upset, 'go and pick some daisies or something. Let me talk to your sister.'

Horace looked at him for a moment and then left.

'Come,' said Toby, holding out his hand. 'Let us sit on this stone.' They sat down. 'Listen, Sylvia, I don't think you realize the implications of what you say sometimes. If I am honest with you, will you keep silent about it?'

Sylvia nodded, sniffed and blew her nose.

'I have guessed that your sister is up to her neck in this . . . activity. She has said nothing and I have said nothing, but it became obvious to me when Sir Veryan was speaking on Tuesday night. Furthermore, I'll bet you anything that she does not mean this meeting of the militia and the smugglers to take place.'

Sylvia said nothing.

'But, Sylvia, if I were a different sort of man with, let us say, a more conventional outlook and a vague unease that something illegal was about to happen, you bringing up the topic at all would arouse my suspicions immediately. I could threaten you, blackmail you with some farrago about your brother's safety perhaps, and you would give in and tell me all. Do you understand me?'

'Yes,' whispered Sylvia.

'Good. And you forgive me for speaking like this?'

Sylvia nodded.

'One more thing.' She will not forgive me for this, he thought, but who else will say it? 'If a man teases you in a way that makes you feel awkward and embarrassed, believe me, that man is up to no good.'

Sylvia's head shot up at this. Her eyes flashed. 'You mean Bram Gunthorpe, don't you?'

'If the cap fits,' said Toby, rising. He gestured to Horace.

Sylvia had gone over to her pony. 'Help me up, please,' she said furiously.

Toby did so. The moment she was mounted, Sylvia shook the reins and galloped off. Horace hurried over.

'She accepted my first warning,' said Toby tersely.

'Unfortunately, she was in no mind to accept the second.'

'Gunthorpe?'

'Who else?' He eyed Horace and added, 'I know you enjoy a game of cards. You'd better watch out, too. I knew of him in London. He was not above cheating.'

'Oh, I know that,' said Horace. 'Come on. If Sylvia gets back before us they'll send out a search party.'

* * *

Sylvia possessed to the full that adolescent ability to create an atmosphere. She was sitting on the window seat, glowering out at the fast approaching dusk. Every now and then she gave an exasperated sigh. The air was thick with a sort of sullen defiance. The rest of the party was attempting to ignore it.

Toby was talking to Fanny and complimenting her on her exquisite darns. He was aware that every now and then Sylvia was darting him furious glances, but took no notice.

Horace was reading an old copy of the *Times*. His eye darted over its pages: *An American vessel has been lately captured by the* Crescent *Privateer* . . . And on another page: *On Tuesday last three French prisoners made their escape from the* Batavia *in Gillingham Reach* . . . There was a world out there of excitement and adventure and he wanted to be part of it. Action, military action, was what he craved. *The conflict was terrible and the carnage great; but we obtained possession of the fortress, though not without a very heavy loss of brave men.* But there was no use thinking of it. Even in a line regiment a commission could cost a hundred pounds or more. He had once suggested to his mother that he'd like to take the King's shilling and she had had hysterics.

Dorothea was sitting worrying about how on earth she was going to stop Veryan from going with the militia that evening. And Bram Gunthorpe was coming to dinner. She had had a brief account from Toby of what had transpired at Trespyrion Quoit, and the last thing she wanted to have to witness was Sylvia making a fool of herself over Bram Gunthorpe at the dinner-table — which she was pretty sure Sylvia would do, if only to express her contempt for Mr Marcham's well-meaning interference.

There was a knock at the door and Jack's head appeared. 'Please, Miss Thea,' he said. 'You be wanted in the kitchen.'

Dorothea rose at once. Oh God, she thought, now what? Jack normally kept to his boot cupboard or the lamp room. He was not usually employed in delivering messages to the drawing-room; that was Lucy's or Molly's job.

She arrived at the kitchen to find everybody out in the stableyard. Veryan was slumped over the saddle bow. Josh and Ozzie had come running. As Dorothea arrived, Veryan slid off and was only just caught by Josh as he slumped onto the cobblestones and was violently sick.

Dorothea ran over. He was bent double and still retching. His skin was white and clammy and a brown liquid had come out of his mouth. Dorothea knelt down, sniffed at the liquid, felt his pulse and called to Mrs Kellow, 'Quick, warm milk. Lucy, I want the jar in the stillroom labelled Carbonate of Lime. Can you remember that? It has a white powder in it.' Lucy ran off.

'What be the matter with him, Miss Thea?' Josh had bent down and summoned Ozzie to help lift Veryan.

'Poison. Probably oil of vitriol. Not too strong, thank God, but bad enough. Get the stretcher, Josh. It'll be less painful for him.'

Veryan was groaning and clutching his stomach. His eyes fluttered open and fell on Dorothea. 'Sorry.'

'Shh,' said Dorothea. 'You've drunk something that disagreed with you. You will be better presently.'

Mrs Kellow now came out with the warm milk and a spoon and Lucy with the jar. Dorothea measured some of the powder into the milk and stirred it in. She tilted Veryan's head back against her shoulder and held the cup to his lips.

'Drink. All of it.'

'Hurts.'

'I know. But you must drink it all.'

'What is it?'

'Milk and chalk. Now stop talking. Josh and Ozzie are going to carry you upstairs to bed.'

Veryan closed his eyes.

Josh and Ozzie carried Veryan to his room and carefully lifted him onto the bed. For some time all was bustle. Mrs Kellow and Dorothea stripped off Veryan's boots, trousers and jacket. Dorothea spooned as much milk and carbonate of lime into him as he could hold. Most of it he vomited up again and Mrs Kellow held the basin while Dorothea held back his hair and mopped his face.

'Yes,' she said. 'Oil of vitriol without a doubt. Mr Gunthorpe must have wanted to have made sure that Sir Veryan would be out of the way.'

'Will he be all right? He looks mortal bad.'

'Yes, I hope so. Only milk, gruel or arrowroot, Mrs Kellow. That will counteract the acid. His breathing's not too bad, thank goodness.'

'But what about the militia arriving this evening?'

'Mr Gunthorpe never meant the militia to come here. That idea must have been Sir Veryan's contribution to the plan, I daresay. I shall write a note to say that Sir Veryan has been taken ill and I regret that I cannot offer the militia hospitality in the circumstances. I doubt whether Mr Gunthorpe will be surprised.'

One thing was certain, thought Dorothea, Bram had swallowed the landing at Runrock hook, line and sinker. It looked as though the *Maria* would be able to land at Porthgavern unmolested. She turned to Mrs Kellow. 'Ask Josh to come up a moment, please.'

Now would be a good time for Josh to tell Abel of the change of plan. Sir Veryan had come back, ill, from Quilquin Hall, with the news that the Launceston militia was going over to Runrock. Word must be got to the *Maria* that the landing would be at Porthgavern instead, once the Polperro Revenue cutter was safety out of the way. Josh could say that he would inform Michael Cross on his way back. Naturally, he would fail to do so and Michael would be left in ignorance. And the best of it was that rumour of Sir Veryan's being poisoned would get round. It would not do her cousin's reputation any harm.

She sat by the bed and looked at her patient. His forehead was still in pained lines and he looked anxious. Poor man, hauled from his cloistered existence, thrust into an alien way of life with an estate up to its ears in debt and its inhabitants up to their ears in smuggling, and then to make friends with the one blackguard who was intent on mischief. And to cap it all he'd been poisoned for trying to uphold the law.

Veryan's eyes flickered open. He reached out and groped for Dorothea's hand. 'Drank something. Stirrup cup. Red wine but it tasted funny.'

'The wine contained diluted oil of vitriol. But you'll be all right. Is it still painful?'

'Cramps, but better.'

'Good. You should rest now. You must drink as much as you can.'

'Gruel. Disgusting.'

'You may have some milk if you'd prefer.'

'Please.'

Veryan was still holding her hand and Dorothea automatically felt for his pulse. It was steadier. She would have liked to have given him some laudanum, but wasn't sure how safe it was to do so. Part of her success with her medicines lay in her reluctance to do more than the minimum. She never used the bleeding most doctors would have employed. Nature, if allowed, would do her best was Dorothea's working maxim.

There was silence for a while. Veryan seemed disinclined to let go of her hand.

How strange, thought Dorothea, to be sitting here like this. It felt peaceful and Veryan, lying still under the sheet with his eyes closed, looked oddly defenceless. She turned her head and studied him. He was lighter skinned than her father and his hair was fairer, but she could now see a slight Selwood resemblance. His cheekbones were the same and perhaps the mouth, thin-lipped, but firm.

The intensity of her gaze must have reached him for he opened his eyes again. Dorothea flushed slightly. Veryan's eyes travelled slowly over her face.

'Why do you put your hair back like that?' he whispered.

'It's easier,' replied Dorothea, tucking a stray wisp back behind her ears in some embarrassment.

'Pity,' said Veryan. 'It's beautiful.' His eyes closed again. A moment later his hand relaxed its hold and he was asleep.

* * *

The evening passed quietly. Whatever excitements might be going on outside, the party sitting in the drawing-room that evening did not know of them. Every now and then Horace stared wistfully towards the

223

window, but even he realized that he could hardly leave to help land contraband with a guest in the house. Dorothea had given the key of the gatehouse crypt to Josh and tried to curb her anxiety: her cousin was ill and she had a duty to her guest. Sylvia was still in a fit of the sullens and was finally sent up to bed by her exasperated mother.

At ten o'clock the tea tray was brought in and shortly afterwards the party broke up. Toby, who would have much enjoyed helping to land the goods, realized that his presence was a bar to any activity and tactfully took himself off to bed. Fanny followed shortly afterwards.

'Do you want to come down with me later, Horace?' asked Dorothea. 'I shall have to look in on Cousin Veryan first, but I shall go down to the harbour just to check that everything went as planned.'

'Rather!' exclaimed Horace.

'At about eleven then. By the back door.'

The two set out shortly after eleven o'clock. Dorothea had changed into a dark dress and a hood covered her head. When they reached the gatehouse the door to the crypt was open and Josh was there supervising the unloading of the mules.

'No trouble,' reported Josh. 'Though 'ee'd best be careful down harbour, Miss Thea. It do look like some wild party down there. But Master Horace 'ull look after 'ee.' He frowned at Horace warningly.

'I'll stay with my sister,' Horace promised.

' 'Ee make sure 'ee do,' grunted Josh and turned back to his unloading.

The scenes down in Porthgavern harbour were indeed like an orgy. Somebody had broken open one of the casks of brandy and it was flowing freely. Several men were reeling about arm-in-arm, singing loudly. The *Maria* had anchored a few hundred yards off shore and the last of the galleys was just now coming in with the remaining bales.

Abel was standing by the harbour-master's cottage. He came over when he saw Dorothea.

'We did fool 'n good 'n proper this time,' he said with a grin. 'The Revenue cutter did go past about ten o'clock and as soon as she'm rounded the cape and we'd got the signal we began to land the stuff.'

'What happened there?' Dorothea pointed to the broken cask.

Abel shrugged. 'Fortunes o' war, Miss Thea. 'Ee do know how it do happen.'

'Yes. And it's dangerous.' She gestured towards the drunken men. She looked around. 'Michael not here?'

'Silly *bobba* did manage to stick a pitchfork

225

through 'is foot,' replied Abel. He had little time for his half-brother.

Yes, thought Dorothea, that fits. She had been expecting something of the sort, some excuse to be out of it. Michael was a timid man and, as Josh had said, not cut out for spying. However, she merely replied that she'd go over in the morning and take some healing salve.

There was a burst of drunken singing behind them. Dorothea turned to Horace. 'I think we'd better be off. Things will get pretty rowdy.' Out of the corner of her eye she could see the last of the ponies winding up the track to the gatehouse. There was nothing more for her to do here.

'Don' 'ee fret, Miss Thea. I'll see to everything,' said Abel.

★ ★ ★

The following morning, Sylvia was once more her usual sunny self. She had got up early and had been down to the stables to groom her pony and worm out of Ozzie what had happened the previous evening. She had always been able to find out things and this morning she imagined that she was the sole possessor of the good news.

Later, her mother would want her in the

prior's room for her lessons, but she had an hour or so free after breakfast and she skipped down to the gatehouse to see if she could help Dorothea in the herb garret. There was usually some little job that needed doing and Sylvia was pretty sure that either Abel or Daniel would come.

Dorothea was grating a lump of chalk when Sylvia arrived and she promptly directed her to spoon it carefully into a glass jar. Her supply of carbonate of lime was running low and she had used most of it on Veryan the previous day. She would have to order some more from the druggist in Plymouth.

'I wish I'd been there!' Sylvia began breathlessly. 'The whole of Porthgavern turned out to give a hand, Ozzie said. It was the most exciting thing. Oh Thea, why won't you ever let me go?'

'It's no place for women,' replied Dorothea, grating the last of the chalk and wiping her hands on a damp cloth. 'Brandy flows freely and things can get rough.'

'You go,' argued Sylvia.

'I go for the landing and then I leave. When a man is drunk, Sylvia, he is beyond knowing whether a woman is respectable or not.' It was one of the few things she disliked about smuggling. It brought much needed money in but it also brought drunkenness and debauchery.

There was a knock downstairs. Sylvia ran to the window and peered out. 'It's Daniel!' she cried, and ran down the stairs to let him in. A moment later she came up holding his hand and laughing.

Dorothea smiled and came forward. 'Daniel, I hoped I should see you today.'

'I did bring a small present for the little maid if she'll just let go of my hand.' Sylvia did so. Daniel reached into his greatcoat pocket and took out a small packet. Sylvia pounced on it, opened it and took out a garnet pendant.

She jumped up and kissed his cheek. 'Oh, you are kind. Isn't it lovely, Thea? Oh, thank you.' She was very fond of Daniel.

'You've heard how it did go, I daresay,' Daniel said to Dorothea. She nodded. 'It were like a proper party. You did never heard such cheering. In a twinkling the goods were off the ship and safe in your crypt, Miss Thea.' He paused, then continued, 'I were sorry to hear that Michael had an accident. Poor soul, he always were an unhandy sort of fellow.'

'Ozzie says that everybody's sleeping it off this morning,' said Sylvia.

'Aye. There be plenty of drunken fools

around,' said Daniel sharply.

'But you made the excisemen look so silly,' laughed Sylvia. 'And I bet the Launceston militia were furious.' Serve them right, she thought, trying to get the better of Cornishmen. She had already decided in her own mind that Bram had not had anything to do with it. He had not informed on the smugglers, after all. Maybe he was trying to stop Cousin Veryan from becoming involved, in which case they should be pleased instead of always warning her against him.

Dorothea looked up at the clock she kept on the shelf. 'Your mother will be waiting for you, Sylvia,' she said. 'It's nearly eleven o'clock.'

'Lessons!' Sylvia made a face. She thanked Daniel again for the pendant, blew him a kiss and darted down the stairs.

Dorothea and Daniel dealt with the *Maria*'s business with their usual expedition. The *Maria* was going down to Plymouth, said Daniel, where he had business with his retired admiral. After that he would be returning to Roscoff. But he'd call again before he went and settle up.

Dorothea let him out and then went down to the crypt. There were two bales of fine Brussels and Valenciennes lace as well as some exquisite Flemish bobbin lace collars and cuffs. There was also a small consignment of Sèvres china. She should do well. Lady Shebbeare had asked discreetly about some collars when they met after church on Sunday and a number of other ladies had let it be known that they would pay well for top quality lace.

At last, she thought. Even after paying everybody who had helped last night, she should clear about £800. She could begin to put something aside for Horace's and Sylvia's future.

The only thing that concerned her was her cousin. She had begun to realize it for some time, but seeing him slumped over his horse had confirmed it. There was something about the intimacy of pulling off his boots and getting him out of his vomit-spattered clothes which had precipitated them into a different relationship. Her usual exasperation seemed to have vanished and had been replaced by a sort of sympathy and even tenderness.

Dorothea was not at all sure she wanted this. It was bad enough having a secret from a man she disliked. How much worse would it be if she found that she had come to care about him?

Nevertheless, she found herself going back to the house and making her way up the stairs to see him with surprising eagerness.

Mrs Kellow was there washing his face and hands. There was a bowl of soapy water on the table.

'He do want to be shaved, Miss Thea,' she exclaimed, the moment Dorothea entered. 'I've said, no; Miss Thea won't hear of it.'

Dorothea laughed. 'Quite right. Not today, Cousin. You may be smooth again tomorrow if all goes well. I take it you are feeling better?' The sight of Veryan's stubble gave her an odd sense of pleasure. She would have liked to touch his cheek. She put her hands firmly behind her back.

'Fragile, but better. Thank you, Mrs Kellow, that will do for now.'

Mrs Kellow, a slight smile on her lips, picked up the bowl of water and left the room.

Feeling strangely self-conscious, Dorothea said, 'Have you been drinking enough?'

'If I drink any more milk I'll turn into a cheese.'

'May I take your pulse?'

Veryan held out his hand. Dorothea put two fingers on his pulse. It was much improved. 'Tongue? Hm.' She pulled down his eyelids and looked into his eyes.

'Anything else you'd like to look at?'

'No thank you. You have an astonishingly strong constitution, Cousin Veryan.' When he came, she thought, he looked so thin that a puff of wind would blow him away. Now, his muscles had developed, his skin had a healthier tinge of colour and even his hair seemed to have thickened up. 'In fact, in spite of your unfortunate experience, I would say that this last month or so in the country has done you a lot of good.'

'Yes, I think it has,' said Veryan. He pulled himself up and Dorothea put another pillow behind him. 'I've noticed that my eyes are getting better. When I first got my spectacles I was told to use them only for reading. But I was lazy and I couldn't be bothered to take them off. When my eyes got worse I thought that was what happened if one was a scholar. Since stepping on my spectacles I've noticed things are getting clearer again. You used to be surrounded by a fuzz. Now I can see you better.'

'I hope that's a good thing,' said Dorothea, trying to shrug off a faint feeling of embarrassment.

'In a metaphorical sense,' said Veryan seriously, 'I doubt whether I've seen you clearly at all.'

Dorothea was standing by the bed. Veryan reached out and took hold of her hand.

'Why are you holding my hand?' she asked, startled by this turn of events.

'I find I like doing it,' said Veryan simply. Strange, he thought, I always assumed that a classical education fitted one out for life. I'm beginning to see that it isn't so at all. 'What nice long fingers you have.'

For a man who didn't like being touched he was not doing badly.

'This cannot last,' said Dorothea with decision. 'In another day or so you will be back to your usual impossible self. But in the meantime, Cousin, nothing but milk or gruel for the next twenty-four hours.'

Veryan sighed and released her hand. Dorothea did not know whether to feel relieved or sorry.

★ ★ ★

Bram had set out the previous evening in an optimistic mood. He met up with the Launceston militia at Tideford and escorted them to Runrock Cove. As he went he toyed with the idea of diverting some of the contraband goods into his own keeping but discarded it. Probably too risky. But there would be prize money of up to £1,000 for the capture of the smugglers' ship and £20 reward for each smuggler convicted.

Of course, that money would have to be shared between the men on the Revenue cutter, the militia and himself. Even so, a useful sum should come his way.

If the militia did their work then they would bag a number of landsmen, including, he hoped, Michael Cross. Michael was hopeless as an accomplice, Bram decided, chicken-hearted and a bad risk. A quick knife thrust during the struggle in the shore would sort him out. He would be no great loss.

When the militia arrived they comprised two dozen men and their captain. None of them were local and they stumbled over the unfamiliar ground making, Bram thought savagely, enough noise to alert any number of smugglers. Fortunately, there was an onshore wind which blew away any sound.

But there was no ship, no smugglers, no goods. The Revenue cutter came on time, the militia lined up as they were told, but then nothing. Midnight came and went. Eventually, after much stamping around to keep out the cold, the captain said, 'I reckon we were misinformed, sir. Or else they got wind of us.'

Misinformed, thought Bram. He'd get Cross for this.

'All right, lads, about turn. Back to barracks.'

There was a lot of grumbling and a sarcastic cheer or two, but they were cold and it was dark and the thought of hot rum beckoned. Bram watched them go and then watched the Revenue cutter turn round and head back to Polperro. He remounted his horse.

The next morning his mood was so savage that neither Isabel nor Mrs Gunthorpe dared address him. His valet had stumbled from the bedroom with a bruised jaw and when Sukey accidentally spilt a drop of coffee on the table, Bram had lashed out and given her such a kick that she'd dropped the coffee pot and fled limping from the room.

Isabel, her mouth dry with fear, nibbled at her toast, which turned to ashes in her mouth. She didn't dare move. Her mother, she could see, felt the same. What had gone wrong last night?

Eventually, Bram came round sufficiently to look at them across the table. 'You two look like a couple of dummies.'

'We are concerned about you, dear,' said his mother tremulously.

Bram grunted. He enjoyed it when they were scared. He'd leave them in suspense for a while. He rose to his feet. 'I am going out. I don't know when I shall be back.'

A few moments later they heard the front door slam. Isabel went to the window. Bram was walking fast. In his hand he carried a lead-weighted cane. Isabel had once seen him hit a recalcitrant horse so hard that the animal had had to be put down.

'Where is he going?' asked Mrs Gunthorpe, staring at the dented silver coffee pot which still lay on the floor.

'Towards Egloscolom. I wish I knew what has happened.'

Mrs Gunthorpe closed her eyes for a moment but said nothing. She had learned not to ask.

★ ★ ★

Veryan spent the next two days keeping mainly to his room. Occasionally, he moved carefully to sit by the window for a few moments, but movement was still painful.

He thought over what Dorothea had said. Could he really have taken oil of vitriol? Was she really suggesting that he had been poisoned? He was well aware that she disliked Gunthorpe, but this was outrageous.

And yet, he had undoubtedly taken something. The nuncheon he had eaten had consisted of no more than some ham and bread with a few slices of cucumber. Mrs Gunthorpe had eaten much the same. He had had an apple, but so had Miss Gunthorpe and there was a bottle of wine that they had all enjoyed.

The only thing that he had had that the others had not was a glass of wine just before he left — a glass that Gunthorpe pressed on him almost as his foot was in the stirrup, which he'd tossed off in a hurry. He had begun to feel ill almost immediately. But why would Gunthorpe want to poison him? The thing was impossible.

The thought crossed his mind that Gunthorpe had not wanted to come to Selwood Priory with the militia, but he, Veryan, had insisted. He'd wanted to show his commitment and share the responsibility. But surely he wouldn't . . .

Since then he'd heard nothing. No word from Gunthorpe on the success or otherwise of the mission and his cousin had kept quiet, too. When he'd questioned Mrs Kellow all she would say was, 'I'm sure I don't know, sir.'

Miss Selwood must be mistaken about the poison, Veryan decided. Probably the ham had been off. Perhaps Mrs Gunthorpe had been ill too. By the end of the second day he was feeling desperate with anxiety for news and rang the bell. He then got out of bed, put on his dressing-gown and sat on the day-bed.

'Molly, ask Miss Selwood if she would

be so good as to come up for a moment, please.'

Molly curtseyed and left.

Dorothea appeared looking grave. She exclaimed when she saw him. 'Cousin Veryan, what have you been doing? You shouldn't be up. Get back into bed this instant.'

'I want to talk to you.'

'Very well. But get back into bed.'

Veryan did so. Dorothea automatically felt his pulse, poured him some more milk and watched him while he drank it and only then allowed herself to draw up a chair and sit beside him.

'You said I'd drunk oil of vitriol,' began Veryan abruptly. 'How can you be sure?'

'You had all the symptoms. You vomited a brown liquid flecked with blood; your pulse rate was dangerously low, your face was pale and covered with sweat, your stomach very tender and the skin on the roof of your mouth had been burned. Do you want any more?'

'Could it not have been caused by some tainted ham?'

Dorothea gave a short laugh. 'No.' She paused and added, 'There are various acids that are poisonous, Cousin, and the effects are broadly similar. It can only have been administered deliberately. I am sorry.'

'I know you dislike Gunthorpe . . . ' began Veryan.

'Of course, I dislike him,' snapped Dorothea. 'He's tried to poison you; his behaviour towards Sylvia, according to Mr Marcham, is not that of a gentleman; he is horrid to poor Fanny and he has succeeded in manipulating you into coming down on the free-traders so that he can boost his own ambitions in that direction.'

Veryan sat up. 'This must be nonsense.'

'Cousin, Gunthorpe has a part share in a smuggling enterprise in Cawsand,' said Dorothea impatiently. 'He wants, and always has wanted, an outlet nearer home, Porthgavern, to be precise. My father never trusted him in business, he always said the man was a shark. Look, if you don't believe me, ask Sir Thomas Shebbeare.'

'But he's a Justice of the Peace,' protested Veryan.

Dorothea laughed. I just don't care, she thought. Let him hear for once what his precious Gunthorpe is like.

There was a long pause. 'Are you saying I've been gulled?'

'I'm afraid so.'

'But why didn't you tell me?'

'Cousin, when the mood takes you you

are as stubborn as a mule,' said Dorothea roundly. 'It has not been easy to tell you anything once you've made up your mind.'

Veryan digested this. He held out his hand and Dorothea took it. 'I know,' he said. 'I'm sorry. My father used to fly into these terrible rages and beat me. The only way I could cope was by digging in my toes. If I'd knuckled under I'd have felt destroyed. And once I'd made my stand, of course, I had to stick to it. Does that make sense?'

'And you've been doing the same ever since?'

'I suppose so. Though I was never really conscious of it until I came here. Academic stands, somehow, are rather different.'

'Cousin,' said Dorothea earnestly, 'please believe me. Bram Gunthorpe is a dangerous man. Has it ever occurred to you that it is he who is like your father?'

'What!' Veryan released her hand abruptly.

Dorothea leaned forward and placed a finger over his lips. The action shocked Veryan into silence.

'Shh,' she said. 'Just think about it and I'll talk to you later.' She left the room.

8

Dorothea sat in the dining-room with Fanny at breakfast the following morning. She was in an unusually pensive mood and whatever she was thinking about was pleasant enough, thought Fanny, for every now and then she smiled to herself. She looked well, too. Not that Dorothea usually looked ill, but normally she ate perhaps half a slice of toast with her coffee, but today she had a whole slice followed by an apple with every appearance of appetite.

Fanny was still puzzling over this when Mrs Kellow came in looking upset.

'Yes, Mrs Kellow,' said Fanny. 'Is anything wrong?'

'Indeed it is, ma'am. We have just had word that the Crosses have suffered a fire. They do say that neither Mr nor Mrs Cross survived.'

Dorothea, suddenly pale, pushed away her coffee and rose to her feet. 'I'd better go over. Tell Josh to saddle up Copper, please. And he'd better come with me. I'll be down in about twenty minutes.' She left the room.

'Does Sir Veryan know?' asked Fanny.

'Not yet, ma'am. I didn't like to tell him without Miss Thea's say-so.'

'No, you are right. It would only worry him. Send Molly up, please, Mrs Kellow. There are the blue-room curtains to be mended and she may as well help me.'

'I'm sorry, ma'am, but Molly be indisposed. She had a fit of the hysterics this morning. Threw herself all over the place, she did. Lucy and me could scarce restrain her.' In the end Lucy had slapped Molly's face hard and Mrs Kellow had dosed her with laudanum. It was all that business with Michael Cross, she didn't doubt, but she wasn't going to worrit Miss Thea with the silly giglet.

Up in her room Dorothea changed swiftly into her riding habit, jammed her hat onto her head and went down to the stables. I should have thought of this, she said to herself, that something might happen to Michael Cross. But what could she have done? If she'd warned him, then he would have known that his secret was out and perhaps told Bram.

Josh was already in the stable-yard with her mare, Copper, and his own mount, a shaggy roan that was used for odd jobs about the estate.

'Tell me more,' began Dorothea, when

242

they had left the Priory behind.

'One of the lads did bring the news in about nine, Miss Thea. The cottage be burnt down. It do seem to have started in the thatch. Maybe an oil lamp knocked over by one of the animals. The hens did escape, but the pig 'e be roast to a turn.'

'Michael and Mrs Cross both died?' Dorothea ignored his levity.

'Aye, Miss Thea. They been overcome by the smoke. Bill Kellow was over in Egloscolom last night and did come home late, about midnight. 'E did say 'e noticed nothing amiss.'

'Hmm.' Cottages, especially those built of cob and thatch, were particularly vulnerable to fires, she knew. It had happened many times on the estate; a child knocking over a tinder-box, a drunken man coming in after a Saturday evening in the kiddley-wink; it was fatally easy to set the buildings alight. But all the same, could it be entirely coincidence that the Cross cottage should burn down so soon after the hoax on the militia?

As if reading her thoughts, Josh said, 'I did hear that Mr Gunthorpe did go over Plymouth this morning, Miss Thea. 'E do plan to stay a day or two.'

'That was sudden.'

She said nothing more. She was pretty sure

Josh shared her suspicions, but until they knew more nothing could be substantiated. They had been climbing up and now reached the top of the slope. Egloscolom with its squat church tower rose up in the distance. To the left, Dorothea could see a drift of smoke. She urged her horse to a canter.

When they arrived, the cottage was still smouldering and a group of villagers from Egloscolom were standing about. A small pile of objects, obviously rescued, was being guarded by Diggory Watson. Abel Watson came forward and took Dorothea's bridle and helped her to dismount.

''Morning, Miss Thea. 'Morning Josh. Bad business this.' His face looked strained. 'Me and Mike didn't see eye to eye, but 'e did be my brother when all be said and done.'

Dorothea nodded and touched his arm briefly. 'I know. I'm sorry, Abel. Do you know more of what happened?'

'Tom here did see flames at about four o'clock when 'e were up with a sick cow. 'E did rouse the neighbours, but by the time they arrived 'twas too late.'

'Did he notice anything suspicious?'

Abel looked surprised. ''Ee be thinking of a tramp, Miss Thea?'

'Possibly. Mrs Cross was always very

careful about lamps and such. But, of course, accidents do happen.'

Large hoofprints, thought Dorothea. She could not help but wonder whether Bram had ridden this way on his big bay. But with half the village tramping about, any hoofprints would have been trodden over long ago.

'You seem to have half of Egloscolom here,' said Dorothea dryly.

'Pickings,' retorted Abel. 'And come to gawp.'

Dorothea sent them packing and with some muttering, they slowly moved off. 'Do you need any help?'

'Tim Wilcox be bringing some mules from Porthgavern,' said Abel. He indicated the pile of implements guarded by a determined Diggory. Dorothea noticed, without much surprise, that the hens were all missing. Folks were desperately poor around here: they took what they could. 'But Michael's cows and sheep be vanished. And donkey, too.'

'Don't worry,' said Dorothea. 'I'll recognize Michael's cows and sheep — and the donkey. I'll put the word round and get them back.'

'Thank 'ee, Miss Thea.'

Dorothea nodded and Abel moved away. 'Josh, we're going over to Quilquin Hall. I think we'll go by St Petroc's well.'

Josh put her up on Copper, mounted the roan and they set off.

'Why this way, Miss Thea?'

'We know things about Michael that Abel, thank God, does not. I cannot help thinking that Mr Gunthorpe may have had a hand in this. If he were here at about four o'clock this morning, he need not have ridden through Egloscolom at all. He could have come through the wood and by St Petroc's well.'

They rode on and turned up past the well. Under the trees the ground was still damp. They went slowly, scanning the ground. Then Josh pointed. Large hoofprints were neatly etched into the mud and then more pointing in the opposite direction. 'Mr Gunthorpe's bay, I reckon,' said Josh.

'Undoubtedly,' said Dorothea. Bram was a heavy man and rode at fourteen stone. His horse was correspondingly large. 'There are few horseshoes that large around here.'

'And 'e did come and go back.' Josh pointed to a pile of horse-droppings. 'Fresh, too.'

'I doubt whether Mr Gunthorpe would confirm it for us,' remarked Dorothea, 'but I think the evidence is pretty conclusive. He's a man to bear a grudge and he may have believed that Michael had double-crossed him.'

'Why be we going to Quilquin Hall, Miss Thea?'

'Just a courtesy call as I was so near,' said Dorothea blandly. 'And if you happen to hear something below stairs . . . '

Dorothea never rode up the drive of Quilquin Hall without a lowering of her spirits. There was something about the neat, regular façade, the unerring quiet taste of the decor, not to mention Mrs Gunthorpe's attitude of moral superiority and Isabel's classic good looks, that made Dorothea feel dowdy and uncomfortable. At Selwood Priory, for all its shabbiness, she was useful and knew herself to be essential to the well-being of those under her care. At Quilquin Hall she was nothing but an ageing spinster, too long on the shelf, whom life had passed by.

Not unnaturally, she seldom visited, or only when courtesy demanded. Moreover, she resented Mrs Gunthorpe's constant denigration of Fanny and any attempt to defend her had always been met with horror and a wonder at the laxity of her morals.

It was Sukey who opened the door. She was still limping and in answer to Dorothea's enquiry said tersely, ' 'E did do it. Saturday morning. And 'e did be in a right temper.'

He would be, thought Dorothea. She expressed her sympathy and promised to send over a salve.

When she was a little girl, brought here to visit by her mama, Dorothea had always had an urge to draw on the walls. There was something about the tasteful expanse of Wedgwood green in the entrance hall which made her want to scribble all over it. Something of that same emotion came back to her; a wish to tear away the complacencies and expose the ugly reality. But, of course, she never did.

Sukey took Josh down to the kitchen and in due course Dorothea was shown up to the pretty drawing-room. Only Mrs Gunthorpe was there and she greeted Dorothea with an anxious civility.

'My dear Dorothea, how kind in you to call. But . . . ' — she glanced at the clock — 'is not this a little early? I hope nothing is amiss?'

Dorothea explained. 'So very sad a tragedy,' she finished. 'Michael Cross was a good tenant and will be much missed.'

Mrs Gunthorpe responded suitably but without any particular consciousness, and then continued, 'But Sir Veryan. We were so sorry to hear that he had been taken ill.

But indeed, dear Dorothea, I do not think it could have been anything he ate here. We all partook of Cook's ham. And we have all been quite well.'

It seemed to Dorothea that her hostess was not at ease and that she was talking as much to reassure herself as to enquire about her neighbour.

'What caused it, do you know?' It seemed as if she was unable to stop probing. Dorothea could see her hands twisting nervously in her lap.

'Oh yes, I know.' Dorothea watched her closely. 'He was given oil of vitriol.'

Mrs Gunthorpe's colour drained away and her lips trembled. 'No! No!' she whispered.

'I'm afraid so.' Dorothea came over and sat beside her hostess and took her hand comfortingly. 'He was given a weak dose of oil of vitriol, probably administered in some wine. I do not think it was meant to kill him, the dose was not strong and he had eaten enough to absorb some of the poison.'

Mrs Gunthorpe clutched at her guest's hand. 'Oh, Dorothea! I was so afraid of . . . Sir Veryan was so insistent on having the militia at Selwood and I could see that Bram didn't like it . . . Oh, what have I done to deserve this? Bram has been so . . . He had everything he wanted. Everything. And now, you don't know, Dorothea . . . He's always asking for money . . . threatening . . . and I have to give it. But there's Isabel to think of and . . . ' She gave way to her feelings.

Dorothea sat in silence. In her view the indulgence shown towards Bram as a spoilt child had been disastrous. But her own father must take some of the blame. He had always encouraged Bram's excesses, clapping him on the shoulder and telling him he was as game a young cock as ever strutted. But the poor lady had done her best, however mistakenly, and must now pay the price.

Eventually, Mrs Gunthorpe mopped her eyes and sat up. 'It's Isabel I am concerned about,' she confided. 'She's frightened of him and it's affecting her health. She is not sleeping well. She told me this morning that she heard Bram get up in the small hours and go out. Of course, he does go out sometimes to . . . well, I don't know what he does. Gentlemen do such . . . But I think she was mistaken. He was here this morning, though now he has gone off to Plymouth. There's a group of men he consorts with there whom I do not like the sound of.'

'Why do you and Isabel not go away, Mrs Gunthorpe? If you are not here then Bram cannot ask you for money. The season is over in Bath, I know, but there are some seaside resorts, Lyme or Sidmouth, for example, that I hear are very pleasant.'

'Oh, if only I could,' sighed Mrs Gunthorpe. 'But two ladies, you know, travelling alone. It would never do. You, dear Dorothea, are so inexperienced in these matters. It would look so odd.'

Mrs Gunthorpe blew her nose firmly. Dorothea could see that normality had returned and that her hostess has reassumed her mantle of superiority. The conversation they had just had would be expunged from her mind. Personally, Dorothea felt that the oddity of two ladies travelling without a male escort would be amply compensated for by Bram's absence from the scene.

She left soon afterwards and she and Josh rode home thoughtfully. They were in agreement, for Josh's conversation below stairs had confirmed Dorothea's own findings. Bram had been out riding that night, but had returned in time for breakfast, apparently in a good mood. He was now in Plymouth, for what purpose nobody knew. Gambling possibly.

'Be 'ee minded to tell Sir Veryan of the note about Master Horace?' asked Josh. ' 'E should be warned. A man who will poison and murder will stop at nothing.'

'Difficult. I can't tell him about Michael

without revealing about the smuggling.'

'But 'e didn't put 'is name to 'n, Miss Thea. Who's to say 'n came from Michael?'

'But if Sir Veryan takes it into his head to cross-question Molly? My God, Molly! She'll be in a state at this news, I don't doubt.'

''Ee do think Molly would let on?'

'There's no saying what Molly would do,' stated Dorothea. 'She blurts out anything. She has no discrimination. No, Josh, I'd rather not tell Sir Veryan unless I have to.'

But she would like to, she thought. She would like a relationship with her cousin where she did not have to watch every word and where her views were respected. Unfortunately, to speak freely was a luxury she could not afford and which she did not think would be offered to her.

★ ★ ★

Dorothea did not arrive home until nearly two o'clock and the family was assembled for luncheon. She sent her apologies and told them not to wait for her; she would come down as soon as she had changed out of her riding clothes. She was in a hurry and, instead of putting on one of the interminable grey dresses which filled up her

252

wardrobe, chose the nearest to hand, a rich, dark-brown dress, which set off her fair hair and her dark eyes.

Dorothea had never cared much about what she wore. There had never been anyone who had noticed, but today, as she entered the dining-room, there was a gratifying murmur of appreciation.

'I say, Thea,' exclaimed Horace, 'you look tip-top, doesn't she, Mama?'

Toby had risen to his feet as Dorothea entered and he now came round and held her chair for her as she sat down. 'You look quite beautiful, Miss Selwood,' he said. 'You should come to London and stun them all.'

'Th-thank you,' stammered Dorothea. Then she caught sight of Veryan. He was dressed in a crimson brocade dressing-gown that had belonged to Sir Walter (it had been cleansed of the port, snuff and brandy stains) and he looked surprisingly raffish. He was staring at her in undisguised appreciation and for some reason this disconcerted her far more than Horace's or Mr Marcham's compliments. 'Ought you to be up, Cousin?' she asked, striving for a normal tone.

'Certainly,' said Veryan. 'I appeal to Mrs FitzWalter. I was going mad up there. Anyway, I'd have missed seeing you looking so wonderful if I'd stayed upstairs.' He spoke without a trace of self-consciousness. Toby stared at him in amazement and looked across at Fanny to see how she was reacting to this interesting development.

'Surely it is all right for him to be down, Thea,' pleaded Fanny. 'Look at him, he's so thin. And we'd just started to fatten him up a little.'

Dorothea laughed. 'You let him twist you round his little finger, Fanny.' She pushed her chair back and walked round the table. Veryan obediently held out his wrist for Dorothea to feel his pulse. 'Very well,' she said. 'Yes, I think you might risk something. Are you hungry?'

'Not for gruel.'

'Mrs Kellow shall do you a baked egg and a slice of bread and butter. No wine, it's too acidic. And you are to eat it slowly.'

'Stop fussing, Thea,' put in Horace. 'You're like a mother hen. She means well, Cousin Veryan, but she does go on a bit.'

'I'm very grateful to her and so should you be, Horace,' retorted Veryan. He smiled at Dorothea and there was a warmth in his eyes that made her colour faintly.

Toby observed this interchange in some amusement. Veryan allowing, nay enjoying, the cosseting of two women! He treated Mrs FitzWalter as he might a favourite aunt. But his remarks to Miss Selwood? Veryan plainly was not immune to feminine attractions after all. Toby couldn't help wondering if his friend were more taken by his cousin than he realized. He was looking at Dorothea across the table with an expression Toby had never seen on his face before: a sort of amused tenderness. He glanced across at Fanny. She, too, was looking at them and, as she turned away, caught Toby's eye. He cocked his eyebrow in a question and gave her a suspicion of a wink.

After luncheon, Veryan asked for a moment of Dorothea's time. 'In the library, if you please, Cousin.'

He seemed determined to be up and about and, as he had eaten his egg and bread without ill effects, Dorothea did not protest. She noted that he was glad enough to sit down on one of the leather-covered armchairs.

'About Michael Cross,' he began. 'I gather you were up there this morning.'

'Yes. I sent your condolences, of course.' Dorothea outlined a suitably censored account of what had happened.

'Is there anything you think that I should do?'

It was so unlike Veryan to ask her advice that at first Dorothea could only stare. 'Er . . . I believe that Abel Watson would appreciate a guinea or so. He is the next of kin — Michael was his half-brother — and it is Abel who will have to arrange the funerals.'

Veryan made a note. 'Anything else?'

Dorothea explained about the missing animals.

'Are you sure that you will get them back?'

'Oh yes,' said Dorothea serenely. 'You must know that local opinion has it that I am something of a witch. I am not often crossed. And I threatened something very nasty if they weren't returned here for safe-keeping.'

'What on earth was it?' Veryan was amused.

'Modesty forbids me to divulge it. But I can assure you that it was most unpleasant.'

Veryan laughed — carefully, for he was still sore. Toby was right, he thought, she has an unusual beauty, when she takes the trouble — and part of her attraction is that she is so completely unaware of it. She is not traditionally pretty — her colouring is too unconventional, but she is definitely beautiful. How strange that he had never noticed it before.

All he said was, 'I would like one thing from you, Cousin, when you have the time.'

'What is it?' asked Dorothea cautiously.

'A family tree of those in Porthgavern and on the estate. And I'd like all the Watsons underlined. They are plainly important and I need to know who they are.'

'I can do that. But the picture is more complicated than you think, for my grandfather was equally prolific, only he didn't give his by-blows his name.'

'Good God, but surely there is a danger of incest?'

'I doubt whether they worry too much about that,' said Dorothea. She saw Veryan was looking shocked and added, 'Much like the ancient Greeks, by all accounts; Zeus and my father would appear to have had much in common.'

There was a moment's stunned silence, then Veryan gave a reluctant laugh. 'I see. I'm being a prig again.'

'Oh no, no! Indeed, I do realize how shocking it is. But I've grown up with it and Abel and the others feel like kin to me. And Horace and Sylvia, of course.'

'Am I included in this family web?'

Dorothea looked at him. His tone was neutral, but there was something that belied this in his eyes. He had been a lonely little boy, she realized suddenly. At some level he wanted to belong. 'You were not eager at first to be kin to any of us,' she said carefully. 'I hope you have changed your mind. Horace and Sylvia are not responsible for their condition and nor are any of the Watsons.'

'I accept that.'

'Then they'll accept you.' She did not say 'I accept you', Veryan noticed and some of his warmth of feeling began to fade. Dorothea paused and added, 'People down here don't think of themselves as English, Cousin. I think as soon as you understand that the sooner you'll belong.'

'Not English!' Agincourt, the Armada, Trafalgar flashed through his mind. 'But that's absurd . . .'

Dorothea said nothing.

Typical, thought Veryan crossly. They had been getting on better and suddenly she had come up with something so ridiculous that it seemed as if they were speaking different languages.

Dorothea rose. 'If you will excuse me, Cousin,' she said formally, 'I must see Molly, who is indisposed. I shall order some baked fish for you this evening. I trust that will meet with your approval?'

'Oh, very well,' snapped Veryan.

The mood of intimacy had vanished.

★ ★ ★

The next few days passed quietly. Horace's head and arm were now well healed but Veryan made no mention of his returning to school and Horace did not remind him. He, Sylvia and Toby went out most afternoons and rode about the estate. In any case, Horace thought, he was needed to chaperone Sylvia. Not that she needed it with Mr Marcham, but his sister could certainly do with somebody to see that Bram Gunthorpe did not come too close.

Horace knew his sister better than anybody and he was aware that she was still in the throes of a violent calf love, which was fanned still brighter by opposition. He just hoped that she had enough sense not to do anything foolish.

Veryan, somewhat shakily, went to the Crosses' funeral, accompanied by Josh and Horace. He offered Abel his condolences and arranged a time to discuss the sale of the farm stock. (The cows, sheep and donkey had all been returned with commendable promptitude. The hens had doubtless filled various cooking-pots.)

Dorothea duly drew up the family tree and was somewhat stunned by the Selwoods' contributions over several generations. She showed it to Sylvia.

'I hope Cousin Veryan doesn't add to it,' observed Sylvia. 'A lot of little Veryansons would be too much.'

'Surely not!' Dorothea found herself revolted by the idea.

'Well, he's a man, isn't he?' said Sylvia cynically. 'And if you haven't seen Lucy eyeing him. I have.'

'Sylvia!'

'Well, it's true.' She looked at Dorothea's stricken face and said hastily, 'Don't look like that, Thea. I was only funning.'

'If Cousin Veryan . . .' A black hole seemed suddenly to have opened up at her feet.

'I said Lucy eyes him, Thea,' said Sylvia impatiently. 'Not that he eyes Lucy. If he eyes anybody, it's you.'

'You cannot be serious?' gasped Dorothea. She had put away her dark-brown dress and not worn it again. She had felt too exposed.

Sylvia laughed. 'Honestly, Thea, what's wrong with that?' She felt immeasurably superior. At least she knew when she had aroused a man's interest; Bram's, for example. And where was he? She'd managed to have a word with Jane, Miss Gunthorpe's maid, after church but Jane had reported that nobody had seen him for over a week.

★ ★ ★

April had passed with its usual showers and sunshine and it was now May. The evenings were perceptibly longer and the weather took a turn for the better. The swallows returned and were once again building nests in the old stable block and the cuckoo's call echoed in the wood behind the Priory.

Veryan recovered and resumed his rides around the estate and now Dorothea often went with him. They had visited Mrs Tregair several times and little Jenny had become used to Veryan. She seemed fascinated by his deep voice and would creep nearer and nearer to him, until, finally, one small hand would rest on his knee for support.

At first Dorothea noticed that he tensed up whenever Jenny touched him, but gradually he relaxed and one day he absently reached out and stroked her hair.

There was not much he could do for Mrs Tregair immediately, he told Dorothea.

There was simply not enough money to rebuild all the cob and thatch cottages with good stone and slate. 'I am concerned about them, though,' he finished. 'That cottage cannot be healthy for them, particularly Jenny. Did you see the bucket to catch the rain? And that sodden mattress.'

'I know,' said Dorothea. 'But you are doing what you can. And a straw mattress on a new wooden frame must be better than one on the bare earth.'

'Another thing,' said Veryan. 'I couldn't help noticing last time we went that there was a brandy bottle hidden in a corner. I didn't say anything. To tell the truth I wasn't sure what to say. It seemed so cruel to upbraid her for it with Jenny ill and the cottage so in need of repair.'

'I do not think Mrs Tregair does more than accept the occasional bottle.' Dorothea chose her words carefully. 'If she decides to sell it on, she may make a small profit and I am sure she spends any spare money on the children.'

'That's it,' said Veryan. 'How can I stop something when I have nothing to offer in its place? Abel was telling me the other day how chancy the fishing is and how hard it is to make ends meet, though I must say that he seems to do all right.'

'He and his wife have a small chandler's shop,' said Dorothea. And a large cellar underneath it, she thought. She knew very well that Abel and some friends occasionally rowed a galley over to Roscoff and came back with as much brandy and geneva as they could hold.

'And the drunkenness in Porthgavern,' went on Veryan. 'God knows how they find the money to do it, but on some nights it's like, well, Bedlam: fighting, drinking men, and women too. It can't be right.'

'Have you any ideas?' asked Dorothea, curious to know what he would come up with. Drunkenness was very bad, she supposed, but it had always been there.

'Yes, I thought I'd build a road.'

'A road!'

'I was thinking of trying this seaweed manure and pilchard leavings, if I can get them, on the fields this autumn. Of course, they could be carried up by mule and pony, but by cart would be more economical.'

'Carts! I don't think there are any hereabouts.'

'Exactly, and that's because the roads, such as they are, are scarcely more than mule tracks. So far as I know the only road that will take any wheeled traffic around here is the Torpoint — Liskeard road, the one the

Mail uses. If we could have a proper road to link up with that, just think of the benefits to Porthgavern. And I could use it for my seaweed manure as well.'

Dorothea was silent. To build a road had simply never crossed her mind. And yet she could instantly see the advantages. Building it would employ a number of men during the slack months. Cattle and sheep would get to Bodmin market in better condition. Carts would mean fewer mules and ponies, which were expensive to feed. It would also mean quicker transport for smuggled goods coming into Porthgavern or Morvoren Cove and possibly a wider distribution area. On the other hand, it would also mean easier access for the militia.

'Would the road go through Egloscolom as well?' she asked.

'Oh yes. It would follow the existing track.'

'But can you afford it?'

'Ah, there's the rub. A large portion of the rents from the estate goes into paying this mortgage your father took out. I have fifteen hundred pounds coming in annually from the funds, together with the income from my own inheritance, which is three hundred pounds a year. On the other hand, if I do it and the place prospers, then we shall prosper with it.'

'You could make a start at least,' said Dorothea, having turned it over in her mind. The money from the *Maria*, if she ever dared to tell him about it, could make a real difference to such a project.

'So you approve?'

'Indeed I do. I'm most impressed, Cousin. Truly I am.'

They had reached a small wood. Last time Veryan had been there it had been barely spring; now the oaks and beeches had come into leaf and the ground was carpeted with bluebells. There was a blue haze as far as the eye could see, interspersed with patches of pink and white from the campion and wild garlic. They reined in their horses.

'It's beautiful,' said Veryan. 'I'd no idea.'

'Yes, isn't it? I always love it at this time of year. Everything is so fresh and green.'

I've missed this, thought Veryan. As a child he had noticed and enjoyed the seasons. He remembered Matty making him special Easter eggs to roll down the hill behind the house. She'd wrapped decorative leaves around them tied on with cotton and secured tightly in muslin. They were then hard-boiled in water and onion skins. When they were unwrapped there were the leaf patterns now miraculously on eggs which had become golden-brown.

In Oxford all he'd been aware of was the need for a fire when damp threatened to curl up his books.

And all this was his! Without his wanting it he had been thrust into the ownership of this run-down estate with its myriad problems and here, like a surprise present, was this bluebell wood.

For the first time Veryan began to feel cautiously content. He sniffed the air appreciatively. It smelled of earth and bluebells and the occasional tang of wild garlic. It was the latter which made him remember something.

'What on earth were you doing yesterday afternoon?' he asked. There had been the most obnoxious smell. Mrs Kellow and Dorothea were running round with aprons on and looking so busy that he hadn't liked to interrupt.

'Making soap. Quite a business I do assure you.'

'What sort of soap?' asked Veryan curiously.

'Different sorts. Some green soap for household use, but other better soap, too. In fact, I meant to ask you whether you liked rose water or elderflower. I can scent it with either.'

'Elderflower. But ought you to be doing such things, Cousin?' He saw the look in Dorothea's eye and added hastily, 'I meant no offence. But surely that sort of hard, dirty work could be left to Mrs Kellow and Molly and Lucy?'

Dorothea laughed. 'Indeed it could not. Soap-making is highly skilled and easily goes wrong. Besides, for a house the size of the Priory, we have very few servants. Fanny and I have to do a lot. That is why so many of the rooms are under dust covers.'

'We can't afford more servants. Maybe when the last of the Watsons have grown up.' Veryan had discovered that Sir Walter gave a shilling a week to support any by-blow of his. The sums amounted to about twenty-five to thirty guineas a year, enough for an extra four or five servants.

'Look at it this way,' said Dorothea, 'that money helps every child in the family.' In fact, the allowance could be said to have made Sir Walter's 'convenients' more eligible. Abel's mother, for example, had borne Sir Walter two children and the two shillings a week that had come in until they were thirteen had been enough to bring in a host of suitors — including Michael Cross's father.

'At least the numbers will decrease with

time,' observed Veryan.

'Provided you don't start,' murmured Dorothea. The moment she'd said it she wished she hadn't.

Veryan said in a voice of thunder, 'What!'

'I'm sorry.' Dorothea whispered. She had turned scarlet.

'You think that I . . . ?'

'Oh please . . . I'm sorry. I don't know what made me say it.' She had never felt so mortified in her life and longed for the ground to open and swallow her up.

Veryan looked across at her. She was still scarlet. Veryan's experience with the fair sex was limited to a few embarrassingly inept episodes he preferred not to think about. He remembered Sir Walter's taunts when they had met at the Mitre in Oxford all those years ago. At least his cousin thought him capable of following in Sir Walter's footsteps. Suddenly he found that he was smiling.

★ ★ ★

The spring weather, however, was destined not to last. A strong wind from the south-west blew up and it became colder again. The barometer in the hall dropped alarmingly. Now, when Dorothea looked outside, instead of blue sky and blossom, she could see dark scudding clouds and white flecks of foam on the sea. Thank goodness Sir Veryan had sent somebody to patch up the rotting reed on Mrs Tregair's roof.

'Looks like we're in for a storm, Miss Thea,' said Josh. 'The horses be all restless.'

The few fishing-boats that were out battled their way back. Horace, Toby and Sylvia went down to Porthgavern harbour to see what was happening. There was a lot of activity. Anything movable was being taken somewhere sheltered. Masts were lowered and boats moored fast inside the harbour wall built by Sir Walter. Small boats were hauled right out of the water. Shutters were shut and barred. The sky had turned a heavy leaden colour.

'I love a storm!' cried Sylvia.

'She'd like a good wreck, I expect,' said Horace. He glanced up at the sky which was becoming darker by the minute. 'Come on, we had better be getting back.'

'I wouldn't,' protested Sylvia. 'At least not when people are drowned.'

'Are there lots of wrecks around here?' asked Toby. They had turned back and were walking towards the gatehouse when there was a loud crack of thunder and a simultaneous streak of lightning split the sky.

'Oh my God,' cried Horace. 'We'd better run.' As he spoke, the first fat raindrops fell.

Toby reached out and grabbed Sylvia's hand. By the time they reached the house they were all soaked. A clucking Mrs Kellow ushered them in and Jack carried off sodden cloaks and hats. There were wet puddles on the stone flags and Mrs Kellow directed Molly to fetch the mop and bucket. The hall had become so dark that Lucy was already lighting lamps and candles.

The storm rumbled on throughout the day and by the evening it was rising in intensity. Everybody was restless; it was impossible to settle to anything. Even Veryan, who was quite capable of becoming totally absorbed in a book to the exclusion of everything else, was reading Pindar with less than his usual attention. Dorothea paced up and down the drawing-room, every now and then going to the window to look at the streaming water outside. The angry roar of the sea seemed to penetrate everywhere and the wind howled down the chimney sending gusts of smoke into the room. The tapestries billowed against the walls.

Suddenly, there was a noise downstairs, a furious knocking followed by confused voices. Dorothea almost ran out of the room. It was Abel, dripping and with water running in rivulets down his face.

'There be a ship, Miss Thea,' he gasped. 'Trading brig by the look of 'er. They think she'm being driven onto Morvoren Rock.'

'We'll be down. Thank you, Abel.'

She went back to the drawing-room. Horace leapt up. 'A wreck, Thea?'

'I fear so, on the Morvoren Rock. Sylvia, Fanny, do you help Mrs Kellow in case there are any survivors. Cousin Veryan, Mr Marcham, do you want to come down? You'll need warm clothes and boots. Horace, fetch the ropes, please.'

'You're not going down, Miss Selwood, surely?' said Toby.

'Of course I am. Medical skills are needed. You don't have to come, Mr Marcham. It will be a long and very exhausting night.'

'I'm coming. Veryan, what about you?'

Veryan closed his book and rose to his feet. 'I'll go and change,' was all he said.

Some fifteen minutes later Veryan, Horace, Toby and Dorothea set out. Dorothea had changed into a serviceable grey gown and a warm pelisse. She had gloves on and thick boots and carried her medicine bag. Outside the wind shrieked and howled. It was almost impossible to walk and they had to cling on to each other to battle down to the

271

gatehouse. Once in its lee, there was some shelter.

The sea sounded very close, thought Veryan, with a sudden surge of apprehension. He hoped he was not a coward, but he had never liked heights. The sky was lit every now and then by a sheet of lightning and he wasn't comforted by what he saw. Horace, unconcerned, was going on ahead down the gully path by the side of the cliff and Toby followed. Veryan looked across at Dorothea and squared his shoulders.

She was holding out her hand to him. 'It sounds worse than it is,' she shouted above the storm. 'Come with me.'

Veryan took her hand and allowed himself to be led towards the abyss. The waters crashed into the chasm below them, there was a dull boom underneath their feet as the wall of water hit the back of the cave and then a spout of water shot up into the air through a vent as if it were boiling.

'Oh my God!'

Dorothea turned and smiled. 'Magnificent, isn't it? Don't worry, that's all it does. Come on.'

There were about fifty people on the beach when they got down. Some, like Horace, were carrying ropes, others had what looked like grappling irons. Somewhere out there in the night, amid the shriek of the wind, was a vessel with poor souls aboard her desperately trying to avoid the rocks.

A cry went up as the crowd on the beach caught sight of a brig silhouetted against the sky. One mast had already gone. Either they had not had time to pull in all the sails or, more likely, they had broken loose, for one of the mainsails was streaming out in ribbons. She was inexorably being driven towards Morvoren Rock.

There was a sudden crunch, the ship juddered and lurched. She was on. Each succeeding wave seemed to pound her more. Dorothea could see frantic figures on board running this way and that.

Another crack and the ship slowly capsized and water surged over her.

'Oh God,' cried Veryan. 'Can nothing be done?'

Several men, tied together, rushed out into the raging surf grabbing the bits of wood that began to be driven ashore. Then came boxes and barrels, then more wood; it seemed as if the whole ship were breaking up. The sky was lit by explosions of lightning, which caught the white foam as it was tossed up into the air until it looked as if it was raining white fire. It was like a scene from Hell.

Suddenly, a cry went up; the rescuers

could see a man clinging to a plank, his head and hands appearing above the foam. Eager hands rushed forward and pulled him from the sea. The man was retching and shivering and a cut over one eye was bleeding sluggishly. Horace and Toby grabbed him and carried him over to Dorothea, who had wedged her medicine bag between two rocks and was prepared as well as she could be for any emergency.

She looked the man over briefly, gave him a slug of brandy and examined the cut over his eye. 'He'll do.' She gestured to Bill Kellow and Ozzie to carry him up to the house where Mrs Kellow was waiting.

Other bodies came in. Some Dorothea could help, others were not so fortunate. The dead were laid to one side. Nothing could be done for them now.

There was a lull. Dorothea wiped the water away from her eyes and looked around. Veryan was thigh deep in the water helping Abel to pull in a heavy chest. Horace and Toby were carrying some wretch to the row of bodies higher up the shore. Her eye moved to the ship and suddenly she saw a woman, a child clasped in her arms, perilously clinging to a spar and being pulled into the undertow.

Without thinking, Dorothea grabbed the

rope Horace had left and ran. Darting from rock to rock she tried to reach her. There were shouts behind her but she ignored them. Again and again the woman was swept forward only to be sucked back.

She must get her, she must. If she could just reach the rock in front, the one with seaweed, then she had a chance.

Suddenly a huge wave swept in, Dorothea lost her balance and was pulled into the water. She tried to clutch at the rock, but it was too late and she was sucked under. Several times she came up, but she could not get a purchase on the slimy surface. Her arm was hurting desperately and she realized that her strength was going.

She began to lose consciousness. Then there was a jerk and a pulling and something was hurting abominably. She groaned. Veryan, seeing the danger, had tied a rope round a pinnacle of rock, then round himself and jumped into the raging sea. He just managed to grab her dress and haul her up onto the rock before another wave broke over them. Using every muscle he possessed, Veryan clung on to Dorothea with one arm and the rock with the other.

Abel and several others rushed over and dragged them back onto the shore. Dorothea pushed Veryan away and struggled to get up.

'The mother and child,' she gasped. 'I must get them.'

'You can do nothing for them.' Veryan was trying to get his breath back. He was soaked and his arm was grazed where he'd rubbed it against the rock in his efforts to haul Dorothea out of the water. If she'd drowned, he kept thinking, what would I have done if she'd drowned?

'But the baby . . . I must.' Distracted, Dorothea had risen and was trying to stumble back towards the sea.

Veryan jerked her back and into his arms and held her tightly. 'Oh Thea! I thought I'd lost you. Don't you realize, I thought I'd lost you!' The relief just to hold her and to know that she was alive. He could feel her heart beating against his and hear her sobs. He cupped her head in the palm of his hand and held her close.

9

Dorothea remembered very little of the night of the storm. She had somehow stumbled back to the house, supported by an anxious Veryan and Abel and handed over to Mrs Kellow's ministrations. Mrs Kellow took one look at her and threw up her hands in horror.

'The state of 'ee!' she cried. 'What have 'ee been doing?' She shooed Veryan and Abel away and told them that if they wanted a hot drink Lucy had some mulled wine in the pantry. There were some pasties there too, but they were to go away for now and leave Miss Thea to her.

Dorothea was only vaguely aware of everybody's concern. Even after Mrs Kellow got her into a nightgown and Molly had run the warming pan over her sheets and she was warm and dry, all she could see were images of the drowning woman and her child. She slept badly, tossing and turning, and was only vaguely aware of Mrs Kellow holding something to her lips and Fanny sitting by her bedside and cooling her forehead with a damp cloth.

The morning found her still slightly feverish and feeling weepy. Sometimes she felt as though she were being sucked under by the water and was drowning, at other times she was being pulled out of the sea and her lungs were aching with the effort to breathe.

'What happened to the baby?' she whispered to Mrs Kellow.

'What baby, Miss Thea?'

Dorothea subsided into a feverish sleep, but always when she awoke came the same question.

When, after breakfast, Veryan asked Mrs Kellow how his cousin was, she told him of Dorothea's question.

'I can set her mind at rest,' he said. 'Let me see her.'

Veryan was shocked to see Dorothea lying flushed and hot, her hair matted from where she'd tossed and turned. She scarcely recognized him. Veryan sat down by the bed and took hold of her hand. Formality was forgotten.

'Thea, it's Veryan.' His other hand reached out to stroke her hot forehead.

The deep voice had its effect. She opened her eyes and tried to focus.

'The baby?' she whispered. 'There was a baby, wasn't there?'

'I am sorry, the baby died. It is lying

with its mother in the harbourmaster's shed together with the others from the brig. I went to see them this morning. They both look very peaceful.'

There was a pause. Dorothea's brows knit slightly, then she closed her eyes and two tears slid out from under her eyelids.

'You won't let them be thrown into the pit?'

Veryan turned to Mrs Kellow for elucidation.

'There do be a bit of field where they bury strangers, Sir Veryan. Mr Normanton won't bury them in the churchyard. He do say he don't know if they be infidels and he be not paid to bury such-like.'

'Does he indeed? We'll see about that!' He turned back to Dorothea.

'Thea? Can you hear me?' She nodded. 'They will get a proper Christian burial in the churchyard, if I have to take the service myself. I promise.'

'Thank you.' It came in a wisp of a voice. 'I think I'll sleep now.'

Veryan let go of her hand and stood looking down at her for a moment or two before leaving the room.

So that's the way the wind blows, thought Mrs Kellow. I wonder if Miss Thea knows? Later she thought, I wonder if Sir Veryan does?

★ ★ ★

Bram spent a profitable week or so in
Plymouth. He made sure that he won, but
unobtrusively and with enough losses to calm
any questions. The storm prevented him
from going home earlier but he did not waste
his time. He made the acquaintance of the
captain of a receiving vessel, which had just
arrived from Portsmouth with instructions to
see about recruitment in the area.

Recruitment, as Bram well knew, was a
euphemism for impressment. There were
certain strict categories that were supposed
to apply. The men had to be between
eighteen and fifty-five and usually sailors in
merchant ships or fishermen. The pressgang
were warned not to impress gentlemen's
sons, or any man who might have the
influence to make things unpleasant at the
Admiralty, but these guidelines were often
honoured more in the breach than in the
observance.

The captain, over several bottles of port,
told Bram that it was a job his men disliked.
They were unpopular and it was a business
capturing enough men without risking the
wrath of the local community. Several of his
men had been attacked.

Bram expressed a suitable sympathy and

refilled the captain's glass.

'I might be able to help,' he said. 'I have a young relative who has recently been in trouble with the law. Nothing serious, I assure you; a spot of smuggling and a tendency to get into dangerous scrapes.'

'Shounds like a likely lad,' slurped the captain.

'A splendid fellow. Just needs a bit of naval discipline.'

'Howsh it to be managed, though?'

'Leave it to me,' said Bram. 'I think I can promise you a fine haul.'

★ ★ ★

The following day Dorothea was feeling well enough to rise, albeit shakily, and come down to the drawing-room in her dressing-gown and with a shawl over her shoulders. Veryan and Toby had ridden out to inspect the storm damage on the estate and Veryan was then going to oversee the service for those who had died in the shipwreck.

'He really told old parson off, Miss Thea,' Mrs Kellow confided when she'd seen Dorothea earlier that day. 'He did say he be a disgrace to his profession and ordered a mass grave to be dug at once.' Eight of the crew had perished in the storm, as well as the captain and his wife and child.

'Will he really take the service, do you think?' asked Dorothea.

'He did say he would if Mr Normanton wouldn't. He be a clergyman, after all.'

'Yes, I'd forgotten.'

' 'Tis good to see he be taking charge, if you know what I mean, Miss Thea. Many's the time I've seen parson so drunk he could scarce climb the pulpit stairs.'

It was somewhat improper for Dorothea to leave her room dressed only in her nightgown, dressing-gown and slippers and with her hair loose, but as the gentlemen were out, she felt she might risk it. Fanny and Sylvia were in the drawing-room when she entered. Sylvia was sitting at a small round table by the window and attempting to translate a passage into French. Fanny was marking an earlier exercise of her daughter's.

'I'm sorry I gave everybody such a fright, Fanny,' said Dorothea, bending over Fanny's chair and kissing her cheek.

'Ought you to be down, dearest?'

'Oh yes. Though I must admit my legs felt very wobbly coming downstairs. Sylvia, Mrs Kellow said you did sterling work the night of the storm.'

Sylvia was looking blooming. She had noticed a letter with Bram's seal addressed to Sir Veryan Selwood in the hall and was longing to know what it said. She had heard, of course, of Veryan being poisoned, but how could it be possible that Mr Gunthorpe had anything to do with it?

Thea must have got it wrong. Her mind was so full of her potions that she saw poison everywhere and probably it was just an ordinary stomach upset. Cousin Veryan seemed to be all right now so it couldn't have been very serious.

'Mr Marcham has been showing me how to play shuttlecock and battledore,' she said. 'We practise in the hall. I hope we didn't disturb you.'

'No. How are you getting on?'

'Oh, it's tremendous sport. Mr Marcham's really agile, he leaps about like anything.' Sylvia's eyes were shining.

'He's been very kind to Sylvia,' said Fanny. 'It must be very dull for him here. No company and no outings.'

'Well, thank you!' Sylvia flared up.

'I'm sure your mother didn't mean that your company was a makeshift, Sylvia,' said Dorothea mildly. Poor Fanny felt that the lack of company was due to her irregular position — for who would visit whilst Sir Walter's erstwhile mistress was still there? Sylvia was too young to understand that. 'I scarcely think he can have found it dull with a wreck to cope with. I daresay he enjoyed it tremendously.'

'He was very brave too,' cried Sylvia. 'He and Horace brought in three men, you know. Horace said that one of them would have drowned if it hadn't been for Mr Marcham.'

'Are the men all right?' Dorothea was conscience-stricken. Usually this was her job and she had not given them a thought.

'You are not to worry, dearest,' said Fanny soothingly. 'Two of them only suffered cuts and bruises. Sir Veryan sent them off with a crown each when they had recovered. The third had a broken arm and is being cared for by Mrs Fawley. The ship was going home to Portsmouth. Poor things, so terrible a tragedy.'

'I know,' Dorothea sighed. 'It happens all the time, of course, but one never gets used to it.'

The door opened and Veryan, hat in hand, came in. Dorothea clutched her shawl to her and sank back against the sofa and tried to become invisible. She felt horribly embarrassed; to be caught thus in her dressing-gown and with her hair undone! What would he think of her?

'How did the service go, Cousin Veryan?'

asked Sylvia eagerly. 'Did you have to take it?'

Veryan laughed. 'In the end, no, I'm glad to say. I've never taken a service in my life.'

'But I thought you were in holy orders?' exclaimed Fanny.

'Oh yes,' said Veryan cheerfully, 'but that is just a formality if you accept a fellowship. I was summoned to see the bishop, we exchanged a few words on my old school — I was at Winchester with his nephew — and then he said, 'Familiar with the thirty-nine articles, are you?' I said yes I was and that was it.

'Next Sunday, after Holy Communion, I was ordained along with half-a-dozen other fellows.'

Sylvia giggled. 'It can't really have been like that, Cousin.'

'I do assure you it was. Good Heavens, Th — Miss Selwood! I didn't see you there.'

'You must forgive my state of undress, Cousin,' said Dorothea awkwardly. 'I didn't think you'd be back yet.'

'How are you feeling?'

'Shaky, but better, I believe.' Veryan was staring at her and her colour rose. He seemed transfixed.

'I've never . . . ' he began. He swallowed

and added simply, 'What wonderful hair. It's like spun gold.'

'Thank you,' Dorothea managed.

★ ★ ★

Half an hour later, Veryan was reading Bram's letter aloud to Toby in the library. It had taken Bram an hour or so to compose to his satisfaction and managed to combine a no-nonsense, man-to-man heartiness ('*So sorry, old fellow, to hear of your indisposition*') with a touch of injured innocence ('*damfool servant — in his cups — must have added the oil of vitriol by mistake. I have disciplined the wretch severely, naturally. Wouldn't have such a thing happen for the world. I hope you won't allow this unfortunate matter to injure our friendship*').

'I suppose it could have been a mistake,' said Veryan worriedly. 'Gunthorpe is a gentleman, after all, and my nearest neighbour. I can scarcely credit that he could have wished to poison me. What do you think?'

'I think the whole letter is humbug from start to finish,' said Toby at once. 'I never cared for Gunthorpe. In London he had the reputation for being none too scrupulous in matters of play and he kept some very odd company. What I want to know is what he is after?'

'Miss Selwood told me that Gunthorpe is part of a smuggling enterprise down in Cawsand,' offered Veryan.

'That fits,' said Toby. 'And I daresay he wouldn't mind expanding business in this direction. I'd be very surprised if he isn't deeply under the hatches.'

'Hm.'

At least Veryan wasn't throwing out the idea thought Toby, encouraged. Maybe he was learning at last. 'Miss Selwood doesn't trust him, does she?' he added. 'She seems to be a lady with a good understanding. I doubt whether she can be so very amiss in her judgement.'

'No, it is I who have been woefully amiss in mine,' said Veryan apologetically. 'My fault entirely.' For a moment he seemed to be about to say something more about his cousin and Toby waited hopefully, but in the end all he said was, 'What do you think I should do about this letter?'

'A non-committal answer? You don't want to start a feud with a neighbour, but you can scarcely return to the old intimacy.'

Veryan sighed. 'Do you know, Miss Selwood suggested that Gunthorpe was like my father!'

'A bullying streak, perhaps? If I'm not mistaken, Miss Gunthorpe is frightened of him. This letter proves his hide is thick, at any rate. I can't see any suggestion that he would understand it if you wished to drop the acquaintance. No, it's all about Gunthorpe getting what he wants. Your father, if I remember rightly, was very good at that.'

'True,' said Veryan. 'We all scurried about like mice to do his bidding.' He, too, had noticed Miss Gunthorpe's unease in her brother's company. Perhaps Miss Selwood was right: it was no mark of a gentleman to intimidate anybody. His father and Gunthorpe were equally at fault.

After some thought Veryan wrote a simple acknowledgement and, without committing himself to believing Bram's story, suggested that neighbours should be on good terms. An amicable neutrality was all that he was prepared to offer.

Bram, however, had other ideas. His first reaction on receiving Veryan's letter was to swear volubly. Either Miss Selwood or Mr Marcham had put him up to this. Left to himself Selwood would have been glad to get back onto the old terms, and probably apologized to boot. Well, he would get his revenge and Selwood would be sorry he hadn't been more co-operative.

If Selwood would not come to heel voluntarily, then Bram would have to try other methods. He told his mother and sister exactly what he expected them to do and accompanied them to church the following Sunday to keep an eye on them.

After the service Mrs Gunthorpe and Isabel, mindful of their instructions, went up to Sir Veryan and expressed their pleasure at seeing him recovered. Poor Mrs Gunthorpe was overcome with shame as Bram had known she would be.

'Oh, dear Sir Veryan! Thank goodness you are up and about again. The shame of knowing . . . but servants will be so careless. Isabel, come and tell Sir Veryan how upset we've been.'

Veryan could not snub so apologetic a lady and found himself weakly saying that of course he would visit when he was fully recovered. His cousin and Mrs FitzWalter had looked after him admirably and he believed that he was on the mend. Such was Mrs Gunthorpe's remorse that she allowed the reference to Mrs FitzWalter to pass unchallenged.

Bram, meanwhile, had stepped behind a pillar and gone in search of Sylvia. She was still standing by the pew, Prayer Book in hand, and looking enviously at Isabel's smart new hat with its elegant ostrich feathers.

Bram glanced up the aisle. His mother, sister and Sir Veryan were in the porch and had moved out of sight. Mr Marcham, Mrs FitzWalter and Miss Selwood had left the church.

'Miss Sylvia!'

Sylvia gave a very creditable start. 'Mr Gunthorpe!' He'd come in search of her!

'Your poor cousin,' said Bram. 'I am upset that, unwittingly, he was struck down at my house.'

'I knew it must be so,' said Sylvia, relieved. 'I couldn't believe that you would deliberately poison him.'

'I am delighted to have retained your good opinion,' said Bram. 'Believe me, Miss Sylvia, I value it.'

Sylvia blushed and studied the floor. Delicious, thought Bram. She'd shot up in the last few months and was on the cusp between girl and woman, just how he liked them. He reached out and took her hand, noticing how her fingers trembled underneath her cotton gloves. He could see the colour coming and going in her cheeks. Could he risk a kiss?

'Sylvia!' It was Horace, his eyes shining with indignation. 'Mama's been looking for you.' It was all Horace could do not to plant a facer on Bram's mouth.

Bram's eyes narrowed. Young Horace was decidedly *de trop*. He tucked Sylvia's hand in his arm, pinching her fingers lightly as he did so. 'Then we must not keep her waiting.' He led Sylvia towards the porch and Horace had no option but to follow behind.

Bram thought it best to release Sylvia before they came in sight of the others and allow Horace to take his place. He turned to say a few words to a surprisingly sober Mr Normanton and fell behind.

'He was holding your hand!' hissed Horace.

'So?' flashed Sylvia. 'We were in full view of everybody.'

'No you weren't. I tell you, Sylvia, he's a bad man. Do you want to go the way of poor Mary Pengelly?'

Sylvia tossed her curls. 'If talking to a man in church is a sin, then we're all guilty.'

'Mama wouldn't like it, I tell you, and neither do I.'

'Oh, don't be so stuffy. Do you think I haven't seen you stealing a kiss from Lucy?' Sylvia pulled her hand free and went to join her mother.

★ ★ ★

The following day Veryan received another letter from Bram. He was delighted to see Selwood on the mend, he wrote and hoped that he'd be himself again soon. He was going to a cockfight down near Cawsand tomorrow and wondered if Horace and Mr Marcham would like to accompany him? He knew Selwood did not care for such things. There would be a Short Main starting at three o'clock at the back of the White Boar. It promised to be a good afternoon.

Veryan frowned down at it. Somehow, Gunthorpe seemed to have manoeuvred himself back into a position of ordinary intercourse with the Priory and put Veryan in a position where he had no option but to respond. Could it be a genuine olive branch, and meant to reassure him that he had no intentions towards Sylvia? (The row between Horace and Sylvia had been long and vociferous on the way back from church and Veryan was left in no doubt that Sylvia had constituted herself Gunthorpe's champion.)

Cockfighting was for men only and, whilst Veryan personally found it barbaric, he was well aware that Horace was an enthusiast. Veryan would have liked to have thrown the invitation away, but he had a suspicion that Gunthorpe would find other ways of seeing that Horace knew about the fight.

On the surface the invitation seemed to be open and straightforward, but Veryan felt curiously uneasy.

Horace was enthusiastic. 'I should say I would!' he exclaimed. 'Gunthorpe has the most spanking Crele game-cock that you ever saw. I wonder if he's taking him?' Bram's iniquities were instantly forgotten.

Veryan turned to Toby and showed him the letter. Toby raised an eyebrow; too smoky by half the look said. 'Yes, I'll accompany Horace — if he has no objection.'

Toby did not particularly care for the sport. He knew cocks fought naturally, but all the same, in spite of the birds' undoubted courage and mettle he found the inevitable slaughter distasteful and he certainly didn't care for the company that frequented such occasions. He would go to keep an eye on Horace.

It was arranged that Bram should meet them at the White Boar shortly before the time stated.

'Have you been here before?' asked Toby, when they were riding along the cliff path towards Cawsand the following day.

'Oh yes. The White Boar is well known around here. I used to go with my father.'

For the rest of the journey Horace talked enthusiastically of Welsh Mains and Battle

Royals he had witnessed and of the particular points to look out for in your true fighting cock. The White Boar, when they reached it shortly after half past two, was a rough-looking building of dubious respectability situated above the harbour. Toby wondered what Sir Walter was about to allow an impressionable young boy into such a place. But there was no help for it, Horace was already greeting various men he knew.

'I can't see Gunthorpe anywhere,' said Toby.

'I daresay he'll be along,' said Horace. 'We'd better go in to be sure of good seats.'

The cockpit was a temporary construction inside the stables. Tiered wooden seating went round a central pit which was lined with turf. A referee stood by with scales and the first two feeders were ready with their birds in sacks. The birds had been shown earlier and the betting was heavy.

Eventually, a big burly man stepped into the ring and held up his hand for silence. 'Fletcher, the landlord,' whispered Horace. Fletcher welcomed the company, cracked a few jokes and read out the list of mains.

'Gunthorpe's birds aren't here,' said Horace disappointed, 'though I can see Sir Thomas Shebbeare's blue-reds.'

The referee was now measuring the cockspurs to check that neither bird had the advantage. The feeders reached into the sacks and pulled out their respective champions. Each was carefully weighed and checked against the entry form.

'I was here once when they discovered a bird had been substituted,' whispered Horace. 'The feeder barely escaped with his life.'

The feeders walked round the ring exhibiting their birds. The referee raised his hand to give the signal and the crowd fell silent. The birds were placed beak to beak. The feeders prepared to let go.

Nobody noticed the stable door open and a dozen men enter. Every eye was on the two birds on the turf. Suddenly there was a loud voice intoning: 'His Majesty's Navy hereby declares . . . ' He got no further.

Instantly there was pandemonium. 'The press! It be the pressgang!' Everybody was pushing to get out. The feeders had grabbed their birds and were struggling to put them back in the sacks. The referee had disappeared. Men were shoving and clambering over each other in their fight to escape. In the scrimmage Toby was knocked down and lost sight of Horace.

The dozen men were backed up by more outside. Bruised and bleeding from the tread of hobnailed boots, Toby picked himself up. The place was empty. All that remained were a few feathers, smashed wood and the bootmarks of desperate men. He limped out. Where was Horace?

In the inn, the landlord had disappeared and the landlady was in hysterics. 'They do usually give warning,' she wailed. 'That it should happen to we!' She had obviously been drinking, for a glass of geneva stood nearly empty on the bar in front of her. When she saw Toby she sobered up enough to say, 'No, I haven't seen Master Horace, sir. Ask Jim.' She indicated the ostler.

Toby limped over. Jim shook his head. 'Master Horace, 'ee been taken, sir,' he said. 'Seemingly they did want 'im, for I did hear one say, 'That's our lad, the one in the black jacket'.'

'But . . . but this is outrageous,' gasped Toby. 'To impress a gentleman's son. Why, it's unheard of.' He tried to think clearly. 'Where will they take him?'

'The receiving ship do dock at Plymouth, sir.'

Toby sank down onto a settle. His head was swimming. He was in no state to deal with the authorities, he realized. It would be better coming from Veryan. He must get back to Selwood Priory as soon as possible.

He must . . . but the world began to spin in front of him and he slumped to the floor.

Some fifteen minutes later, Toby was tucked up in the land-lady's best room with a stiff dose of laudanum inside him.

Bram had watched the pressgang's attack from the safety of the first-floor window of a ropemaker's shop opposite the White Boar. It had all gone remarkably well. Horace and about two dozen others were taken, tied up and frogmarched down the hill. They would be rowed in fast galleys to the receiving ship in Plymouth and thence to Portsmouth. When everybody had gone, Bram went downstairs and strolled over to the stable-yard, where he met the shaken landlord who at once poured out his woes.

'They've taken young Horace? Don't you worry, Fletcher, I'll see to it.'

'Thank 'ee, sir. And the poor gentleman that was with 'm be upstairs.'

'Hurt is he?' said Bram with satisfaction. 'I'll call in at the Priory on my way back; I'm sure Selwood will sort it out. No need for you to send anybody.'

That disposes of Horace, thought Bram, as he turned his horse towards Quilquin Hall. Marcham wouldn't get home until tomorrow and by that time Horace's deposition would have been signed and it would be too late:

he'd be on his way to Portsmouth.

Bram promised himself an enjoyable time comforting Sylvia.

★ ★ ★

When Horace came to he was lying in the hold of a ship with his ankles and hands tied securely. His head hurt and he felt horribly sick. What had happened? The last thing he remembered was a man with a swarthy face and a black beard grabbing his collar and shouting, 'This is our lad.' He had yelled and struggled and then something hit him on the head and he knew no more.

He moaned and struggled to loosen the ropes which were cruelly tight round his hands. A rough voice spoke in the darkness,' 'Tis no use crying, boy, we been pressed.'

'Pressed! But . . . '

'Aye, and it do seem they did plan 'n good and proper. Usually Fletch be warned, but we did be caught like rats in a trap.'

A trapdoor above their heads creaked open and they could see feet and a swinging lantern descending the ladder. The man stopped in front of Horace.

'You look bad, cully. You was hit pretty

298

sharp, I reckon. You feeling sick?'

Horace nodded carefully. The man had a damp rag tucked into his belt and he wiped Horace's face. He then undid the ropes around Horace's wrists, and gave him a drink. The blood coming back into Horace's hands was agonisingly painful and it was all he could do not to cry. The man held up his lantern to Horace's head. 'A lump as big as an egg,' he said. 'Well, they say Gunthorpe don't make no mistakes.'

'Gunthorpe?' echoed Horace. 'Gunthorpe had me pressed?'

'I ain't said nuffin',' said the sailor, alarmed. 'It slipped out like.'

'Where are we?' asked Horace, struggling to sit up. The man had gone over to tend the other prisoner.

'In Catwater, Plymouth. This is the receiving ship, see. You'll both go with the others before the captain and the doctor tomorrow and then down to Portsmouth.'

Catwater, thought Horace. A faint hope entered his mind. 'Is the *Maria* docked here, by any chance? A cutter. Belongs to Daniel Watson?'

'Don't know, sir. This ain't my part o' the world.'

'But you could find out?' pleaded Horace. 'Daniel Watson's the name, of the *Maria*.

He'll make it worth your while. He's my half-brother.'

The sailor spat. 'Can't promise, but I'll see. Lor', here comes old short arse.' The sailor vanished up the ladder and the trapdoor fell with a crash.

'Some people have friends in high places,' remarked Horace's companion sourly.

Horace gave a short laugh. 'And enemies,' he said. Bram had done this. Doubtless the whole thing was set up. He wondered how long it would take Marcham to get back and would Veryan be able to do something in time? He doubted it. Pressed men were usually got on board pretty sharpish, that way they'd be in the navy before their folks could do anything. Horace knew he was under age — he wouldn't be eighteen until October — but somehow he couldn't see the captain of the receiving ship admitting it, especially if he'd been well greased in the palm by Gunthorpe.

No, practically speaking, his only hope lay in Daniel and the *Maria* being there.

★ ★ ★

That morning Dorothea had awoken feeling better. She had slept well and her head had cleared. As she lay in bed hearing the early morning sounds of Lucy and Molly clattering about with brooms and brushes, she began to go over the night of the storm. She remembered her strange feeling of desperation at seeing the woman with her baby struggling in the raging waters and then stumbling across the sand and rocks to try and reach them.

Dorothea knew perfectly well that the first rule for anybody at a wreck was to make sure that they did nothing foolish to endanger more lives. She had broken all those rules. She had behaved, however understandably, in an irresponsible fashion and, had it been Horace, she would have been furious. It had felt so much worse that a mother and baby should drown. She had no children of her own and a child in danger was especially precious to her.

Other moments were returning. Was it really Veryan who had rescued her? Increasingly, that was who it felt like. But he had said nothing and neither had anybody else. Perhaps neither Mrs Kellow nor Fanny knew. All the same, if her memory was right, then she owed him a debt of gratitude that could never be repaid. Dorothea was well aware that she had been very close to losing her life. And whoever had pulled her out of the sea had done so at considerable personal risk.

There was one more recollection which she found it much harder to understand. She was standing within the circle of somebody's arms and being told over and over again how precious she was to him. She could recall a thudding heart and the wet salty tears, or was it just spray, running down both their faces? And she had clung to him. The next thing she remembered was being helped by Abel and Veryan up to the Priory and Mrs Kellow coming forward and the candlelight flickering wildly as the door opened.

It must have been a dream. And yet, it felt so real. She could still feel the buttons on the man's coat pressing against her cheek, hear his ragged breathing. But was it Veryan? He had been very reassuring about the burials and very kind, and then he had complimented her on her hair, but that had been all.

She shook herself firmly. What was she thinking of? They had, she hoped, come to a better understanding of each other recently, but there was surely nothing else? Dorothea was so unused to thinking of herself as essential to anybody that she found it hard to comprehend the degree of desperation in that voice. She must be mistaken.

The memory, however, would not go away,

and in the end Dorothea decided that, if she felt strong enough, she would go down to the herb garret and send a message to Abel asking to speak to him. He was there the night of the storm. He had helped her cousin bring her back to the house. Perhaps he could tell her.

Breakfast that morning had been full of Horace's excitement at the forthcoming cockfight. It was difficult for anybody else to get a word in edgeways.

Fanny and Toby didn't even try. All Sylvia said was, 'Cockfights? Horrid things, I wonder you will like them,' and turned her attention to her breakfast.

Veryan said very little. He seemed somewhat abstracted, though he enquired kindly after Dorothea's health and said that, when she felt up to it, he would like to discuss the possibility of moving the Tregairs into Tamsin Wright's newly repaired attic rooms in Porthgavern. There was no hurry.

This hardly sounded like the distraught man of the storm, thought Dorothea, and wondered why the thought depressed her. Naturally, she was interested in the Tregairs and anything that promoted their welfare concerned her, but somehow she couldn't find the enthusiasm for it just now. She managed to smile and say something suitable.

That afternoon, after Toby and Horace had set off for Cawsand, Dorothea escaped Fanny's well-meaning fuss and walked slowly down to the herb garret and sent Ozzie off with a message for Abel. It was a relief to sit down in the gatehouse and smell the pleasantly astringent smell of dried herbs and the subtle undertones of the more exotic spices. This was who she was, this was where her life lay, not in some half-remembered dream about something which couldn't possibly have really happened.

Abel's words, however, dispelled that.

'It were Sir Veryan who rescued 'ee, Miss Thea,' he said. 'I reckon 'e belong here after all. 'E be so brave as a lion, for all 'e be so quiet.'

'I never thanked him,' said Dorothea, conscience-stricken. 'I've only just remembered it with any clarity. He never said anything.'

Abel hesitated and then he said,' 'E do be mortal fond of 'ee, Miss Thea.'

Dorothea looked across at him. 'I . . . I thought I remembered . . . ' she began. 'But it's all so hazy . . . '

'Aye, he did cuddle 'ee, if that's what 'ee be trying to say,' said Abel, smiling. It amused him to see Miss Thea stumbling like this. She was usually so collected. 'In full view of half of Porthgavern too!' Speculation had been rife ever since and the taverns and kiddleywinks had been full of it.

'Oh no!' Dorothea turned scarlet.

'Don't 'ee take on so, Miss Thea,' said Abel kindly. 'Sir Veryan be a good man. 'E just be mortal shy with women. 'E'll have to help 'n'.

'I?' exclaimed Dorothea, with such a note of incredulity in her voice that Abel chuckled. Dorothea allowed herself to smile. 'Well,' she said crisply after a moment, 'I know the truth and that is what I wanted.' Whether she could cope with it, she thought, was quite another matter. But she could hardly discuss that with Abel.

★ ★ ★

Dinner that evening was a quiet meal. Veryan had arranged with Mrs Kellow that something should be saved for Mr Marcham and Master Horace when they came in: he did not expect them until late, he said. Doubtless Master Horace would want to stay as long as possible.

'I'll heat up some stew when they do come in, Sir Veryan,' promised Mrs Kellow.

Privately, Veryan was worried. He hadn't liked the invitation and now Toby and Horace had both actually gone he liked it even less. He was not a suspicious man, but something about it had not smelled right, even though he could not possibly see what. It was a public cockfight, at a known place and Toby was with Horace. All the same he was uneasy and on edge all afternoon and as evening drew on the feeling increased.

He tried to allow nothing of this to appear at dinner however, simply saying that he'd instructed Mrs Kellow to save something for Horace and Mr Marcham. He asked how Sylvia had found Tamsin Wright and about the progress of Mrs FitzWalter's sewing. He hoped Miss Selwood had taken the opportunity to rest a little.

Something's the matter, thought Dorothea. He's trying to disguise it, but he's worried. After dinner Veryan excused himself and retired to the library and, as soon as she felt she could leave Fanny and Sylvia without remark, Dorothea followed him.

She found him, not reading as she'd expected, but pacing up and down.

'Cousin Dorothea? Is anything wrong?' Veryan ceased his pacing and went to offer her a chair.

'That's what I've come to ask you,' replied Dorothea, sitting down. 'You may tell me that it is none of my business and, of course, I shall accept that, but you have been on edge all evening and I wondered if something was worrying you? If there's anything I can do to help . . . ?'

Veryan looked at her for a moment and then crossed over to Sir Walter's old oak desk, took out Bram's letter and handed it to her. 'It seemed preferable that Horace went with Toby to him going on his own. But I didn't like it and if I could have found some way of preventing it I would have done so.'

'Oil of vitriol, perhaps?' said Dorothea dryly.

Veryan gave a short laugh. 'You may think I'm being fanciful . . . '

'No, I do not,' said Dorothea at once. 'I think you should send Josh over. Now. He may meet them coming back, in which case all's well, but if not he will be able to tell us what, if anything, has happened. Of course, you may prefer to wait until morning.'

'One thing I have learned about the Cornish,' said Veryan, 'is that being out after dark holds no terrors for them — provided they can avoid the headless horsemen, spriggans and what not that abound in these parts.'

'So you've learnt that, have you?' said Dorothea smiling. 'I was wondering how long it would take you.'

'I didn't notice you enlightening me,' retorted Veryan.

Dorothea opened her eyes wide. 'But Cousin, surely so well-educated a man as yourself never believed such things?'

'Perhaps not. But it took me some time to work out why I was being fed all these taradiddles.'

'Ah!' said Dorothea. So he knew about the smuggling then, or at the very least, had a good inkling.

'Is that all you have to say?' demanded Veryan, smiling.

'No,' said Dorothea, suddenly serious. 'No, it isn't. But it will have to wait.' She realized suddenly that she had made up her mind: Sir Veryan must be told the truth about the *Maria*. She owed him her life; it was unthinkable that he should continue to be deceived.

'I'd better go and have a word with Josh. Would you like to come?'

★ ★ ★

At nine o'clock the following morning Horace and the other pressed men, about thirty in all, were escorted down the gangplank to a room set aside in Mayoralty House, for the cursory medical examination and their being sworn

308

in as recruits to His Majesty's Navy. The room was dusty and smelled of stale beer. There was a curtained screen, behind which sat the doctor, a desk for the captain and a number of benches for the recruits. Horace eyed the captain. He had wondered during the night whether he might have seen him in Gunthorpe's company before and, if so, whether he could risk an appeal, but the man, large and with a bulbous red nose and mottled hands, was a stranger.

The pressed men were in various stages of shock. Some were slumped on the benches, staring at the floor, some were near to tears and a few were openly pacing up and down. Horace was still feeling sick and giddy. He'd vomited up the skilly last night and had been unable to eat this morning. The petty officer had taken a dislike to him and every time he saw Horace he aimed a cuff at him. 'Playing the gentleman, eh?' he sneered.

'FitzWalter?' barked the doctor.

Horace stood up and one of the guards pushed him behind the curtain.

'Strip! Huh! Fought like a demon I see. Cuts and bruises, he'll do. Next.'

'But . . . ' began Horace.

He was jerked back and told to shut up.

At the desk, the captain was taking notes and filling in forms.

Horace was pushed towards him.

'Name?'

'FitzWalter. But sir, this is . . . '

'Age?'

'Seventeen.'

The captain wrote down 'Eighteen.'

'I said seventeen,' cried Horace. He was clouted over the ear by the guard.

'Place of residence?'

'Selwood Priory. I am the ward of Sir Veryan Selwood.'

The captain looked up. 'That's a new one!'

'It's true!' cried Horace, ignoring the guard who was twisting his arm behind him. It began to feel like some dreadful nightmare where you were caught and nobody could hear you cry for help although people were all around.

The door opened and two men entered. One was a burly figure with a white moustache and a rolling gait. The other was Daniel Watson. Horace closed his eyes with relief.

The captain lumbered to his feet and saluted. 'Admiral.'

'Sit down, sit down,' said the admiral testily. 'Come to see about a young man you've taken. What's his name, Watson?'

'FitzWalter, sir.' Daniel indicated Horace.

'Hm.' The admiral looked Horace over. 'You've been in the wars, lad. How old are you?'

'Seventeen, sir.'

The admiral turned to the captain. 'You'll have to let this one go. Under age. Besides, he's the ward of Sir Veryan Selwood. We can't upset the county.'

'He's been passed as fit and his name's down, sir,' said the captain huffily. His nose had turned purple.

'He's seventeen, dammit. Cross him off!'

'Sorry sir, can't be done. It's against regulations.' The admiral was retired, the captain knew. He doubted whether he still had much pull. The captain wasn't going to get into trouble because of some old buffer. In any case, he'd been promised twenty guineas by Gunthorpe to see this FitzWalter on his way to Portsmouth and he wasn't going to risk losing that.

Daniel moved forward and bent over the captain's desk and whispered a few words in his ear. The captain looked thoughtful. Gunthorpe badly dipped? He had heard rumours, and once young FitzWalter was signed up there was nothing anybody could do, money or no money. Daniel spoke again. The captain screwed up his eyes and looked at him.

'A case?' he said at last.

'Of the best, Captain.'

'Very well.' He scratched irritably at the form and crossed out 'Eighteen' and substituted 'Seventeen. Discharged'.

A few moments later, Horace, with Daniel's hand steadying him, was escorted from the room.

10

It was a long and anxious wait for Veryan and Dorothea. Josh and Ozzie had both set out the previous evening and it wasn't until about eleven o'clock the following morning that they heard anything when, to their enormous relief, Toby and Ozzie appeared, Toby, still looking somewhat shaken, and Ozzie leading Horace's horse. Veryan had given orders that they were to come straight to the library; he did not want to distress Mrs FitzWalter and Sylvia unnecessarily.

On their arrival at Cawsand, Josh had cross-questioned the Fletchers and had come to a reasonably accurate knowledge of events. They discussed Mr Marcham's condition and decided that Ozzie should stay at the White Boar and return with Mr Marcham, who plainly ought not to travel alone, in the morning. Meanwhile, Josh would get a lift on a boat going over to Plymouth and see what news he could gather about Horace.

Veryan was all for going over to Plymouth himself immediately, but Dorothea dissuaded him. If Josh had gone over to Plymouth, she thought, he probably had some plan up his sleeve. It was possible that Daniel was there. If Josh came back empty-handed then it would be time for Veryan to act — and he would have to go straight to the Admiralty, for she knew that pressed men were sent to sea as soon as possible.

But Veryan did not know about Daniel. His was the one Watson name that did not figure on the family tree she had so carefully drawn up.

Veryan reluctantly agreed to await Josh's return. When Ozzie had gone back to the stables and Toby, after allowing Dorothea to deal with his cuts and bruises, had retired to bed, Veryan said, 'I have the feeling, Cousin, that you know more about this matter than you are prepared to let on.'

'Oh?' said Dorothea.

'Do you not trust me?' It was spoken lightly, but there was hurt there, too.

'Yes, I trust you,' replied Dorothea. 'God knows, I owe you my life.'

Veryan made a gesture of dismissal.

Dorothea added, 'I know that Josh has a number of contacts in Plymouth who he might not want you to know about, that's all. I did not wish to jeopardize anything he might have planned.' She smiled and added, 'Josh is very resourceful.'

'I see.' He paused, as if waiting for Dorothea to continue. When she said nothing he went on, 'We shall have to think about Horace's future. Plainly, he is not safe here. Has Horace told you of his wish to join up?'

'Yes. I think it's an excellent idea, if his mother could be brought to agree. Just what Horace would like and the discipline would be good for him.'

'It will have to wait until he is eighteen, though, which won't be until October,' said Veryan worriedly. 'And I daresay a second lieutenancy would cost a hundred pounds or so, but I could probably find that from somewhere. I wish I knew what to do about him until then. He will scarcely want to go back to school.'

Dorothea was silent. She was thinking fast. She must tell Veryan about the *Maria*. It was quite wrong that he should be left in ignorance when he was shouldering all the burdens of Horace's support — particularly when she knew that she had easily enough money from her free-trading to pay for Horace's commission.

But supposing he decided to inform on her? Could she trust him not to do that? Abel had said that he was 'mortal fond' of her. If that were true, how true would it be after she had told him?

'You are very silent,' said Veryan. He had been watching her frown of concentration. 'Is anything amiss? You know that I will help if I can.'

Dorothea drew a deep breath. 'Cousin, there is something I've been wanting to tell you for a long time.'

'Oh?' Veryan turned and looked at her.

'It's difficult to know where to start . . . '

There was a noise outside, cries of welcome followed by a brisk knock at the library door. Veryan went to open it. In the doorway stood Josh, Horace and Daniel Watson.

'Oh, thank God! We've been so worried.' Dorothea ran up and hugged first Horace and then Daniel.

'Daniel, I hardly dared to hope that you might be in Plymouth.'

'Whoa, lass,' said Daniel. 'There, there. Master Horace is back safe and sound. Naught but a few bumps and bruises.' He looked up. Veryan was standing rigidly, staring at him. Daniel looked across at Dorothea. 'You'd best introduce us, Miss Thea,' he said.

'Of course.' Dorothea looked at her cousin. He doesn't like it, she thought. She must tread warily. 'Cousin Veryan, this is Daniel

316

Watson, the captain of the *Maria*. I . . . I have known Daniel all my life.'

'So I see,' said Veryan dryly.

★ ★ ★

Over the next few days, the cockfight and its aftermath were gone over exhaustively. Horace and Toby were made much of and sat of an evening looking interestingly pale and bruised. It came out that it was Josh who had found Daniel on board the *Maria*. She was preparing to sail and Josh arrived in the nick of time. Together they had decided that Daniel should approach his friend, the retired admiral, and see what could be done. Veryan absorbed himself in the *Meditations* of Marcus Aurelius, whose austerity suited his mood, and appeared not to listen.

'I knew Daniel would help me, if only I could tell him somehow,' cried Horace.

'Of course he would,' said Sylvia. 'He's always helped us, hasn't he, Thea? Do you remember when I was little and he brought me that doll from France after I'd been ill?'

'Yes,' Dorothea said reluctantly. She was all too aware of Veryan's rigid figure behind her.

317

'Who exactly is this famous Daniel?' asked Toby.

'He is one of the Watsons,' replied Dorothea, suddenly realizing that this was an opportunity to clear things up a bit. 'His mother was a laundress here and they lived in the cottage next to Bill Kellow's. Daniel was father's favourite Watson; he certainly helped him more than he did the others and, as Daniel showed early promise, he enabled him to go to sea.'

'So Daniel now owns the *Maria*?'

Dorothea didn't answer. Horace and Sylvia shuffled awkwardly. Toby, realizing too late that some questions were better not asked, changed the subject.

'Thea was always very fond of Daniel,' put in Fanny, looking up from her sewing. 'As was Sylvia.'

'I've always thought of him as my older brother,' said Dorothea firmly.

Veryan continued to read Marcus Aurelius. Whatever he was feeling he was not going to discuss it. Several times Dorothea tried to talk to him and each time he avoided her. He took Josh or Ozzie with him on long trips round the estate, went to Bodmin market, called on Sir Thomas Shebbeare for his advice on switching from ploughing with oxen to ploughing with horses, and he kept

318

his cousin at arm's length.

There seemed to be nothing that Dorothea could do. Such was her state of anxiety that she failed to notice Sylvia's growing fantasy that all Bram needed was the love of a good woman.

Sylvia was increasingly disinclined to join in the general condemnation of Bram's behaviour. Of course he was wrong, she thought, very wrong. But perhaps he had never truly been understood? She had heard from his own lips that the poisoning of Cousin Veryan had been an accident — which nobody else seemed to believe. Surely, he could not have meant Horace to be pressed? It was so unfair that he should not be allowed to give his side of the story.

Sylvia resolved that, if the chance arose, she would give him that opportunity.

★ ★ ★

A couple of days passed and Dorothea was feeling desperate. Somehow it had become an absolute necessity that her cousin should know the truth. How odd that only a few months ago it would have been a matter of complete indifference to her what he thought. Now, being estranged from him was acutely painful.

319

It was obvious that he would not allow her near enough for them to talk. She would have to find other means. In the end she decided to give him the *Maria*'s ledger. It went back a long way, ever since her father had first bought the ship, in fact. There was the original bill for her construction, the deed naming Dorothea herself as the owner, and all the various transactions over the years, initially in her father's scrawl and, over the last year or so, in her own writing. The ledger named names. If only he would look at it, it would explain everything.

She would just have to trust that when he had read it he would not inform against her.

She went down to the herb garret and took it out from its hiding-place. Then she sat down and wrote a brief letter.

Dear Cousin Veryan

When we were interrupted by Horace's return, I had been about to tell you something. As I have not had the opportunity to continue our conversation as I had hoped, this ledger will have to explain for me.

I am sure that you will understand why I was reluctant to tell you at first, but

320

please believe that I have long wished to rectify the omission. I have learned to appreciate your integrity and to admire your dedication and discernment in dealing with the estate's many problems.

Yours etc.
D. Selwood

It was rather balder than she liked, but it would have to do.

She sealed the letter, wrote *Sir Veryan Selwood* on the front and put it, together with the ledger, on the oak desk in the library.

★ ★ ★

There followed three days of awful suspense. Veryan said nothing. He gave no sign at all of having even noticed the ledger and he continued to treat Dorothea with cool politeness. Dorothea's appetite vanished. Had she made the most dreadful mistake? Was her cousin even now with the authorities in Launceston? Had she condemned Daniel, Abel and a host of others to transportation or even the gallows?

She began to have nightmares of warders coming for her, holding out handcuffs and the people of Porthgavern pelting her with filth; 'There goes the woman who betrayed us!'

On the afternoon of the fourth day, unable to bear being in the house a moment longer, she escaped down to the herb garret. There was not a lot to do there at this time of year. In a month or so she could begin to harvest the herbs growing in the garden — if she wasn't languishing in some prison — but she found the presence of her jars and dried herbs comforting.

She sank wearily down on the window seat and stared unseeing out to sea. Her reverie was broken by a sharp knocking at the door downstairs. She peered down and saw Veryan's fair hair. He was alone. There were no officers of the law accompanying him. She rose slowly, took the key from its hook and went down to open the door.

'May I come up?' Veryan held the ledger under his arm.

Dorothea swallowed and nodded. She could not have said a word. She indicated that he go in front of her.

Veryan had avoided making an issue of the herb garret. He had realized early on that to insist on having the key would be an unforgivable invasion of her privacy and the gatehouse alone had escaped his eagle eye and his notebook in that first inspection of the Selwood inheritance.

Silently he took the ledger from under his arm and handed it to her. Dorothea looked at him fleetingly, she had never felt so vulnerable or so exposed in her life. She put the ledger down on her desk with hands that trembled and then, as her legs would no longer support her, sat down abruptly.

There was another oak chair at one side and Veryan pulled it round and sat facing her. He could see her hands clasped together so hard that her knuckles were white. There were dark rings under her eyes and her hair was escaping in a number of fair wisps from an awkwardly knotted bun on top of her head. Veryan had expected her to be defiant or even angry but now, for the first time, it occurred to him that she was frightened.

Any lingering resentment that he felt over having been duped so successfully, vanished.

'That was a very brave thing to do,' he said gently.

Dorothea looked up and gave a deep sigh of relief. 'I could not bear to go on lying to you.'

'I'm sorry it has taken me so long to come to you, but I wanted to talk to Daniel and Abel and it took a day or so to arrange.' He saw her colour drain away and added hastily,

'I was very ungracious towards Daniel when he brought Horace back, and I wished to remedy that. But he was very kind and he showed me over the *Maria* and explained the arrangements to me. I think we reached a good understanding.'

Dorothea stared at him. He'd spoken to Daniel? Daniel had shown him over the *Maria*? Surely that meant that they had got on? She couldn't imagine Daniel allowing her cousin anywhere near his ship if he had not believed him to be trustworthy.

'But one thing I must say, Cousin, and Daniel agrees with me in this, your father treated you abominably in using your money for the *Maria*. Good heavens, if she were to be impounded, you would be left without a penny to your name!'

'I know,' said Dorothea. 'But whilst Father was alive I could do nothing. I planned eventually to pay myself back. Though I am sure I may always command a home with Fanny.'

'I see that you are putting money aside for Horace and Sylvia. Do you not think that should be my business?'

Dorothea swallowed. 'It should have been Father's business,' she said. 'And I wasn't sure at the beginning how much you were willing to do for them. Then it began to seem unfair that you should have to take on Horace and Sylvia as well, when you had the mortgage on the estate to pay off and all the problems of years of underinvestment. You forget that I am well aware of your financial situation. At this present moment I probably have more ready money than you do!'

Veryan smiled. 'I agree that getting Horace settled is a priority, but after that either the *Maria* or I must pay you back the seven thousand pounds that was left to you by your mother. I have inherited your father's obligations as well as the estate and it is against my principles to allow so disgraceful a debt to stand.'

Dorothea was not used to thinking of herself as being entitled to anything very much, so she said, 'But is that so very important just now? Sylvia will need a dowry, you know.'

'That is not the point,' said Veryan. 'Your inheritance belongs to you and you must have it. Good God, surely you don't imagine that your mother would have agreed to such an arrangement?'

'No, of course not.'

'Well then.' He saw that Dorothea was still looking uncertain and decided that she had had enough for the moment. 'Come, Cousin, may I ask you to show me round?'

Dorothea took him up onto the leads and they admired the view. Then she took him down to the crypt. 'The last secret,' she said penitently, as she handed him a lantern, 'You may as well have the whole picture.'

'An astonishing picture too,' commented her cousin. 'Lace for Mrs Gunthorpe, tea for Lady Shebbeare, tobacco for Sir Thomas, brandy for practically everybody . . . There can scarcely be a person in the county who isn't involved in some way or other. I can quite see how my arrival caused you some alarm.'

Veryan was most impressed by the crypt. He walked around holding the lantern up high and admired the corbels and the fan vaulting. 'Amazing!' he said enthusiastically. 'I have rarely seen anything so fine. It is quite unspoilt, too.'

Dorothea was amused. It was typical that he should admire the architecture rather than be interested in just how much contraband it could hold. How much he has changed, she thought. She could not imagine the Veryan Selwood of a few months ago taking all this so calmly. Greatly daring, she said so.

'I know,' Veryan smiled. 'Crossing the Tamar has been a voyage of discovery. I suppose you could say I have grown up. I hadn't really thought about it before, but

Oxford is such a restricted world and it allowed me to ossify. Very pleasant in many ways, but once you are out in the real world and have to cope with real problems and your eyes have opened, there is no going back.'

'So you are not sorry that you came?'

Veryan turned to look down at her. 'No,' he said seriously. 'No, I'm not sorry. Are you?'

The air seemed suddenly full of some other, hitherto unexpressed emotion. Dorothea found she could not speak. Silently she shook her head.

★ ★ ★

The atmosphere at Selwood Priory assumed an air of holiday. Veryan, at Horace's and Sylvia's request, reread *The Lay of the Last Minstrel* to them of an evening. Toby's cuts and bruises healed and laughingly he shrugged off Fanny's anxieties that he must have a very poor notion of Cornish hospitality. He had been vastly entertained, he told her: he could not remember having had so adventurous a time in years.

Veryan and Dorothea embarked on a cautious intimacy. Veryan told her of his lonely childhood and how lost he would have been without Matty. He told her of

Oxford and how he had chosen, wrongly he now saw, to opt for a disengagement with the outside world. It was, thought Dorothea, like being invited into a private garden, where you could wander round and ask about this and that. Sometimes there were places that you learned were special, whose secrets were perhaps painful and still tender; at other times there were patches of weeds or nettles to be negotiated and talked of only with difficulty.

They talked endlessly about plans for the estate and Dorothea confided various smuggling exploits and all the background information she had previously kept hidden. Quite where all this was leading, neither of them considered. The pleasure was in being able to talk freely and without reserve of what mattered to each of them.

By contrast, the atmosphere at Quilquin Hall was almost murderous. Bram beat up one of the grooms for some imagined impertinence and the man was left with a broken jaw and three cracked ribs. Mrs Gunthorpe and Isabel crept round and avoided him whenever possible and one of the kitchen maids, who had been kicked once too often, ran away.

Bram, however, still had his spies and one of them, Isabel's maid Jane, brought him news after church that interested him very much.

Usually Mrs Gunthorpe ignored Sylvia's presence at church but today, such was her distraction, she spoke to her quite kindly and even asked Isabel to chat to Miss FitzWalter for a moment. Knowing that her mother wanted to talk to Dorothea uninterrupted, Isabel drew Sylvia aside and, accompanied by her maid, sought the quiet of the back of the church.

Isabel had always known of Sylvia's admiration and she couldn't help but be flattered when Sylvia burst out, 'Oh Miss Gunthorpe, pray let me say what a beautiful hat! I was admiring it throughout the sermon — though I know that was wrong.'

Isabel laughed — the first time she had done so for many a day. 'You must praise Jane here, for hers was the inspiration.'

Jane came forward for her share of Sylvia's youthful enthusiasm. After they had discussed hats for a while, Sylvia shyly asked after Mr Gunthorpe.

'My brother is very well,' said Isabel shortly. 'Business occupies much of his time.'

'Oh,' said Sylvia disappointed. 'I had hoped he would come riding with us again soon. I wanted to show him Trespyrion Quoit.'

'That be old druid's stone, miss?' put in Jane.

'Yes. It looks like a funny sort of three-legged table. Underneath it's like a bed, all grassy. I used to play at doll's tea-parties there when I was little.'

At this moment Isabel's attention was claimed by her mother and Jane, after a swift look round, whispered, 'I could tell Mr Gunthorpe that'ee be there sometimes, miss.'

Sylvia's eyes lit up. 'Oh, would you!' she exclaimed.

★ ★ ★

The following afternoon found Bram at Trespyrion Quoit. So it was like a bed, was it? Bram peered inside and saw that once in they would be more or less hidden from prying eyes. She was only thirteen, but already she was showing herself to be a knowing little thing. Bram didn't doubt that she'd be able to evade any number of would-be protectors and come here.

And he would have first bite at the cherry. It would make up for his disappointments in other areas and Bram was determined that Sylvia would pay for the slights he had received. She would cry and beg and he would pretend to consider, but in the end he would take her just the same. But she'd crawl first. He'd make as if to let her go and just when she thought she'd got away he'd go for the kill.

There was a fluttering of white ribbons and dancing brown curls, and here she was on cue. Bram straightened up and came forward.

'Well, well,' he said, 'what have we here? A little sprite come to the fairy mound.'

'Good gracious!' Sylvia's hand went to her slight breasts in well-simulated surprise. 'Mr Gunthorpe!' Then she spoilt it by giggling.

'I've never been here before,' observed Bram, 'you must show me round. But first of all I must exact a penalty.'

Sylvia put her head on one side and peeped at him from under her lashes. 'And why should I pay a penalty?'

'You kept me waiting for ten whole minutes,' responded Bram. 'Ladies who do that pay a price.'

Sylvia took a step forward. 'Oh?' she said hopefully.

Bram reached out lazily, took hold of her and pulled her towards him. His grip was surprisingly strong and Sylvia knew the first tricklings of fear. 'Ow! That hurts!'

Bram took no notice. He brought his mouth down hard on hers and cupped one hand under her buttocks to hold her to him. Sylvia began to struggle. Bram raised his head momentarily. 'Stop that!'

'What are you doing?' Sylvia's mouth had gone dry. Her voice was scarcely a whisper. Why hadn't she heeded the warnings? She'd crept out unobserved and nobody would know where she was.

'What you asked for, my dear, what else?'

'But . . . I never . . .' Sylvia began to cry. 'Please, Mr Gunthorpe, I . . . I made a mistake. I'm sorry.'

'Oh no you didn't, Sylvia. You came here of your own free will, didn't you? Well, now it's my turn and you will dance to my tune for a change. Understood?'

Sylvia's head went up. 'I won't. You can't make me and if you were a gentleman you'd let me go.'

Bram laughed. 'A gentleman! That's rich. I gave that up a long time ago, my dear. And you'll find that I can make you.'

Sylvia tore herself free and began to run. But it was too late. Bram caught her, slapped her face hard a couple of times and dragged her back to the quoit. Sylvia stared at him in shock, then she began to scream. Bram hit her again and, taking hold of her bodice, ripped it open. With his other hand he began to unbutton his trousers.

Veryan, Toby and Dorothea were in the knot garden enjoying the early summer sunshine. Veryan was much absorbed by the problem of the oxen. They gave a mediæval feel to the place, he said, which he quite enjoyed, but they were simply uneconomic. If only the soil could be improved then they could use horses, who could plough twice as much in a day.

'Oxen can go to market after five years or so,' put in Dorothea. 'You can't eat horses, though I believe they do so in France — at least, so Daniel told me. He said it gave him the shock of his life when he saw a horse's carcass, hanging up outside a butcher's shop.' She looked up. Fanny was coming into view.

'Have you seen Sylvia?' she asked. 'I wanted her to try on a gown I've been letting down, but she's nowhere to be found. She said she was helping you.'

Dorothea shook her head. 'I haven't seen her this afternoon. I thought she was with you.'

Veryan looked up, suddenly tense. 'I saw her slipping out earlier. She was heading in the Egloscolom direction.'

There was a short silence. Eventually

Dorothea said, 'I don't want to worry you, Fanny, but I'd be happier if we found her. She's been unwontedly docile ever since church yesterday. I wondered if she were planning something.'

Toby got to his feet. 'If she's escaped I think I may know where to,' he said. 'Trespyrion Quoit.' Oh my God, he thought, if she's offered to show Gunthorpe the bed underneath it . . .

Veryan rose. 'I'll go. I was going that way anyway to see Mrs Tregair. Do you want to come, Toby?' He exchanged a concerned glance with Dorothea, who at once turned to Fanny.

'Come Fanny, let's go into the house. It's too hot out here.'

The moment they'd gone Veryan hastened his step. 'I smell trouble,' he said. He almost ran into the stable-yard. 'Josh! Ozzie! Saddle Sir Walter's chestnut and the cob. As fast as you can.' In a matter of minutes they were off.

For a while, nothing could be heard but the thundering of hooves and the creaking of leather. When they came to the field with Trespyrion Quoit they reined in. There was a distant flutter of some white material on the ground and then, faintly, on the breeze, a scream. Veryan clapped his heels into the chestnut's side and the horse broke into a gallop.

Sylvia was inside the quoit. All they could see was a pair of bare legs, bruised and blooded. They could hear her strangled screams. But they could see enough of Bram. His boots were lying on the ground and his trousers were round his ankles. Without a second's thought Veryan sprang off his horse, lifted his riding crop and slashed at Bram's buttocks with such fury that great weals instantly appeared which oozed globules of blood.

Bram crawled out to meet the cold anger in Veryan's eyes. He was at a disadvantage, but he managed to say, as he fumbled with his trousers, 'She's a right little bitch. A real cockteaser.'

'Get off my land,' said Veryan, his voice icy. 'And I advise you to leave the county.'

'Pooh!' sneered Bram. 'You'll keep your mouth shut if you know what's good for you, unless you want the little bitch exposed. Like mother, like daughter they'd say and they'd be right.' He stooped, wincing as he did so, picked up his boots with what grace he could muster and walked off.

Toby dismounted and bent down to peer inside the quoit. Sylvia was curled up into a ball at the far end, shaking uncontrollably.

'Come on,' he said gently. 'It's all right. You're safe now.'

Sylvia curled herself up tighter and didn't respond. All he could hear was terrified gasps.

'Leave this to me, Toby,' said Veryan, in a tone Toby had never heard before. 'Sylvia,' he commanded. 'Come out at once!'

There was a sob and a scrabbling sound and Sylvia crawled out. She was filthy. Her dress was ripped and her face was bruised and bleeding where Bram had hit her.

Toby remounted. 'Hand her up to me, Veryan,' he said quietly. 'The cob will take two of us.'

Veryan, his face still set, picked her up as though she weighed nothing and placed her in front of Toby. He then climbed into the saddle and, without a word, set off for home.

'I'm sorry,' whispered Sylvia, so low that Toby had to bend to catch it. 'You did try to warn me and I didn't listen.'

'I'm sorry too, sweetheart,' said Toby. 'I should have tried harder.'

Sylvia shook her head. 'My fault.'

★ ★ ★

Dorothea, alerted quietly by Toby, had gone at once to Sylvia's room where Veryan had

336

carried her. The two men left and Dorothea did what she had to do. The moment they were alone, Sylvia broke into a storm of tears. It took a long time to get the whole story out of her but eventually Sylvia told it all. 'I thought he meant to kill me,' she sobbed. 'He had his hands round my throat.' Molly and Lucy brought up the tin bath and Sylvia was cleaned, examined and doped and when she was finally asleep Dorothea went down to the library to speak to Veryan and Toby.

'You arrived in time,' she said without preamble. 'She has been terribly frightened and shocked. There are a number of nasty cuts and bruises, but they will heal in due course. Otherwise she is unharmed.' The emotional scars, she thought, may take longer to heal.

Veryan closed his eyes in relief. 'If I'd had a gun I would have shot him,' he said.

'Let's hope he does the sensible thing and leaves the county,' said Toby.

Dorothea said nothing. She was well aware that in this place of close kinship and family loyalties, there was little chance of Bram getting away with it.

The next few days passed quietly. Sylvia spent most of her time in the prior's room with her mother. Fanny had always felt diffident about talking to her daughter intimately; she was too aware of the shame she had passed on to feel comfortable discussing it. But now, urged gently by Dorothea, she did talk more and Sylvia began to understand things that she had scarcely thought of before.

There was no excuse for Mr Gunthorpe, Fanny said firmly. Nothing could excuse a man who tried to rape a 13-year-old girl, however coming that girl appeared to be. He was perfectly capable of understanding her innocence and he deliberately chose not to do so. But, all the same, her dearest Sylvia must be made aware of how provocative she sounded and that an unscrupulous man would take advantage of it.

All this was a great comfort to Sylvia who was plunged into guilt. 'Mr Marcham did try to tell me,' she confessed, 'but I thought he was just being stuffy.'

There was comfort, too, in the number of posies of flowers and leaves full of early strawberries that she received. Everybody seemed to wish her well. Slowly, Sylvia stopped feeling like a pariah and began to come to terms with it.

It helped that Bram had left. He had not been seen since the night after the attack. Sukey reported to Mrs Kellow at church on Sunday that he'd come back in a real state and had locked himself in his room and allowed nobody in but his valet. The following day he was gone, nobody knew where. 'Good riddance,' said Sukey. She was sorry Sir Veryan hadn't killed him.

It was a week after the attack that Abel came up to the Priory and asked to speak to Sir Veryan. Veryan was in the library with Dorothea discussing crop rotation, a topic both seemed to find so fascinating that they didn't hear Abel's first knock.

'Oh Abel, come in,' said Veryan.

Abel came in, hat in hand. 'How be the little maid?' he asked, when the first courtesies had been exchanged.

'Doing well, thank you,' said Dorothea.

' 'Ee don't have to worry no more about Mr Gunthorpe, Sir Veryan,' said Abel. ' 'E won't trouble Miss Sylvia again. We'm taken care of 'e.'

'Thank you, Abel,' said Dorothea, seeing that her cousin was speechless.

'That be all right, Miss Thea. We be kin after all.' He ducked his head briefly at her and left the room.

'Oh my God,' said Veryan. 'What have they done?'

'Nothing more than he deserved,' said

Dorothea crisply. 'But if I were you I wouldn't ask.'

'But . . . but I can't leave it like that!' Veryan exclaimed.

Dorothea reached out and touched his arm briefly. 'You cannot force any Cornishman to tell you anything he doesn't want to,' she said. 'Leave it, Cousin. What good would it do to stir up a hornets' nest? Abel has told us nothing specific, after all. They may simply have taken Bram and dumped him on some beach in France and he is now languishing in some prisoner-of-war fortress. We just don't know.' Personally, she thought it more likely that he'd been coshed and later dropped over the side of a boat. She doubted whether he were still alive.

'I suppose you're right,' said Veryan after a moment. 'I would have killed him myself if I'd had the means.'

Their talk turned to Sylvia.

'She really ought to go to school,' said Dorothea. 'She needs the companionship of other girls of her own age. Girls to giggle with and who would tell her that she mustn't say some of the things she comes out with. It's no good my telling her, she sees me simply as an ageing spinster who knows nothing.'

'Is that how you see yourself?' asked Veryan. It seemed to him intolerable that she should have such a low opinion of herself.

Dorothea shrugged. 'Yes and no. I am thirty years old and unmarried. That, in Sylvia's eyes, makes me scarcely human. But I know that I am not as ignorant of the world as she would like to think.' She paused and then went on. 'When we were both sixteen Bram tried to attack me. I bit his earlobe so hard that he nearly lost it. You may have noticed the scar. I must confess it gives me a quiet satisfaction whenever I see it.' And I can still taste the horrible saltiness of that blood, she thought, with a mental shudder.

'The scoundrel!' Veryan was incensed. 'Did your father not do anything? I'd have had him thrashed at the very least.'

'I never told anybody,' Dorothea confessed. 'Children don't, you know. This is the first time I've spoken of it.'

Veryan reached out, took hold of her hand and raised it to his lips. Dorothea smiled shyly at him.

★ ★ ★

Sylvia was to go to school. There had been much discussion and argument but in the end it was decided that a few years at a seminary for young ladies in some pleasant

341

healthy town, some place where there would be no gossip about her, would be the best restorative for her spirits and give her the experience and companionship she needed.

Fanny tearfully agreed, but only on condition that she was allowed to go with her and lodge nearby. She could not bear the thought that Sylvia would be so far away and that she might only see her once a year when she came home for the summer.

'A child of thirteen needs her mother,' she protested and, in the end, Veryan agreed. He had missed Matty terribly when he went to Winchester and he did not want Sylvia to suffer as he had.

A suitable school was found in Harrogate. A young cousin of Toby's went there and her mama spoke highly of it. Letters of enquiry were written, the terms proved to be reasonable and all was arranged. Sylvia and Mrs FitzWalter would go up to Harrogate in September. Veryan agreed to make Mrs FitzWalter's income up to £200 a year. She would lodge nearby and be able to see her daughter after church every Sunday and Sylvia would stay with her mother over the Christmas and Easter holidays. They would come back to Cornwall for the summer.

There was, however, a problem and it was Toby who mentioned it to Dorothea.

'Miss Selwood,' he said one day. Dorothea was in the stillroom making lavender bags. He paused and sniffed. 'Wonderful smell.'

'What is it?' Dorothea smiled at him. She liked Mr Marcham. She admired the tactful way he dealt with Sylvia, treating her more as a grown-up and yet allowing himself to tease her gently if she needed it.

'I'm sorry to mention this, but neither Mrs FitzWalter nor Veryan seem to have thought of it.'

'Oh?' Dorothea's mind was engaged with her work.

'My dear Miss Selwood, has it occurred to you that your own position here will be most awkward when Mrs FitzWalter goes?'

Dorothea looked up. For a moment she stared at him and then realization, like a black pit, opened up in front of her. She could almost feel herself falling. When she spoke her voice sounded distant as though it were somebody else talking. She dropped the lavender bag.

'You mean that I shall lose Mrs Fitz-Walter's chaperonage, I presume?' Toby nodded. 'But surely, I . . . Mr Marcham, I am past thirty and . . . ' Her voice trailed away.

'I am sorry,' said Toby. 'You and I know that any suggestion of impropriety would be ridiculous. Nevertheless, Miss Selwood, there would be gossip. And I think you would find it most unpleasant. You might well be isolated as Mrs FitzWalter has been.' He paused and looked at her stricken face and added gently, 'I think you must consider leaving Selwood Priory.'

He could see that she was looking stunned as if a heavy blow had fallen, but there was nothing he could do to help. It seemed unimaginably cruel that she should be banished from the only home she had ever known, but what else was possible? If she stayed there was no question but that she would be ostracized: the assumption would be that she was Veryan's mistress. Like father, like daughter, people would say.

The only person who could do anything was Veryan himself — and it had plainly not occurred to him that there was anything to do. Toby did not doubt that Veryan was fond of his cousin, but he'd been a celibate academic for most of his adult life, how far would he want to change that now?

Dorothea fiddled with the lavender bag for a moment, then she said tonelessly, 'I believe you are right. I hadn't thought of it. I would not want my cousin to lose the goodwill he has won. After all,' she tried to smile, 'I shall be able to visit when Sylvia and her mother come down.'

★ ★ ★

The little community at Selwood Priory seemed to be breaking up. Veryan had remembered that his colleague at New College, John Norton, had a brother in the 95th Rifles and wrote to him. Correspondence between them flowed back and forth. His brother Arthur was currently adjutant to General Crauford, wrote John Norton, and they were expecting him back in England in September. He was sure he'd be happy to help Selwood's young ward. Why didn't Selwood bring him to visit and they could meet?

Horace was ecstatic. 'Join the 95th? I should say so!' The 95th was a new regiment, one of the most modern in the army.

Fanny was less easily persuaded, but in the end she agreed. Horace was not cut out for a sedentary life, she knew. A good regiment, with a kindly mentor keeping an eye on him, would be just what he would like. She bravely quelled her maternal anxieties and gave it her blessing.

'What about you, Toby?' asked Veryan one evening when they were together in

345

the library. 'What are your future plans? I hope all the goings-on here have not made you miss the London season?'

'I was happy to miss it anyway,' replied Toby. 'It palls. I shall go home, for a while at any rate, see how Papa is, and, I suppose, to London. On to fresh fields and pastures new.' His tone was not very enthusiastic.

'Fed up with chasing other men's faithless wives?' quizzed Veryan. 'Why don't you get married and settle down?'

'I'm only twenty-five,' retorted Toby. 'I don't want to settle just yet.' He stopped and looked at Veryan half-embarrassed, half-defiant. 'No, I believe I'll wait for Sylvia. I really like that girl.'

'Good Heavens,' said Veryan faintly.

'But she's very young,' went on Toby. 'We'll see. Anyway, she may not want me.'

Sylvia, naturally, knew nothing of this conversation, but she was not happy about going away to school. 'I know I was wicked,' she said tearfully to Toby, 'but do I have to be *banished*?'

'Of course, you weren't wicked,' said Toby robustly. 'Just inexperienced. But you do need to go away, Sylvia. A good education and learning how to mix with girls of your own sort is important.' He began to feel about a hundred — he hoped she didn't regard him as a sort of uncle, proffering good advice. 'Why don't you view it as an adventure? Of course, you'll miss your home, but it will still be here, and you will come back for the summer. You'll meet new people, make new friends, will that really be so bad?'

'I suppose not,' she sighed. 'And Mama and Thea will be there. But oh, Mr Marcham, poor Thea! Does she really have to go? Why can't Cousin Veryan marry her? Surely that would make it all right?'

'Sylvia,' said Toby sternly, 'don't you dare say one single word, even the tiniest hint, to either of them about that.'

'But why not?' Sylvia was puzzled. 'Cousin Veryan is so cross with Thea. He hardly ever talks to her now and they were getting on so well before. He thinks she's doing it deliberately and it hurts her. Could somebody not explain?'

Toby sighed. 'No,' he said. 'I mean that, Sylvia. Look, if you were Miss Selwood would you want Sir Veryan to propose because he felt it to be an obligation? Something expected of him?'

There was a pause while Sylvia mulled this over. 'No.' She put up her chin. 'I would have my pride.' Toby smiled. 'But it does seem very hard.'

'Let us hope that they can find their way through,' said Toby. 'And you can always talk to me about it, if you must.'

* * *

Veryan had reacted to Dorothea's declaration that she would go with Mrs FitzWalter to Harrogate, with the same cold fury as he had shown at Daniel Watson's sudden appearance. Dorothea had expressed no emotion at all, merely stated it as something that she would do. He was hurt and angered to the most painful degree.

'Very well,' he'd said coldly. 'Do as you wish.' He'd turned away at once and from then on had scarcely spoken to her. It was a mad idea, he thought. How was she going to manage? Her fortune was tied up in the *Maria* so how was she intending to support herself? Did she think the £200 a year that Mrs FitzWalter had would support them both? She would be leaving everybody in the lurch. Poor little Jenny Tregair, what would become of her? It was arrant selfishness.

He had begun to think that she was somebody special. He was glad to have been enlightened as to her true character. Part of him was aware that he had closed down his emotions so fast that he had not even enquired why she had decided on this step, but he was unable to help himself. He felt such a mixture of pain and rage and the only way he could cope was by excising her completely from his mind.

It wasn't until he paid a call on Sir Thomas Shebbeare that the truth struck him. He'd gone over to see Sir Thomas's red Devon cattle and to ask him about their upkeep. He was invited to take a nuncheon with them and there he met Lady Shebbeare.

Lady Shebbeare was an ambitious woman whose one aim in life was to marry off her three daughters. The only reason she had not sought out Sir Veryan's acquaintance before had been the contaminating presence of Sir Walter's mistress at the Priory. She listened to Sir Veryan's arrangements for the FitzWalters with relief. At last the man was doing as he ought. Veryan then mentioned that Miss Selwood would be accompanying Miss FitzWalter and her mother to Harrogate.

Lady Shebbeare's eye brightened. 'Poor Miss Selwood,' she said, 'she will feel the loss, I know. But, of course, it cannot be helped. She could scarcely stay at Selwood Priory unchaperoned! Indeed, I said to her when Sir Walter died that she would have to go, but she paid no heed. 'Miss Potter is all the chaperone I need', she said.

'I'm relieved that wiser counsels have prevailed. Of course, Miss Selwood is a dear girl but she is hardly eligible. Why, she must be knocking thirty, and that peculiar colouring! So unfortunate. Not to mention living in that ramshackle household . . .' She laughed and patted Sir Veryan's unresponsive arm. 'You were quite right to see that she went.' She leaned over and confided, 'Between you and me, my dear Sir Veryan, you can do a good deal better for yourself!' She smiled archly at him and added, 'Some of Cook's excellent ham, or could I tempt you to a slice of our pigeon pie?'

★ ★ ★

Dorothea was up in the herb garret. She often took refuge there nowadays. She found she simply couldn't bear to be near Veryan in this mood; it was too acutely painful. And she found Horace's enthusiasm for the 95th Rifles and Sylvia's endless queries about her new school and where they would live difficult to cope with.

It was, she thought, far worse than the months after her mother's death. That had been dreadful and she had missed her mother most acutely, but there had been Fanny's

350

loving support and the home she loved and people she knew. In due course there was Horace and Sylvia and gradually colour came back into her life. This was different. She felt as if she had fallen into some desert place, dry, barren, lifeless, where nothing existed, or ever could exist.

She was in the herb garret because she knew that she ought to be sorting things out there. Daniel had promised to deal with her financial affairs. She was not too surprised to learn that he had a substantial account with Hoare's Bank. If she let him know her direction in Harrogate, he told her, he would see that she received whatever sum she cared to name. She must make some decisions about that.

Then there were her medicines. What should she do about Jenny's tonic and the salve for Tamsin Wright's rheumatism? Perhaps she should leave recipes for each? But who would make them up?

There seemed no answer to any of these questions and she was too tired to think anyway. She was living in a grey limbo where it was difficult even to move around. She sighed and dropped the measuring spoon she'd been holding and moved to the window where she gazed out to sea but could see nothing. She did not hear the knock downstairs, nor the footsteps coming up.

Veryan saw her figure framed in the window as he came up the stairs. She was not crying but every now and then a tear ran unheeded down her cheek. He had never seen her look so forlorn. As he moved forward there was a creak of a floorboard and she looked round, gasped and tried desperately to compose her features into the neutral mask she'd been wearing all week.

Veryan came straight over, took her into his arms and kissed her. It was not an activity he was used to and he was apprehensive as to how she might react. After a moment he raised his head and looked at her. She appeared more bemused than cross and his earlobe seemed in no immediate danger. He kissed her again, more purposefully and then, with a surge of joy and relief, felt her arms creep round his neck.

He began to tell her, in between exchanging kisses, how precious she was, how beautiful and how much he loved her.

When they finally let each other go, Veryan said in a rush, 'Oh Thea! I'm sure I'm doing this all wrong, but please won't you consider marrying me? I cannot bear you to go away and I love you so much.'

Dorothea reached up to kiss him. 'Yes, I'll marry you,' she said. Her tears had dried on her cheeks and her eyes were glowing. 'I don't know where you get this idea of doing it wrong. You seem to be managing pretty well to me!'

Veryan gave a rueful smile. 'It must be the triumph of Nature over inexperience!'

'I love you just as you are, Veryan,' said Dorothea. 'I'm not complaining.'

THE END

We do hope that you have enjoyed reading this large print book.

Did you know that all of our titles are available for purchase?

We publish a wide range of high quality large print books including:
Romances, Mysteries, Classics, General Fiction, Non Fiction and Westerns.

Special interest titles available in large print are:
**The Little Oxford Dictionary
Music Book
Song Book
Hymn Book
Service Book**

Also available from us courtesy of Oxford University Press:
**Young Readers' Dictionary
(large print edition)
Young Readers' Thesaurus
(large print edition)**

For further information or a free brochure, please contact us at:
**Ulverscroft Large Print Books Ltd.,
The Green, Bradgate Road, Anstey,
Leicester, LE7 7FU, England.
Tel: (00 44) 0116 236 4325
Fax: (00 44) 0116 234 0205**

Other books in the
Ulverscroft Large Print Series:

HIJACK
OUR STORY OF SURVIVAL

Lizzie Anders and Katie Hayes

Katie and Lizzie, two successful young professionals, abandoned the London rat race and set off to travel the world. They wanted to absorb different cultures, learn different values and reassess their lives. In the end they got more lessons in life than they had bargained for. Plunged into a nightmarish terrorist hold-up on an Ethiopian Airways flight, they were among the few to survive one of history's most tragic hijacks and plane crashes. This is their story — a story of friendship and danger, struggle and death.

THE VILLA VIOLETTA

June Barraclough

In the 1950s, Xavier Leopardi returned to Italy to reclaim his dead grandfather's beautiful villa on Lake Como. Xavier's English girlfriend, Flora, goes to stay there with him and his family, but finds the atmosphere oppressive. Xavier is obsessed with the memory of his childhood, which he associates with the scent of violets. There is a mystery concerning his parents and Flora is determined to solve it, in her bid to 'save' Xavier from himself. Only after much sorrow will Edwige, the old housekeeper, finally reveal what happened there.

BREATH OF BRIMSTONE

Anthea Fraser

Innocent enough — an inscription in a child's autograph book; a token from her new music teacher, Lucas Todd, that had charmed the six-year-old Lucy. But in Celia, Lucy's mother, it had struck a chill of unease. They had been thirteen at table that day — a foolish superstition that had preyed strangely on Celia's mind. And that night she had been disturbed by vivid and sinister dreams of Lucas Todd . . . After that, Celia lived in a nightmare of nameless dread — watching something change her happy, gentle child into a monster of evil . . .

THE WORLD AT NIGHT

Alan Furst

Jean Casson, a well-dressed, well-bred Parisian film producer, spends his days in the finest cafes and bistros, his evenings at elegant dinner parties and nights in the apartments of numerous women friends — until his agreeable lifestyle is changed for ever by the German invasion. As he struggles to put his world back together and to come to terms with the uncomfortable realities of life under German occupation, he becomes caught up — reluctantly — in the early activities of what was to become the French Resistance, and is faced with the first of many impossible choices.